BEVERLEY GREEN FINDS TRUE NORTH

BOOK THREE OF THE BEVERLEY GREEN ADVENTURES

ANDREA C. NEIL

ISBN: 978-1-7334154-2-2

Cover Design by Cynthia Frenette.

Edited by Three Point Author Services, LLC.

1631 Press, LLC.

For Deepti, who has helped guide me through stormy seas to calmer waters and balmy climes.

1

"What do you mean, 'step away from the chicken'?" I asked, my hands raised above my head. It was pitch black out here except for one bright light shining right in my face. I heard a little scuffling noise and looked down. I was able to make out the shape of a chicken scratching at the ground by my feet. What was the voice talking about? Step away from the chicken? Seriously. What harm could come from standing near a chicken? I looked closer and saw that the chicken wasn't just any chicken; it was Beryl—evil genius hen and leader of the avian gang that lived in my backyard.

Oh.

"Ma'am, please. Just move slowly away from the chicken," the voice said again. It was a smooth, deep voice; it wasn't unkind, but it definitely had an authoritarian edge to it. I liked it. "Don't make any sudden moves and keep your hands up where I can see them," the voice continued with so much command that I dared not do as it insisted. Things were definitely headed in a promising direction. Maybe I'd get an idea for my romance novel out of all this. Then I looked down again at Beryl and thought that a romance novel probably wouldn't have a chicken in it. Maybe this wasn't quite what I'd been hoping for.

Dang.

Beryl looked up at me and started laughing her evil chicken laugh.

Double dang.

Beryl was dangerous and I definitely didn't want to be standing too close to her in case she was getting ready to attack, so I started sidestepping slowly into the darkness, away from the light and away from Beryl. What do I do now? As if reading my mind, the deep voice started talking again.

"Here you go," it said, and a piece of paper appeared in front of me. I reached out and took it, hoping that this move didn't put me in violation of the earlier command to keep my hands up. Squinting in the bright light, I saw the words *CITATION* along the top of the paper and underneath that, the words *UNLAWFUL WRITER'S BLOCK.*

Triple dang. The Novel Police had found me.

"Please remit payment by Memorial Day," the voice continued. "Otherwise you will be subject to stiffer penalties. Thank you."

Stiffer penalties? Maybe this *was* romance novel material! But no such luck. Right before the light shining at me went out, I had just enough time to see the penalty amount of one million dollars printed on the citation. It really didn't pay to procrastinate. I wondered what the *stiffer penalties* might entail.

Right then something rustled the grass at my feet again, and I assumed it was Beryl trying to stir up more trouble. She was probably the one who had called the Novel Police in the first place. I made a mental note to give her a stern talking-to later.

I took a step away from the noise and bumped into something. It was very solid, and very hairy. I could now hear the very solid, very hairy thing breathing softly, rhythmically, and ever so slightly menacingly. The smell of wet leaves and chocolate icing filled my nostrils. I slowly reached one hand out, and my fingers came into contact with warm fur that was rising and falling in time to the sound of the breathing.

Bigfoot.

I jumped about six inches, my arms flailing wildly. *"Squatchie!"* I yelled at the top of my lungs. Then my eyes popped open and I woke up.

My forehead was covered with a thin layer of sweat and my muscles were tense, ready to run from both the terrifying cryptid and the forbidding chicken. I stared at the ceiling, listening to my alarm going off. It was supposed to be the sound of ocean waves, but to a paranoid dreaming person, it could easily have been mistaken for the inhale and exhale of a seven-foot-tall Sasquatch. It seemed like a reasonable interpretation to me, anyway. Good grief. A dream filled with just about everything that scared me the most. All it would have needed to be the ultimate scary dream was a clown and a Sunday *New York Times* crossword puzzle. I needed to stop eating those peanut butter, Nutella, and potato chip sandwiches right before bedtime. Or I should at least stop adding the Cholula hot sauce.

I sighed and started rolling out of my bed. I wanted to keep rolling right onto the floor but at the last second decided to save my dignity and sit up instead. It was Monday morning. Time to start the week.

My name is Beverley Green, and I live in Guthrie, Oklahoma where I own a bookstore. One day, I was a forty-something Gen-Xer working in publishing in Manhattan. The next day, I woke up in my comfy city apartment and decided I needed to get the heck out of Dodge. I spent about fifteen minutes living with my parents in Oklahoma City before heading for open prairie and small-town life in Guthrie. I opened The Book Store soon after that.

My parents still lived right down the highway. They were close enough for me to see them a few times a month, but far enough away that they didn't come over without calling first. Living in Oklahoma again was nice. Things were less stressful and it felt like time moved more slowly, which was good—most of the time. Lately though, things seemed to be dragging.

This morning I was trying to think of positive thoughts that would get my week off to a good start. It was springtime! And sunny! I could enjoy yet another day of selling good books to the fine citizens of Guthrie! I could go get a coffee at my favorite coffee shop! It would be a good day. And perhaps I'd even come up with an idea for my romance novel. Yeah, maybe I would get started today! Uh huh.

After a quick shower and an even quicker breakfast, I went to the backyard to check on my chickens before leaving for work. I let myself into the pen. All of the hens crowded around my legs because they knew I was bringing them treats. Each one came to say hi except, of course, for Beryl, who stood behind the others. She was not only a threat in my dreams, but also a real-life menace. She glared at me warily, the red ring of skin around her eyes implying a touch of malice. She was out to get me; I just knew it. I wondered how many other chicken owners had birds that would hire hitmen if they could. No wonder she and Bigfoot—the thing I'd been afraid of since childhood—haunted my dreams.

I tried to offer Beryl an extra grape as a friendship bribe, but she wanted no part of it and instead strutted off to sulk behind the coop. Well, it was better than her continuing to give me the stink eye. I swear, she had caused me more trouble in the last six months than her weight in scrambled eggs. But I wouldn't want it any other way.

At one point late last year, I'd considered giving Beryl to someone who could provide her with a bigger, better home. A few hundred acres in Wyoming would probably do it, but somehow she had endeared herself to me, even though she looked like she wanted to kill me most of the time. She'd gotten loose several times since I'd gotten her, and she always made it back home again. She was one scrappy bird. She had even survived being held captive by Bigfoot, and that showed some real moxie in my book. Yup, not even Sasquatch had wanted her. Respect.

I double-checked the latch on the pen, said goodbye to the girls, and prepared to leave for work. Technically I wasn't supposed to own chickens because Guthrie had a stupid rule about no domesticated poultry being allowed in residential neighborhoods. It's not like I was harboring show horses in the shed with my lawnmower, for heaven's sake.

So far, I'd managed to elude the authorities, including my landlady. When I first moved here last spring, I didn't know you weren't allowed to have chickens. But I sure as heck wasn't going to give them up now; they were way too cute.

Plus, I love omelets.

Walking to work this morning seemed like a good idea. April in Oklahoma was still pretty chilly at the start of the day and in the evenings, but the sun was out and I really wanted some fresh air. The novelty of sweaters and winter coats had worn off right after Christmas, and this morning I finally opted for a lighter jacket. Because sunshine.

I must have been a little tired from my weird dream, or at least that's what I used as my excuse when my feet mysteriously changed course. Instead of heading to the bookstore, I was now walking towards Missy's Bakery. Sometimes my feet or car headed to the bakery without me consciously meaning to do it. It was like getting lost, only I magically ended up at the same place each time. You would think that after almost a year of walking and driving around town I wouldn't get lost like this anymore, but it still happened. Regularly. So, I might as well support a fellow local business by buying a chocolate old-fashioned donut when in the neighborhood. It was the least I could do.

I got to my shop a few minutes before I needed to open for the day. As I walked up to the door, I glanced at the picture windows spanning the front of the store. The words *The Book Store* had been hand-painted in a plain, white, sans-serif font across the tops of the windows. I'd wanted the logo to be simple to match the name and feel of the shop. I wanted people to walk by and know exactly what was inside and I wanted them to think, *Wow, that's one classy bookstore! I want to go in there.* I felt like I'd succeeded in my goal, for the most part. The lettering was sharp and professional and the display of books in the windows was inviting. This month the theme was Springtime. We had lots of gardening books.

Sometimes when I caught a glimpse of my store this way—like someone who was coming across it for the first time—my breath would catch a little and if no one was around, I'd let myself tear up a tiny bit. It was the culmination of a dream I'd had for a long time. But today when I looked at the storefront, it felt as if something was missing. I couldn't figure out what it was, though.

"Meh," I said to no one and unlocked the front door. Time to get down to business.

Justin and Myrna Miller made their usual Monday morning visit, as soon as I was officially open. They were some of my best customers and had been shopping at my store since I opened. Business had steadily picked up during and after the holidays, but I never took the long-time regulars for granted.

I marveled at the constancy of Justin and Myrna's reading habits. No matter what size book they bought, they always managed to finish it on Sunday night and need a new one the very next morning. Today I showed them a few new titles I'd gotten in the previous week. Justin stood at the counter to look them over while Myrna went to visit Jimmy.

"How has little Jimmy been?" she asked. "He still going strong?"

"Oh, he's doing great," I answered. "He's been eating more. Seems to prefer crickets over earthworms right now." I walked over to where she stood, and together, we peered at Jimmy.

Jimmy was the store's resident pet turtle. I had inherited him from my twin niece and nephew, Meg and Jack, when they came to stay with me for three weeks over the holidays. They lived in Chicago and had somehow managed to smuggle a little turtle onto the plane in Meg's backpack. Since no one had been able to figure out how to get him back to Chicago save for a UPS box with some holes in it, he was now mine.

Meg had named the turtle after Detective Inspector Jimmy

Perez, the lead character in a series of Scottish crime novels. She was eleven but read a tiny bit more advanced than most kids her age. We ended up housing the turtle in a Christmas nativity scene I had bought as a holiday decoration for the store. I had planned to take both the turtle and the nativity scene home after New Year's, but thanks to a few hundred photos of Jimmy that ended up on social media, both the turtle and his heavenly habitat were now permanent fixtures in the store. They were a tourist attraction that definitely hadn't hurt my book business. *#bookstoreturtle* for the win.

A few more people had now wandered in on this fine Monday morning, so I excused myself to greet them and offer help. I loved having groups of people in the store; it made the place feel lively and busy. When Justin was ready to make his purchases, I walked back up to the counter. Myrna followed and placed her book in front of me—a 600-plus page tome of a romance book. It made a heavy *thud* on the counter.

"Goodreads says this is the best historical romance of all-time," Myrna said.

"Well, that might be kind of subjective," I confessed. "But I did enjoy it." I wondered if Myrna was ready for all those steamy bits.

"I like the TV series they made out of it," she added. Oh. I guess she *was* ready for the steamy bits. I slid the books across the counter to ring them up.

"Ever since your Bigfoot article came out last year, I've been looking into these here extraterrestrial beings," Justin said as he handed me his credit card. "Personally, I think Bigfoot is an alien species. I'm working on putting my theory together. This is a tax-deductible research book!" He pointed at the other book I was holding, an equally hefty paperback. That was a science fiction novel. About an alien species sending a microbial bioweapon to our galaxy billions of years ago. Hmm.

"But this is *fiction...*" I wanted to try to explain further but I had a feeling it wouldn't make any difference to Justin.

He leaned over the counter and cocked his head slightly. "Says *you.*" He winked at me. Oh well. It was between him and his accountant now.

"Well, these ought to keep you busy for a while," I said as I made sure his credit card payment went through.

"I'll let you know when I put my theory together. Maybe you could write an article about it for the paper!"

"Okay!" I said, matching the enthusiasm in his voice, but not really meaning it. I was getting used to people constantly talking to me about Bigfoot. I didn't like it much, but I didn't seem to have a choice. Ever since I wrote the article the previous fall about some local Sasquatch sightings, including my own, I'd managed to become a curious sort of local hero. It was a dubious distinction at best, but I also knew I shouldn't look a gift horse in the mouth, especially when said horse was wanting to buy a few books.

So even now, a good five months after the story came out, people were still flagging me down on the street to tell me their Bigfoot stories, or they'd stop me in the grocery store to ask me a question about some obscure Sasquatch fact. I'd even started to receive Sasquatch-related gifts from admirers: a Bigfoot mug, a few stickers, and a slew of blurry black-and-white photos that everyone said they'd taken themselves and adamantly swore were of a Bigfoot. I had hoped people would start accepting me into the community because I was a smart, entrepreneurial small-town leader, but no such luck. I was still considered an outsider, "one of them big-city types," but at least I was gaining a little traction, albeit as the Bigfoot Lady. Oh well. At least people knew who I was.

Justin and Myrna gathered up their books and waved goodbye on their way out of the store. I waved back, sighing to myself. It would be easy to dismiss Justin's theories and call him a wacko. But who was I to say?

As the store quieted down, I took a seat behind the counter to catch up on email and my donut. The donut was much less spammy. I ate it way too fast, and as penance I admonished myself to be more productive for the rest of the morning.

As part of that penance, I spent a little time looking through my bills. No matter how hard I wished they would stop coming, they never did. Sales were definitely trending in the right direction, but I was still at that point where a little extra cushion would be nice. That chicken scratch didn't pay for itself.

I moved on to shelving books, wishing I had another donut. Mostly I wandered around the store looking at book covers and straightening displays. I looked in on Jimmy again and gave him a morning snack of fresh lettuce and a dried cricket. He accepted them graciously and retired to the miniature barn to take a nap with one of the wise men. I didn't judge.

The morning workload ended up being pretty light. I was not at all productive despite my previous self-admonishment to get my act together. I had scolded myself so often about being more productive that even my own brain didn't pay attention to the idle threats anymore. I should have tried to work on my novel, but the early-morning Sasquatch nightmare had rattled me too much. That was my excuse, anyway. I hoped there was no such thing as the Novel Police. I made a mental note to google it. Later.

Around noon, my stomach growled, my built-in food alarm clock telling me it was time for lunch. And right on cue, my part-time employee Julie walked in the door as if it were all being orchestrated by the heavens. I silently thanked the stars above that the store was doing well enough financially that I could keep both Julie and my other part-timer, Chuck, on the payroll past the holiday season.

"You sure it's okay that you leave school at noon on Mondays?" I asked. It seemed a little weird to me.

Julie rolled her eyes at me. "Yes, Beverley. I have a half day on Mondays. Don't worry, 'kay?"

"Hmmm," I said suspiciously. I trusted her though.

Julie was a senior at the high school and had been a big help to me since the shop opened. And I'd hired Chuck right before the holidays. He was a college student who had come back to Guthrie to help out with some family obligations and didn't appear to be in any hurry to get back to school. He'd told me he wanted to be called "Banjo Man," for reasons unknown. Those reasons were likely to remain unknown, because I hadn't yet screwed up the courage to ask why, and he'd never volunteered any more information himself. I had simply told him his name tag would just say "Chuck" for the foreseeable future, and we'd left it at that.

When Julie got situated, I said goodbye and headed over to Stacy's Place to meet Kelly for our standing Monday lunch date.

2

As USUAL, I was early. I slid into our regular booth to wait for Kelly, who, like always, would probably be late. Kelly Passicheck was my best friend in Guthrie, and we'd been meeting for lunch almost every Monday since my bookstore opened the year before. I had hired her as my attorney when I needed help leasing space for the shop, but it didn't take long before we realized we got along like a feminist house on fire. It was probably more a case of me realizing how much I needed and appreciated having a female bestie in town, and her realizing I wasn't the high-strung New York bitch she'd expected me to be. I was definitely a little high-strung, but hopefully not too bitchy.

About a month ago, we also realized we'd finally reached "regular booth" status at Stacy's. Neither of us remembered exactly how it happened; it wasn't like there was an official swearing-in ceremony or anything. We were just sitting there one rainy Monday, waiting for our food to arrive, and it dawned on us that we hadn't had to wait for a table, or even look for one. When we had walked in, our regular waitress Molly had just pointed to the only empty booth in the back, and being obedient customers, we went where we were told. Now here we were.

I always brought something to read with me wherever I went. I tried to read as much as I could to keep up with new releases. If someone came into the store and asked for a recommendation on what to read next, it would be better if I didn't just shrug and say, "I have no idea."

Plus, I figured it would be good to be seen reading in public. It was like free advertising, especially if I made sure to look completely engrossed in my current book of choice. The ol' *I'll have what she's having* tactic.

So, I pulled out my book and opened it up. This week's selection was *The Silkworm* by Robert Galbraith. The first book in the series was a great read and the second was proving to be just as engrossing. I tried to dive right in, but I was having trouble concentrating. The words swam around on the page, and bits of conversation in the room distracted me. I put the book down and observed my surroundings.

Stacy's was always busy during the mid-day hours; it was one of the best places in Guthrie to see and be seen. On any given day, you could spy an eclectic mix of people eating lunch: tourists, cowboys, old-timers, regulars, and business owners. It was as close as you could get in these parts to a power lunch spot.

In a corner booth on the opposite wall I spotted Mark Ellison. He was the editor of the *Guthrie Ledger* and also my boss, since I was a part-time reporter at the paper. He was talking to two grey-haired men wearing khaki pants and golf shirts. A huge platter of chili cheese fries sat in the middle of the table, and I guessed he was trying to convince the two men to buy advertising space. It wasn't technically his job, but he knew everyone in town and often went beyond what his job description called for. He'd been working for the paper for close to fifteen years and knew every aspect of the business. He was a handsome man, in a dark and brooding sort of way. A divorce had left him jaded and guarded, but he still looked good, and when he wasn't really grouchy, he could almost pass for human. A very attractive human. He looked up and caught me watching him. I smiled; he furrowed his brow and kept talking. Message received.

In another booth along the same wall sat three ladies wearing Guthrie High School sweatshirts. I recognized Martha Drake, the head of the PTA at the High School. I had donated some books at the beginning of the semester, and she had sent me a thank you card. She saw me and waved congenially. I smiled and waved back.

It was a good feeling to see so many people I knew, but there was a difference between being seen and feeling like I belonged. I hadn't reached the status of belonging yet. I might as well have been wearing a sign that said *BIG CITY FANCYPANTS*. When I moved back to Oklahoma from New York the year before, I'd chosen Guthrie because of its charming small-town appeal. I longed for a simpler life, one with less cars and less people, but more open space and more freedom. I had been confident I would fit right in. After all, I was born right down the road in Oklahoma City. I had been certain that people would easily accept me. While sales at the bookstore proved no one was boycotting me for being an outsider, I could tell I still wasn't considered a local. Nonetheless, I still felt a sense of community as I sat and looked around the restaurant. It felt more like home than New York ever did.

My brain, the master of the *non sequitur*, chose this moment to remember the previous night's Novel Police nightmare. It was my brain's way of ruining a calm moment. Thanks, brain. *No problem,* it answered cheerily; *I didn't want you to get too carried away with feeling good.*

Recalling the dream reminded me all over again of my lack of writing progress. It felt uncomfortable, like a strand of hair that had blown across my face in the stiff Oklahoma breeze, but I couldn't tell whether it was in my eye or across my nose, and the more I tried to get it out of my face, the more I couldn't grasp it and the more it bugged the living peanut butter out of me.

Writing books had been part of my long-term plan. I originally thought I'd open my bookstore, and when the shop wasn't flooded with adoring customers, I'd use the quiet time to write romance novel masterpieces. But so far, things hadn't quite worked out like my vision. Imagine that! I'd written pretty much absolutely nothing. So far, all I'd done was fill up a few yellow legal pads with some really intricate doodles and various metaphors for certain bits of the human anatomy. There was always something more important to do than sit down and write. I always had a good excuse.

A whole year I'd been here—well, almost a whole year. And what did I have to show for it? Nothing. Okay sure, The Book Store was doing pretty well, and my chickens, except for Beryl, were happy. That beast would never be happy. I was also learning to be a decent journalist by writing for the *Ledger*, but that was different from writing a full-length piece of fiction. In that department, I hadn't written jack cheese. With that thought, I let out a heavy sigh.

I didn't realize my sigh had been so loud until I looked up and noticed a few people at nearby tables were staring at me. But I couldn't help it. I was feeling frustrated the more I thought about it all and I was starting to get mad at myself. Damn Novel Police.

The worst part about writer's block wasn't that I didn't get any writing done; it was how bad I felt about not getting any writing done. I'd heard someone say that writer's block didn't really exist, that it was a form of resistance that could simply be overcome. Well, whatever dope came up with that one obviously wasn't a professional procrastinator. It was probably some skinny, young go-getter who designed inspirational quote notecards on their iPad for a living and ate goat's milk yogurt parfaits out of mason jars. I'd been around the block a few times and I could attest to the fact that the struggle was real—real annoying.

At that moment, Molly came up to the table and dropped off two waters and two iced teas. Her red hair bounced as she stepped back and grabbed her pencil from behind her ear. Sometimes she knew I liked to order before Kelly got there because I was always so hungry."Hiya, Bev," she said, pulling her notepad out of her apron. "You gonna want the usual today?"

I lurched forward in my seat, ever so slightly, as if the earth had just derailed off its axis and I was the only person who had noticed. Everything suddenly went off-kilter and today, there was something different about how she had said "the usual." It wasn't a lunch order this time. No, this time it was a judgment of my character. It was an accusation, a mockery of my mundane existence. This time, it was personal.

"What are you saying?" I asked loudly. "The usual? The *usual?* No, I do not want the usual. I don't know what I want! And I don't know what I want for lunch, either!" A few more of my fellow diners were watching me now.

Molly calmly placed her pencil back behind her ear and carefully slid her notepad back into her apron pocket. As if scared that a loud sound or sudden movement might set me off again, she continued to back away from the table, never taking her eyes off me. When she got to the nearest wall, she groped behind her back, pulled a menu off the stack, and silently brought it to me.

I tried to regain my composure, realizing I might have just put my mental health in question. If I didn't rein it in, she might call the sheriff's department on me. It might be bad for The Book Store's business if I got arrested for being nuts. "Thank you so much," I said as evenly as I could. Molly backed away from the table again.

I stared blankly at the plastic-covered pages of the menu. I felt frustrated and embarrassed. My palms were sweaty, and my eyes felt like instead of pupils, they had those little swirly lines that you see in cartoons. I wondered if this was the beginning of a midlife crisis of some sort. I had left New York in hopes of preventing said crisis. Should I have stayed in Manhattan? Did I make a mistake moving back? What if my new life wasn't enough? What if all this wasn't what I was supposed to be doing, after all? What if I couldn't write a novel? My brain reminded me of that age-old adage about not being able to outrun your problems. But instead of agreeing with my brain, the rest of me just wanted to punch its lights out.

I was still absentmindedly thumbing through the menu when Kelly slid into the seat opposite me and let her book bag full of lawyerly stuff drop heavily on the bench seat beside her. It was the bag I got her for Christmas last year, after I couldn't stand seeing her lose papers out of rubber-banded manila folders anymore.

"What's with the dazed squirrel look?" she asked, putting her phone and keys on the table.

"I was going for more of a 'what the hell am I doing with my life' look," I said glumly.

"What's the difference exactly?"

I opened my mouth to speak but couldn't think of an answer. What was the point? It was all just semantics. I shrugged.

"Well, this is gonna be a fun lunch," she mumbled, squinting at the specials board behind my head. "I'm fine, thanks for asking," she added, leaning back into her seat. "So, what the hell *are* you doing with your life?"

I got a squirmy feeling in my stomach. "I don't know," I whined. I knew whining wasn't my best quality, but sometimes you just had to. A tiny bit.

"It's finally happened," Kelly sighed with an air of resignation.

"What?"

"You haven't been able to adapt to small-town life and you've gone batshit crazy," she said calmly. She never had been one to mince words. "Where the hell is Molly?"

"I think I scared her away," I confessed, looking toward the back of the restaurant. I didn't bother disagreeing with her diagnosis of my condition.

"Oh, for shit's sake," she mumbled. She turned to look around the room, and when she spotted our server, she smiled and waved politely.

Molly approached the table like there might be someone hiding under it waiting to ambush her. Kelly scowled at me across the table, then turned to Molly again and flashed her "impress the judge" smile.

"Yes?" asked Molly.

"Hi, Molly. I'll have the special, please," said Kelly.

Of course, the daily special! That's what I should order, I thought. There was nothing that said "living on the edge" quite like ordering off the specials board without even looking to see what was on it. I felt a little better. "Me too," I said politely.

Molly nodded slowly, eyeing me cautiously before walking away.

"So where were we?" Kelly continued. "Oh yeah, your midlife crisis."

"Does it show?"

"In spades," she said, pretending to inspect her cuticles now.

"But it can't be a midlife crisis! It just can't be. I promised myself."

"Okay, your nervous breakdown then."

"Better, but I prefer to call it an existential funk."

"What brought it on, though? Oh man, you regret those chickens, don't you! They're driving you crazy. I knew it! I told you to get rid of the damn things." She beamed at me triumphantly.

"Try again, Kel. I love those chickens. Best thing that ever happened to me, those chickens."

"Why can't you just have a dog like a normal person?"

"I don't like dogs. Besides, chickens are much more practical."

"Well, I can't argue with that," Kelly agreed. "You can't eat a dog for lunch."

I bowed my head and Kelly picked up on my exasperation. "So, what is it?"

"I've been here almost a year. I still live in a rental house. My parents are still bugging me about being single, and worst of all, I haven't made any progress on my stupid novel."

"For starters, maybe the problem is you're calling your novel stupid." I looked at Kelly like maybe *she* was stupid. "I'm serious! Be careful about the language you use when you talk about this stuff," she cautioned.

"Are you getting all 'woo' on me?" I asked, breaking out the air quotes. She shrugged as if she knew better and I was just missing out. Maybe I was missing out. At this point, I knew I shouldn't rule out anything.

"This town is just boring, I guess," I said by way of a lame defense.

"Oh really."

"Yeah, that's it. It's boring here—no inspiration."

"I thought you moved because you wanted a simpler, slower-paced life," Kelly pointed out. Just like a lawyer to throw what you'd previously said back in your face when you were trying to build a flimsy defense for yourself.

"Yeah. Well. I just need to get over this writer's block."

"Is this all because you don't have a boyfriend?" she asked. "Maybe you just need to get some."

"Some what?" I asked, trying to stay focused on writer's block and pretending I didn't understand what she was saying. She snorted but didn't explain. I could feel myself blushing. "Not everything is about sex, Kelly."

"Are you sure?"

I paused. "Well, no. I guess I'm not one hundred percent sure."

She looked like she had just won her case.

"Gah! I don't need a man!" I said loudly. Heads turned again. I wasn't doing myself any favors here. "You sound just like my parents," I stage-whispered.

"Your parents want you to get laid?"

"My mom calls it something else, but yeah, pretty much."

"What does your mom call it exactly?"

I slapped my open palms on the counter. "Can we just change the subject? You all can stop worrying. I'm doing just fine in the romance department right now."

"It sounds like you can't even find the romance department."

I shot her a look like I wanted to run her over with my car. I knew what she was thinking and I was tempted to follow her line of reasoning if only to let her know that I could most certainly find the romance department and had been successfully doing so for many years now.

"You know what I mean," I said instead. "My trouble is in the fictional romance department. I wanted to write a romance novel. I thought it would be so easy for me to write a book and that I'd have all the time in the world along with a million great ideas. But so far, I've got nothing. Just a whole bunch of super cool doodles and a few pithy remarks about UPS men and their packages. I should be *done* with a book by now."

I lowered my head onto the table and left it there, my forehead resting on the cool formica surface. I hoped I looked as pathetic as I felt. "I was supposed to have a *plan.*"

"Stop being so hard on yourself. So what if you don't write a book right away? You can't plan everything out, Bev."

"Yeah but I *want* to. Aren't I supposed to have like a six-month plan, and a one-year plan, and a three- and five-year plan? Instagram influencers say I need a plan."

"Screw Instagram influencers; their heads are up their asses. You don't need a damn plan. But you do need to know how you want to spend your time. Like right now, for example. You have lots of things going on! Your bookstore is doing great, isn't it? And you've got your chickens and your job at the paper. And what's going on with Danny, anyway?" she asked in a conspiratorial tone.

"What do you mean?" I was getting good at playing dumb.

"It seemed like you and him, you know...after your Bigfoot article came out, everyone was talking...and Christmas..." She tried to ask without asking.

I looked up slowly. "I like Danny, I guess. And we did hang out a few times. But it's never really gotten off the ground." Just like my romance novel writing. No plan, I thought to myself, but knew better than to say it out loud.

"Off the ground? Were you ever trying to get it airborne in the first place?"

I was silent for a moment before continuing. "I don't know." I flinched just in case she decided to punch me for being so evasive. But it was true. I hadn't given it all *t*hat much thought.

"What about Mark?" she suggested. Her voice sounded silly and innocent, like we were in sixth grade talking about the boy at the other end of the lunch table. We both looked over at the boy in question, watching him talk to his advertising prospects. His dark eyes were expressive as he worked to convince them to give him money. I had to admit; he was the best-looking man at the table—possibly in the restaurant.

"He's my boss," was all I said.

"Yeah, but he's liked you since eighth grade!"

"Yeah, and he's also gone through a really bad divorce, and I'm pretty sure that now he thinks all women are evil."

"None of that is insurmountable."

I was still hunched over the tabletop, but when I looked up at her, I couldn't help but laugh. "You're joking, right? That's ridiculous! Mark. No way, I'd never. And Danny. I mean, I wouldn't..."

"Uh huh," she said, not believing any of my BS.

I lowered my head to the table in resignation once again. I hadn't wanted to think about starting a relationship. I was busy. Maybe there was not a single man in town that was good relationship material. Had I just used the phrase *relationship material?* Thank goodness I hadn't said it out loud. Was it really the fault of all the men in Guthrie? Or was it me? Did I care? It was so much easier to simply not think about it.

Suddenly I realized I hadn't said anything for a while and I wasn't exactly sure how long I'd been silent. I had gone off on one of my man-tangents. I must have departed on my man-gent quite a ways back, because when I looked at Kelly, she was staring at me with a big grin on her face that told me I'd been caught. I lowered my forehead to the table once again.

"I just need to write a book," I told the table.

"What about those notes you're always taking? You're constantly writing things down to use in a novel. Surely you have enough material by now."

"I've got nothing."

"What about the story where Bigfoot captures the sexy journalist and holds her captive and makes her his love slave?" I couldn't see her, but I could tell Kelly was silently laughing at me. I didn't care. I groaned for dramatic effect.

I heard a noise and lifted my head as Molly put a huge plate of fried catfish, coleslaw and fries in front of me. Oh great googly-moogly, this was what I got for ordering the daily special without looking to see what it was first.

Many years ago, like when I was probably eight, I had vowed to never eat catfish. They were creepy and gross and even though they were a southern staple, I just couldn't even. I should have known Kelly would go for something like this. The woman ate her own body weight in fried batter every six months. I had no idea how she stayed so healthy.

"Thanks, Molly," I said to our server. I thought I sounded congenial, maybe even sane. She smiled back and I could tell that all was well.

"You're welcome, hon," she said as she left us to it.

I turned back to Kelly. "I appreciate your encouragement," I continued, using the word *encouragement* loosely. "I should have finished writing something by now. Or at least have something started." I stared at the mound of food in front of me. Maybe I could just eat the coleslaw, I thought, as I stuffed some fries in my mouth.

"That's just plain stupid," Kelly scoffed. She appeared to be a third of the way done with her meal already. "You're being way too damn hard on yourself."

I considered this. Was I too hard on myself when I lived in New York and worked seventy hours a week as an editor for a big publishing house? Yes. And didn't I leave because I didn't want to be so hard on myself? Didn't I want a more meaningful, fulfilling, and simpler life? Hell yes. So, what was the problem?

"I don't know," I said out loud. "Things feel stagnant. Maybe there's a middle ground somewhere between my past life and this one. I want to write a book and I want it to be a romance book."

"Why romance? Why not a memoir, or maybe a Sasquatch exposé?"

I didn't say anything, as if I didn't know the answer. But of course, I did know.

"Isn't romance kinda schlocky, escapist fluff? There's already a ton of it out there, and a lot of it doesn't seem to be very good."

"How would you know?"

She frowned slightly, realizing she had given herself away. "Yeah, okay fine. I've read some; I admit it. Everyone has, I guess."

"So why do you read it? Is there something wrong with your life that you feel the need to escape it by reading a romance novel?"

"No..." She couldn't think of anything else to say.

"There are lots of different kinds of books out there and yes, there are a lot of romance novels already. Some are hokey. Some are thinly-disguised porn. But all of them serve a purpose." I scooped some coleslaw up with my fork and then dumped it back into its little ramekin. "Maybe I just want to elevate the genre by adding my own classy voice," I suggested. "Maybe I want to write some subversive fiction."

Kelly let out a laugh. "How on earth is romance considered subversive?"

"You of all people should know the answer to that. You deal with divorce, dishonesty, and grumpy people every day. You help people who have been wronged or hurt. And all we see on the news are scary, depressing stories. A book with a bona fide happy ending is practically a political statement these days. It's a bold move." I ate a few more fries, feeling smug about my philosophizing. "You could call it oversimplifying or idealizing; I call it vital to the survival of the human race."

Kelly said nothing, but I could tell that she was thinking about what I had said.

"Plus, it's an opportunity to rewrite some of the old tropes. Simply put, the world needs more good romance."

"But maybe you're wanting to write it to avoid living it. You think the whole world could use some romance—everyone except for you."

"Pfft! I don't know what you're talking about."

"Oh bullshit, Bev."

"Okay. *Maybe* I need romance too. Possibly. It's just that—" I stopped there, wondering if I should continue.

"Just that what?"

"I don't know. I don't exactly have time for a relationship, you know? I'm so busy between the store and the paper and my house..."

"Don't tell me you're using your damn chickens as an excuse for not having a boyfriend."

It had made sense in my head, but I had to admit it sounded stupid as soon as it came out of my mouth. "Well," I confessed, "I don't exactly have the best track record with guys." That one definitely sounded legit.

"Oh, give me a break!" Kelly laughed outright this time, not even trying to cover it up. This wasn't exactly the response I'd been hoping for when I bared my soul to my best friend. But I wasn't surprised. It wasn't that she didn't care; she just didn't take anything too seriously— like her cholesterol levels. "Everybody has baggage. By the time you get to be our age, if your heart hasn't been stomped on at least once, or if you haven't done any stomping yourself, there's something seriously wrong with you. Of course, it's scary, but dammit, Bev, you're tough. You've got real moxie. You could get any guy in this town you wanted." Kelly finished her sentence and her plate of food at the same time. I hadn't even tried the slaw yet.

"Moxie?" I thought about the word. I did like it. But still. "Meh. I don't want any guy in this town," I muttered in my best pouty voice.

"Excuse me? What's wrong with the guys in this town?"

"Nothing, I guess. I don't know, I haven't met any that are..." I couldn't figure out how to finish the sentence. I was running out of material right quick.

"Up to your impossibly exacting standards?"

"I don't have impossibly exacting standards!" I huffed. "Okay, so I'm pretty sure I probably maybe don't have impossibly exacting standards. But I guess they are pretty high standards. No, it's more like I haven't met a man that's..."

"Interested?"

I sighed. The woman wasn't cutting me any slack, but I couldn't blame her. I knew I was being defensive. And Kelly knew it too. "Raising chickens is way easier," I sighed forlornly. "They may break your heart, but at least they make you breakfast."

She laughed and pushed her plate toward the side of the table. It looked like she had licked it clean. Then she eyed my plate, which still had a large piece of catfish on it, as well as a cup of slaw and a few lonely fries. "You know what your problem is, Beverley?"

"Enlighten me," I said, pushing my plate toward her.

"Now that you've made a big change by moving home, you're wondering what's next. You think you're supposed to have everything laid out all nice and neat. But you don't know what you want. You thought you did. You moved back here because you had a picture of how you wanted your life to be. But now that you're here, you don't have the details of the picture and you're feeling a little lost."

Every fiber of my being wanted to yell at her that she was wrong and stupid and mean and anything else I could think of that sounded accusatory. But I couldn't. All I could do was remain silent and think about what she'd said. And eventually realize she was right.

"I thought I knew," I started. "I mean, I definitely know what I *don't* want. That's why I left New York."

"Yeah, but knowing what you don't want doesn't automatically mean you know what you do want," she pointed out. "But it's a start. Now's a good time to give that some thought. You don't need a big fancy plan, but you do need to think about how you want this to look." She motioned around the room.

We looked at everyone around us. People were talking and laughing and eating together, just living their lives.

"Has anyone told you that you should write a self-help book?" I asked. I didn't necessarily mean it as a compliment.

"It could be another way for me to push my feminist agenda," she remarked, reaching for her glass to polish off her tea. She had finished all the food on my plate before I'd even noticed she'd started. She waved Molly over and ordered dessert, apparently still peckish even after polishing off two specials plates.

"You need to think about what you want, but remember one thing," she said casually as Molly left to get our dessert.

"Oh yeah? What?"

"Just be careful what you wish for, is all I'm saying."

Totally cryptic. Spoken like a true a lawyer.

3

After splitting a gigantic piece of coconut cream pie with Kelly to complete my healthy meal with some fruit, I left Stacy's feeling confused and frustrated. On some level, I knew Kelly was right. I wasn't sure what should come next, or more importantly, what I wanted to come next.

I could blame my lack of writing on all kinds of things, but ultimately it came down to the fact that I simply hadn't done it yet. Maybe I only thought I wanted to write novels, but didn't actually want to spend the time doing it? Maybe I felt the town was boring, but I just hadn't given it enough of a chance? Maybe I kept telling everyone I didn't want a boyfriend, but maybe deep down I did want to find someone to have fun with and share my life and my omelet skills with?

On yet another level, maybe I just wanted to kick Kelly in the shins.

I walked to Hoboken, our local coffee joint, for some caffeinated inspiration. I was still feeling a little shaky from my restaurant breakdown, and I was sure caffeine was just what the psychiatrist ordered. I got a flat white—the hipster version of a cappuccino. No one who was anyone got cappuccinos anymore; they were passé. Instead, the lightly-frothed milk of a flat white was where it was at. While I waited for Seth, the owner and my favorite barista, to make my drink, I listened to him tell me how flat whites were invented in Australia. Apparently, Australia had a huge coffee culture. Who knew?

After a minute or so, my brain tuned out and I started thinking about the very first time I'd met my pal Danny Cadence, right here in this coffee shop last fall. I could remember it clearly: his wind-blown sandy blond hair and the superhuman sparkle in his bright blue eyes, followed by me dropping my phone and spilling coffee all over his boots. I smiled at no one in particular.

Seth put my drink in front of me, and I managed to tune back in for the last bit of his Australian Coffee Culture lecture before leaving him a few bucks in the tip jar and heading out. It was time to get to the *Ledger* offices for our weekly Monday meeting.

Why hadn't things progressed with Danny? This was something to ponder while walking. So far, I didn't have an answer. We had a nice time when we were together, but it was as if we were both afraid of something or we knew that we weren't right for each other. Or maybe, I posited, our Chinese Zodiac signs didn't match up and our planets or chakras weren't aligned properly. Maybe I should see a psychic about it. At that last thought, I almost tripped. It was dangerous for me to posit and walk at the same time.

Last fall, Danny had helped me with "research" for my Bigfoot "article" I had to write for the paper. It was more like he'd helped me with some possible fake journalism. Potato, potato.

The research we did together consisted of going on a Bigfoot stakeout. During that stakeout, we kind of got "close." By close I mean we made out. Twice. I could remember that night very clearly. It had been one of the nicest times I'd had doing research like, ever.

We had also gotten "close" around Christmas, and we'd run into each other plenty of times since, even getting coffee together once or twice. Sure, we always flirted. He was so adorable with his lean, lithe figure and irresistibly sparkly blue eyes. But maybe I didn't want to complicate my new life by adding a man to the equation—even a really cute, nice man. And even if I was willing to give it a try, I wasn't sure that a pair of sparkly blue eyes was enough to base a real relationship on.

Wow. Had I always been this wishy-washy? I sighed and took a sizable sip of my flat white. Probably.

I continued to hoof it over to the *Ledger* building; I definitely didn't want to be late and face the wrath of Grumpy Mark. On my way, I passed by Craddick's Barber Shop. I saw Al Turner and his cousin Bill Turner sitting on a bench outside the shop's front windows. They were both at least in their late 60s with white, thinning hair, but that was where the similarities ended. Al was fairly tall and gangly. If he wasn't wearing his glasses, it would be best if you gave him a very wide berth. Bill was shorter and rounder. He shuffled more than he walked; not because he couldn't get around very well, but more because he couldn't be bothered to lift his feet, which were usually clad in man sandals, with socks if it was chilly.

Bill waved happily at me and I watched as Al leaned over to say something to Bill, who then said something back to his cousin. Finally, Al waved at me too. Al didn't have his glasses on; he must have had to ask his cousin who he was waving at.

Suddenly Bill got up off the bench and looked like he was going to try to flag me down, but Al grabbed his arm and pulled his cousin back down to the bench. I wondered what that could have been about. Then again, I didn't really want to know. It was probably better to remain ignorant.

Those two. Al couldn't tell the difference between a Bigfoot and a 1982 Toyota Cressida if he wasn't wearing his glasses. I knew this for a fact because I'd had to interview both Al and Bill for that Bigfoot article last year. They claimed they saw a She-Sasquatch on their way home one night while Al was driving his Ford Ranger truck. While intoxicated. Without his glasses. And rather than make a big fuss about the contradictions and utter lack of logic that accompanied their accounts of the harrowing experience, I went with it. They, and the rest of Guthrie, had been happy about that.

I personally ended up seeing what could have been one fake and one real Sasquatch while with Danny on our Bigfoot stakeout. I was still convinced he played a joke on me—twice. He admitted that our first sighting was his friend Tom dressed up in a furry suit, but still insisted to this day that the second sighting was the real deal.

I walked up to the *Ledger* building and as I opened the door, I ran into Mark. Literally. I had been looking down and he had been looking back when we collided in the entry. His arms were wide open; mine were trying to hold onto my coffee. His broad chest stopped me in my tracks before his arms automatically folded around me. Even though part of me didn't mind the situation at all, I still went into fight or flight mode. My body tensed up and I did what any sensible woman would have done in my position: everything I could to keep from spilling my coffee. Joes before bros, y'all.

"Well, hello there," I sang, happy to have averted a coffee disaster. "You beat me back from Stacy's!"

"Uh," he said. Our gaze met, and for a split second, his dark brown eyes locked onto mine and I swore I saw a thing there. You know, a *thing*. I knew it was a *thing* because I could feel it in my romance novel body parts. It felt nice to be in his arms and he smelled nice. Maybe someday, if those gloomy, woman-hating rainclouds ever left the airspace above his head...

He quickly looked to his left and then to his right, and finally down at the ground. I stood still and waited, curious to see what he would do next. Eventually he decided to sidle around me slowly, like I was a nuclear bomb and he was trying to avoid setting me off. He made his way all the way around me until he was free, and then slunk out the door.

"Bye!" I called after him happily. I wasn't going to let him rain on my one-woman parade.

"Uh," he said once more before creeping down the street and around a corner.

I shook my head in confusion. Two *uhs?* I might need to look that one up in my Manspeak Dictionary later, although I was pretty sure I knew what had gotten him flustered enough to use the double *uh*.

I walked into the conference room, took my place at the table, and waited for Mark to come back and get the meeting started. Everyone was there already: Grace Mobley, the Assistant Editor who had an imaginary boyfriend which, thankfully, she no longer brought to staff meetings after recently coming to an agreement with him to keep their work and personal lives separate; our Photographer, Max; me; and the other two part-time staff writers, Jade and Brett.

"Hey, Grace. How's the boyfriend?" I asked as I slid into a chair. I feared that her imaginary boyfriend had been the result of a flawed understanding of the Law of Attraction and had now become so real to her that there was no going back. We all went with it and since he couldn't be there in person, I could at least ask after his health.

"He's good," Grace answered, with a decidedly disappointed look on her face, her lack of enthusiasm obvious. Note to self: an imaginary man could only get you so far.

Max and Brett were arguing about something sports-related, and Jade was texting her real boyfriend. Based on her facial expression, I guessed it was something dirty. It inspired me to want to check my own phone, although I doubted anyone had texted *me* anything dirty and if they had, it would have been from a wrong number and therefore, very creepy. Before I could even get my phone out, Mark blew in and tossed a stack of papers onto the table. They flew everywhere. It was his way of handing out copies.

"Sorry I'm late," he said breathlessly. "I had to run out to my truck to make sure my gun was locked in the glove box."

Everyone looked at him with a nod of understanding except for me, who sported more of a *WTF* look. I wasn't used to people taking such a cavalier attitude towards gun ownership, but in Oklahoma, you were definitely the odd one out if you didn't have one. I wasn't a big fan, which never won me many points. Once, I tried to get Mark to let me write an article about the virtues of gun control, and now I understood why he'd never replied back to any of my emails about it.

"So, let's get down to it," he said, jerking his head toward the papers that landed all over the table. Everyone picked up a copy and looked at the story assignments for the following week's issue. "We're about finished editing this week's articles; you guys did a lot better this time around, except for you, Bev."

Oh snap! Busted by the boss. I wondered where I could have gone wrong with my story about the city council's controversial decision to limit downtown parking on Thursday mornings.

"For next week," Mark continued, "I want to change things up a little. Brett, you're still going to handle sports, but Jade, I want you covering local government stuff. Beverley, something different for you too." He turned to look at me; his face was all business, our brief doorway interlude seemingly forgotten. "I want you to write up a couple human interest type stories; highlight a few of our community leaders. The first two people on your list are Leona Tisdale and Sheriff Branch." He turned back to the table. "You'll all work with Max to get whatever photos you need, as usual. Also, we've got a new advertiser, just so you're aware..."

Mark continued to fill us in on our new advertiser, a pet store that opened down on Division Street the week before. They specialized in hamster antidepressants. Or something like that. I had pretty much stopped listening after the words *Leona Tisdale* came out of his mouth.

Leona Tisdale. My landlady times two, de-facto leader of the Guthrie Old Timers, unofficial civic leader, and mean old coot who acted like she really had it in for me. She didn't like chickens, hamsters, or New Yorkers, even if they were born in Oklahoma. She also didn't like know-it-alls, porn, or coffee. She did like Jimmy the turtle, but not the fact that I never wore skirts. She had never been my biggest fan, right from the start, and now I had to write a warm, heartfelt, family-friendly article about her? Great.

And then I had to write about the laconic, cryptic, and frustrating as all get-out Logan County Sheriff. He had been less than helpful when I was trying to write my Sasquatch exposé. However, he may have helped me avoid getting evicted over the holidays. I just couldn't figure that guy out. Writing a whole article about him was going to be about as much fun as figuring out how to knit a sweater.

Once again Mark had made my day. No, he'd made my whole week, and maybe even my whole month, with his story assignments. I was starting to think he was doing it on purpose. It was like he liked me and therefore had to be extra mean. How third grade! Well, two can play that game, I thought to myself. I smiled warmly at him as he continued to talk about the alarming global decrease in gerbil serotonin production.

When the meeting was over, I sashayed out the door and back to my desk where I found a package of Hostess Cupcakes perched atop a stack of papers. I smiled and looked around for Danny. I spotted him leaning on the door frame of Mark's office. They were talking, but he looked over at me and we shared a quick grin.

The cupcakes were a private joke between Danny and me. Well, everyone in town knew that Hostess Cupcakes were Sasquatch's favorite snack food, but only Danny and I knew that when we'd met Bigfoot last fall, I had traded him one cupcake for the safe return of my chicken, Beryl. And *no one* knew how Bigfoot had ended up with her in the first place.

I wanted to leave the building before Mark chewed me out about whatever I had done wrong this week, but I sat down at my desk and pretended to do important stuff until the two men had finished their conversation. I could feel little butterflies in my stomach. I wondered why he always made me feel this way. It was kind of nice, but also kind of annoying. Damn blue sparkly eyes.

Finally, I could see him moving toward me out of the corner of my eye, and I straightened up in my chair but kept pretending to read the piece of paper on the top of the stack for the third time. The words I'd spoken at lunch came back to me about how there were no good men in this town and how I'd never want to date anyone and how I didn't need no one, no how. Suddenly, I became nervous. He leaned over me and my eyes traveled from my paper to his belt buckle, up his chest, and finally to his face, which was framed by those curly, dark-blond locks.

"Hiya Bev," he said warmly.

"Hiya Danny, how's things?"

"Oh, you know, can't complain. You?"

I was a writer. I was a wordsmith by trade. I knew I should have a quick and sassy comeback for his old, overused line. But I was also nervous. "Good! Glad you're cute—I mean, good. Yeah, I'm fine too. Good. Real good. No complaining. You?"

He laughed, to be nice. To his credit, it did sound authentic.

"I haven't seen you around much. Have you been busy?" I asked. I regretted asking as soon as I had finished speaking; I hoped it didn't make me sound like I had been like, you know, paying attention to whether or not he'd been around or anything like that.

"I've been doing some traveling. Went to visit some family, then went to go look at some cattle up north. Why? Did you miss me?" He grinned.

"Pfffft!" I said a little too loudly. I looked down to make sure I hadn't spit all over my desk. "Don't be ridiculous," I admonished him, unable to meet his gaze. I could feel my cheeks getting warm.

"Oh, okay then." He shifted his weight from one foot to the other, and I used the movement as an opportunity to stand up, because I still wanted to try to escape the building before Mark hunted me down.

I pushed my hip out to the side in an effort to be sassy and considered tossing my curls around but knew I could never pull off a move like that in a million years, not at the same time as a hip push. I wasn't that coordinated.

I picked up the Hostess Cupcakes. "Thanks for bringing me these," I said, holding them up before putting them in my bag. "It was nice of you to think of me."

"You're welcome," he said sincerely.

We walked out the front door of the building together and he turned to walk one direction, while I turned to walk in the opposite direction.

"You steer clear of those Sasquatches, okay? And stay out of trouble too." His smile turned a little mischievous.

"No guarantees," I retorted with a similar smile. "Take care, Danny." I continued my path down the sidewalk toward home, hoping he was watching me. Finally, I couldn't stand it any longer and I shifted to look. He was walking in the other direction, but his head was tilted, and he was watching me over his shoulder too. We both laughed before heading off in separate directions alone.

I spent the rest of the afternoon at The Book Store, combining light dusting with heavy procrastination. I had let Julie go home early and at five I closed up before starting my journey home. The weather would be cooling off even more now that the sun was setting, so I tried to keep my pace brisk as I made one quick detour. I needed some food. Since I had only eaten a fistful of fries, a bite of coleslaw, and half of an automobile-sized slice of pie for lunch, I could tell I was going to need an early, healthy dinner. I was craving vegetables, so I stopped at the market to pick up some fresh organic produce to sauté in my cast iron skillet.

There is a hard and fast rule in Oklahoma that you need to own a cast iron skillet and you have to be able to cook edible food in it. You also have to know how to season it and keep it clean. If you don't pass *Cast Iron Skilleting 101* within your first year of residency in the state, they kick you right back out. The test consisted of proficiency in three categories: stovetop deep frying, oven-baked desserts, and bacon. I was still practicing. The stuff that came out of my skillet did count as food in that it was edible for the most part, and I hadn't rusted out my pan, so I was holding my own. They hadn't kicked me out of the state yet. I considered this a major life accomplishment.

On a whim, I changed directions again toward August's Liquor

Store. When in Rome, you pick up some beer, so I bought a local pale ale to restock my Emergency Beer selection. I always had a few in the fridge because you never knew when you might need one and I believed in being prepared for all possible eventualities.

It was slow going the rest of the way home with a bag full of vegetables and beer weighing me down. I regretted not having driven to work, and I chastised myself for not eating healthier at lunchtime so I could have skipped the store and just eaten whatever carb stash I had at home for dinner. The trek was making me hungry. And thirsty. I considered stopping for an Emergency Beer since my thirst could be considered close to emergency levels, but I decided being picked up for "public emergency beer drinking" might not be a great idea.

When I finally set my bag down on the kitchen table, my hands were cold and stiff. I took a minute to warm them up before getting a glass of water to drink. Rummaging around in my bag, I pulled out the cupcakes that Danny had given to me and put them aside before finally locating my phone. I had one new message from my mom.

My parents never called me on Mondays. It wasn't on their social calendar to call me on Mondays. Something was wrong. What was wrong? Who died? Or who was dying? Or getting divorced? Omigod, my mom was dying, and my parents were getting divorced. My life had become so rote that my parents calling on a non-scheduled day sent me into a tailspin. I steeled myself for the terrible news that I just knew was waiting for me on my phone. I listened to the message.

"Hi, sweetie, it's Mom. Listen, we're in Guthrie picking up an oak table for the store, and we want to take you to dinner. Meet us at Luke's at 6:15; we have a 6:30 reservation. Wear something nice, not one of your chicken farmer outfits, okay? See you soon, bye bye now."

My parents were in Guthrie? They lived in Oklahoma City and had come to visit pretty regularly when I first moved to town, but they hadn't been up since mid-January when they got back from all their holiday vacationing. They had visited me to make sure I wasn't starting off the year freezing and starving to death like in that movie *Bridget Jones' Diary* when Bridget imagines herself dying single and alone before her body gets eaten by a pack of wild dogs. It was as if my parents thought my life was exactly like that movie. They might be right. I hadn't been eaten by wild dogs yet, but it still remained a distinct possibility.

I usually went to see my parents every other week on Sunday evening for dinner so we could catch up. It was also a great way of preventing them from coming to visit me. It wasn't that I didn't want them to visit, per se...Well, okay, I didn't want them to come visit. I loved them, but they always had so much to say about how I was living my life. And decorating my house. And dressing myself. And oh lord, how they hated my chickens.

But now they were in town and wanted to see me on an unscheduled day with no advanced notice. Something was definitely up. But what? My mind leapt to all sorts of fantastical possibilities. Like, "picking up an oak table" for their antique store was actually code for "your father is a jewel thief." And "wear something nice" meant "we'll need you to fence some hot merchandise for us."

I looked at the time and realized that I had about twenty more minutes to worry about it before I had to leave to meet them for dinner. I made good use of the time by continuing to fret about their impending divorce, death, and incarceration, while trying to get rid of the dread by feeding the chickens and then cleaning something.

First, I picked the cupcakes up from the table, thinking I could have one as a quick snack before I had to leave. I took them outside with me so I could check on the chickens and make sure everyone was still there. You never knew with Beryl. She was still in the pen, eyeing me suspiciously. She didn't look the least bit worried about my parents.

"What do you think is wrong?" I asked her, setting the cupcakes down on my picnic table. "Am I losing my mother to a rare disease that comes from wearing ill-fitting shoes just like she always warned me about?"

Beryl stared at me. *"Bwwwaaaaaaaak,"* was all she said.

"You're no help." I went back in the house, even more nervous than before.

I looked for something to clean. I always got my best cleaning done while I was trying to write or was worried about something. I kicked it into high gear and cleaned the stove and vacuumed my living room. I was about to start dusting the bookshelves when a quick look at my phone told me I was out of time. I needed to change clothes.

I considered wearing my coop-cleaning jeans to dinner just to annoy my mother. But I couldn't do that to her now that she was dying and everything. Maybe I'd wear what I had on: jeans, t-shirt and Vans. Eventually, I decided to put a little effort out for dinner at a nice restaurant. But just a little. My Mom had told me to dress nice and I couldn't let her down; it might be her dying wish.

When I moved back to Oklahoma, I had become a firm believer in comfort over fashion, preferring jeans and a pair of Vans over pant suits and heels. When I decided to leave big city corporate life behind, I decided to leave it *all* behind, including the clothes. Besides, I could sell books in jeans and a Ramones t-shirt as well as I could in a pencil skirt. Probably better. But I did like to look somewhat nice from time to time so I changed into some cropped chinos, my favorite cardigan sweater and a pair of flats, then took a cursory glance in the mirror. My hair was on strike again, refusing to cooperate with even a very polite, reasonable request to behave. But ultimately, I was too low-maintenance to give a literal flip. I gave up a long time ago trying to tame my curls. We finally came to an understanding in my thirties; I kept them clean and cut and they did whatever the hell they wanted to. Today was no exception.

My stomach growled loudly, protesting the lack of food. "I hear ya," I said as I patted my belly. "And yes, I promise to eat veggies." I was kind of sad I wouldn't get to use my cast iron skillet. I vowed that tomorrow night I'd cook up a huge batch of veggies and eat them all. But not tonight. Tonight was restaurant food and bad news night. I took a deep breath in, exhaled loudly, and headed out the door, bracing myself for whatever horrible announcements my parents had in store for me.

4

I WALKED down the steps and through the basement-level door of Luke's Steak House promptly at 6:10, because 6:15 would have been considered late and would earn me at least three snide comments. Immediately I saw my parents waiting for me at the bar. You could tell they had been together for a very long time because at this point in their lives they almost looked like one person. Their clothes matched and they appeared to be joined at the hip. Neither of them *looked* like they were dying, so that was encouraging.

"Hi, hi, Sweetie Pie," my dad beamed as he gave me my usual greeting. It made me cringe every time, but I had learned to cringe on the inside, not the outside.

"Hiya, Popster," I shot back, because I knew he hated being called Popster. "Hi, Mom," I said cautiously, waiting to see what kind of mood she was in.

"Hi, honey," she said, pressing her hand to the side of my head in an attempt to get my hair to behave. This was a Roberta Green hug.

They seemed in high spirits. If I didn't know better, I'd say they were in too high of spirits. They must have gotten a really freaking great deal on that oak table.

A few minutes before 6:30, the hostess came to tell us our table was ready. My dad reached for his Scotch, my mom picked up her glass of Cab Sav, and we all walked across the front of the restaurant to a table next to the large windows that were actually below street level and looked out onto a small patio filled with potted plants. We sat down and I noticed the hostess had left the table set up for four people. They usually took away one place setting when I ate here with my parents. She was new, so maybe she didn't know.

"So, how's the bookstore, sweetie?" my mom inquired, with a little too much English on her question. I decided they were getting divorced. Yep, it was definitely divorce. Our server Mitch came over to say hi and brought us a basket of the most delicious fresh bread in the entire universe. So much for my healthy all-veggie dinner. I grabbed a big hunk of bread and started attacking it with fresh butter.

"The store is great, mom. Business is good. I've got a book signing coming up next month and I'm thinking about starting a reading group. Are you guys getting divorced?"

My mom almost choked on her wine and my dad started coughing loudly. "Whatever makes you think we're getting divorced, Bev?" he asked incredulously.

I knew it was bad manners, but I pointed my butter knife straight at him and looked him square in the eye. "Something's up. I'm no slouch, you guys. You don't come to town for oak tables. What's going on here?" I started stuffing bread in my mouth. Not that I was prone to stress-eating or anything.

"Sorry I'm late," a voice said calmly, right above my head. It was a man's voice. It was a voice so smooth, you could slide down it without ripping your pants on it. It was so deep that you could drill for fossil fuel in it. And it was so rich, it had three of its own Swiss bank accounts, plus one in the Caymans. I looked up, but all I could see was the dark silhouette of a man. A tall man. A very tall man, wearing a cowboy hat.

"Cal, great to see you!" My dad stood up and shook the man's hand.

"Hi, Cal," my mom purred, staying seated but practically oozing out of her chair. I was momentarily floored by the sultry undertones of her voice. I'd never heard her talk to my dad that way. I wondered if she had meant to do it or if it was some sort of vocal cord glitch.

"Steve, Roberta, good to see you both," the stranger poured his voice all over the table.

"Please, call me Bob," my mom's voice tinkled like piano keys and alarm bells started going off in my head.

My dad gestured to the empty chair on my right, inviting him to take a seat. I didn't want to look at him, but out of the corner of my eye I saw him take off his coat and hat and place them on the back of the chair before sitting down. *What. Was. Going. On?*

Now that he was seated, I could see him better. He was maybe a few years older than me, with a few flecks of grey in his light brown hair. His face was slightly weathered, like he'd spent a fair amount of time outdoors. His cheeks and chin sported a few days' worth of blond stubble, a handsome complement to the angled line of his jaw. He looked tall even seated in his chair, and I could see he had a lean but sturdy frame. I bet myself he was wearing cowboy boots and just as I thought this, I heard them scuff against the wooden floor. Of course. He like a real-life Wild West Sheriff, sitting right at our table. And then I realized why he'd seemed familiar.

Before either of us could say anything, my mom spoke up, sporting a smile that I'd never seen her use before. "Cal, this is our daughter, Beverley. Bev, honey, this is Sheriff Branch."

The tall man turned in his chair to face me. At first his expression was blank, then it turned to surprise, and finally it softened before he smiled. "Hello, Beverley. Callan Branch." He extended his long arm toward me and his hand engulfed mine. His grip was gentle but firm and warm. He kept my hand in his, and I started to wonder if I'd be getting it back anytime soon. "It's nice to meet you."

Right about then, I realized my mouth was still completely stuffed with bread and butter. I couldn't even smile until I'd spent what felt like a lifetime chewing and swallowing what had started out as delicious bread but had now turned to sawdust in my mouth. Everyone at the table waited expectantly, and Sheriff Branch was still holding my hand which I tried to shake, but he was too strong for me; our hands didn't move. It was taking me so long to chew the sawdust bread that I was starting to panic.

"Hello again, Sheriff," I finally said. As I finished saying the word *Sheriff,* a few boulder-sized bread crumbs flew out of my mouth and landed on the table in between us. We both looked down at them, neither of us saying anything. *Well,* I thought, *where does one go from here?* It was an existential question but was also relevant to the current situation. I carefully removed my hand from his and proceeded to turn beet red.

"You two know each other?" my mom asked with what sounded like a tinge of jealousy in her voice.

Before I could spray more bread onto the table, the sheriff began to explain. "Yes, we met last year."

My dad raised his Scotch to the sheriff. "I hope it wasn't because you had to arrest her for something," he guffawed loudly, sending the ice cubes clanking against the side of the glass.

I shot him a killer laser beam stare. "No, I didn't get arrested," I said testily. "Bigfoot—I mean the sheriff, helped me with some research for an article I was writing." As I remembered it, he hadn't been any help at all. I had tried to interview him, hoping for some insight into all of the alleged Sasquatch sightings that had been reported over the years, but he had been the epitome of the word *laconic,* managing to avoid answering all of my questions. Wasn't that like an elected official? Let's just say he hadn't made much of an impression on me at the time.

He turned to me and said as an aside, "You did a great job on that article, by the way."

"Thank you," I said politely.

"Did you just call him Bigfoot?" my mom asked me.

"Funny story—" the sheriff started.

"That we can save for another time," I interjected quickly. The story of how I was so scared of Bigfoot that I kept mistaking Sheriff Branch for a Sasquatch would have to wait for a happier occasion. Like, never. I was still trying to figure out what was going on here.

"Oh," my mom said slowly, clearly confused. But then her face brightened. "Well, isn't that nice that you already know each other!"

"I also helped her save her bookstore," he added casually as Mitch came to the table and brought him a glass of water.

"What?" my Dad asked. "Is that true, Bev?"

I had sort of forgotten about that story. "Uh, yeah I guess so. He kind of smoothed things over with my landlady after the hamster incident."

My parents stared at me. Clearly, I had lost them, and it was really okay with me if they stayed lost. I turned to the sheriff. "Thank you for that, too."

"You're welcome," he said, raising his glass. "I even know where she lives." He quickly took a drink of water, the ensuing silence making a statement. This last piece of information was directed at my parents. Was he stirring up trouble? Sure seemed like it.

As my cheeks grew hot, I glanced at my mom. She was staring at me slack-jawed. Then we all looked at the sheriff, who I noticed wore a tiny glimmer of a smile. It was true, he did know where I lived. He'd given me a ride home last fall after my failed attempt at an interview, but that didn't mean he had to throw that into the first five minutes of dinner conversation. What a smart-ass.

We sat in silence for a few beats and it quickly grew uncomfortable and awkward. What now? Was I supposed to say something? Clearly, he wasn't going to say anything; he never said anything. Should I say something witty? Oh, why did I even care? I didn't ask my parents to set me up on this date, dammit. Oh my *god,* had they set me up on a blind date? I thought I might start crying before we even got an appetizer. Instead, I bobbed my head up and down a few times and started in on another hunk of bread, hoping we'd be ordering soon because I was still so damn hungry and if my face was stuffed with food, I wouldn't have to say anything.

My dad took advantage of the silence and started talking. He began to explain to everyone how he and the sheriff first met. As he gained momentum and had more Scotch, he got so sidetracked that he never got to the part of the story that explained how they actually met. He was saying something about a Chamber of Commerce meeting, a poodle, and a deck of tarot cards. Or was it a grapefruit? Or maybe it was something about ducks. I had stopped listening.

As I sat there watching my dad's mouth open and close, it hit me. They had set me up on a blind date. With the freakin' Sheriff of Logan County. And by set up, I mean they had gotten me good. Oak table, my ass! I hadn't even seen it coming. I was hopping mad, but I was also thoroughly embarrassed. Did the sheriff think I had asked my parents to do this? Oh god. He must've thought I was a total loser, having to rely on my parents to find me dates. I wanted to slide under the table and seep through the cracks in the wood plank floor and disappear.

We ordered our entrées and as my dad continued to talk, I continued to fume. I was so upset I was getting a stomachache. He went on and on about how great the sheriff was and something about crime, then something about antiques, then on to crime and antiques and finally antique crimes. Meanwhile, I stuffed my face with bread and polished off two glasses of water. There wasn't anything else to do but eat since none of us, not even the sheriff, could get a word in edgewise. Maybe if I drank enough water, I could spend the rest of the evening in the bathroom.

As my dad continued to monopolize the conversation, I had plenty of time to study Sheriff Branch. It was either that or watch my mom make googly-eyes at a man who wasn't my dad. I watched the way the sheriff's whole face smiled, even though I knew it was a fake smile, because there was no way he thought what my dad was talking about was actually entertaining. I noticed that when he smiled, the small creases around his eyes grew a little deeper and his mouth widened to display two rows of white, straight teeth. As he deftly buttered some bread, I noted that his hands were strong yet agile.

Wait. This was the guy who had been unhelpful, reticent, and borderline rude. Why did I care how he buttered his bread? Even if he *did* save my bookstore last Christmas. But right now he was kind of charming, and he looked, dare I say it, just a smidge handsome. I guess I hadn't noticed before because I'd been too busy mistaking him for Bigfoot.

I felt bad for him, sitting here having dinner with me and my parents. Maybe he had been duped into it, just like me. Surely he had more important things to do, like arresting purse snatchers or making an appearance at the Elks Lodge. He smiled and nodded his head a lot and continued to pretend to listen intently to my dad. It made me want to crawl under the table even more, but also to take him with me so we could both escape. A fresh wave of embarrassment passed over me. I wondered what he thought of me—a grown woman being set up on a blind date by her parents. So much for successful adulting.

I was studying his warm brown eyes again when suddenly he turned to look at me. My dad was still talking, and Sheriff Branch was still listening, only he was watching me. "Yes, I remember that one," he said to my dad, never taking his eyes from mine. "It definitely was one of the better episodes of *Miami Vice*." One of his eyebrows curved slightly upward as he said this, and I had to look away before I started laughing.

I could still feel his gaze on me for what felt like forever. It was my turn to be observed. I guess I hadn't been as covert as I had thought. Turnabout was fair play, I conceded.

It felt like three weeks since we had ordered our food, and I prayed it would show up very soon in the hopes it might quiet my dad for a few minutes. I sighed loudly, not realizing I'd done it until everyone turned to look at me, and I could feel my cheeks turning red.

"Food!" I pointed across the room at our waiter bringing plates of steaming hot food our way. Saved by the beef.

Mitch placed a big steak in front of each of my parents and a grilled salmon fillet in front of me, and one in front of the Sheriff. There was an extra side of steamed broccoli on his plate instead of a baked potato. Masochist.

As we tucked into our meals, my dad was finally quiet, which gave my mom an opportunity to start up. She began telling everyone about my illustrious former career as a high-powered book editor in New York City and how I came home to Oklahoma to selflessly give back to my home state. She left out any mention of chickens. My parents would have made great car salespeople.

Then my mom started telling the story of how I won my fifth-grade spelling bee. It was an embarrassing story involving me misunderstanding the word *uvula*, and I was starting to feel like I was on the verge of having flashbacks.

Finally, I couldn't take it anymore. "You like mystery novels," I blurted out, cutting off my mom's most hilarious story in her repertoire.

"That's right." He looked at me and his face brightened. It appeared he was also glad to hear someone else speak besides my parents. It occurred to me that I should have tried to save him sooner, but I had been too flummoxed. I resolved to make up for it.

"Henning Mankell," I recalled.

"The Wallander series, yes." He shifted in his chair so that his whole body turned in my direction. "I like all kinds of books, though. Westerns, Greek mythology, history..."

We continued to talk about books, and he told me what he had been reading recently. We listed off some of our favorite crime fiction authors and it turned out we had a few in common. It was a subject my parents knew little about, so they were quiet. Their idea of mysteries was more along the lines of the four hundred different *CSI* shows on TV.

My parents had been quiet, but I'd watched them share knowing looks with each other. At this point, they both looked like they had just invented cake, realized they could trademark cake, and then live off the royalties from everyone baking and eating cake for all of eternity. In other words, they looked pretty damn smug.

We managed to make it through dessert with minimal awkwardness, even though we knew it was getting close to the end of the evening and we were all wondering what was going to happen next. On the bright side, I had managed to avoid spitting any more food on the table, and I even kept my mom from telling more stories about me. I was considering faking a headache and leaving early to avoid further awkwardness, but before I could get my story straight, my dad ordered four herbal teas, after which he and my mom suddenly stood up from the table. They offered some lame excuse like *oh my goodness, look at the time, we didn't realize it was so late and we'd better get going, our oak table is getting cold, so sorry.* They paid the bill for the whole party and then vanished in a puff of cloying smoke, leaving me and the sheriff with four cups of peppermint tea.

We sat and looked at each other, trying to figure out what had just happened. Then we both started laughing.

"I'm so sorry about this," I said finally. I stirred some honey into my tea. He did the same.

"I have to admit, when they told me they wanted me to meet someone, I didn't think it would be their daughter and I definitely didn't realize it would be you." That explained the confused and surprised look on his face when we were introduced. Oh, my manipulative parents. They'd told him about as much as they'd told me. More, actually.

"Well, at least they told you that you were going to meet someone. They didn't even tell me you were coming,"

"Really? Shit. I'm sorry, Beverley."

"Oh, it's not your fault!" I assured him. "I knew they were up to something; I just didn't know what. And you can call me Bev, if you want."

"Okay, but only if you call me Callan. Or Cal. Save 'Sheriff' for when I arrest you."

"Deal," I said.

We both fell silent and stirred our tea. "What was the thing about a cold oak table?" he asked, his brows knitting in confusion as he recalled my parents' hasty exit.

"Don't ask," I advised. He nodded slowly in agreement.

"Well, at least we got a free meal out of it," I said, suddenly feeling uncomfortably full. It had been a very good piece of salmon.

"Yes. That salmon was pretty good. I haven't eaten here in ages."

"I'm stuffed," I muttered as I pushed away from the table.

"Me too. Want to go for a walk?"

"Okay."

We got up from the table and he made sure I had my jacket and bag before he followed me to the door. He placed his hand on the small of my back as he held the door open for me. It had gotten colder, and I shivered as I tried to get used to the cool night air.

We walked past his SUV. I could tell it was his because it was white and had the word *SHERIFF* painted in big black menacing letters on the side. He went to the passenger side, unlocked the door and pulled out a coat which he then draped around my shoulders. Oh, hell yeah. Chivalry was so not dead, at least not in Guthrie, Oklahoma on this particular Monday night. I looked at him with what must have been a weird expression on my face because then he said, "What?"

"Just trying to figure you out," I said before I realized I was talking. "Do you keep an extra coat in your vehicle for this type of emergency?"

"Chivalry's not dead," was all he said before putting his hand on my back again and leading me down the street. When his hand finally did fall away from my back, I found myself feeling sad about it. "Do you like living in Guthrie?" he asked.

Compared to our attempt at conversation last year, the man was being a complete chatterbox. Not that I minded. But I wondered what had changed.

"Yeah, I do," I answered honestly. "So far, anyway. I'm glad I moved back to Oklahoma. New York was amazing, but I do love it here. And I've been lucky the bookstore has been doing pretty well. Are you from here?"

"No," he admitted as we continued to walk slowly down the street, away from the other shops and bars. "West Texas. Hill Country."

"How did you end up here?" I asked, genuinely curious.

He let out a long exhale. "Long story," he said, clearly not about to offer up anything more. His tone implied there was definitely more to the story, but he didn't elaborate, and I didn't press him. I was curious though and made a mental note to try to find out the scoop someday.

"Texas, huh?" I asked. I could wait on the personal story, but I couldn't pass up an opportunity to hassle a Texan. "How on earth did you get elected? Oklahomans aren't supposed to like Texans."

He shrugged his shoulders. "Maybe," he said, "but when the Texan is a kick-ass sheriff, everybody loves him."

"I see," I said, trying to keep a straight face. There had to be something to it, otherwise he never would have been elected.

"Hey, guess what?" I announced, changing the subject. "At the *Ledger* staff meeting, I got assigned to write an article about you. It's supposed to be one of those human-interest stories, like how you enjoy knitting and saving kittens and baking bran muffins for the elderly in your spare time, stuff like that. Just today, this happened. Isn't that funny?"

"Really," he said thoughtfully, rubbing his stubbly chin with his long fingers. "How did you know I like knitting?"

"Oh, I, uh..."

Mercifully, he bailed me out. "This happened today, huh?"

"Yeah! What a coincidence, right?"

"No."

"I know! Wait. What?" I was confused. It wasn't a coincidence? Because it seemed an awful lot like one to me.

"There are no such things as coincidences," he said.

If it hadn't been a coincidence, what the hell had it been? I expected him to explain further, but of course he didn't. "I don't usually give interviews like that," he continued. "I'd think your editor would know that."

I deflated slightly. "Oh."

"But maybe I'll make an exception for you." His smooth voice emphasized the word *you*, and I felt my eyebrows go up involuntarily. He coughed nervously, as if realizing he'd given something away he might not have meant to. "I mean, I'll think about it," he added.

"I hope so, because my boss is a real pain in the ass, and if I go back to him and tell him you said no, he'll cut out my liver with his pencil."

"If Mark gives you any trouble, you just refer him directly to me, okay?"

I laughed. "Okay."

We walked a little further, past the Apothecary Garden. For some reason, this made me think of my weird dream the night before.

"I had a dream about the police last night," I said absently.

"Yeah?"

"Uh huh. The Novel Police. They gave me a million-dollar fine for having a severe case of writer's block."

"You're a writer?" he asked.

"It was part of my trademarked Great Life Plan to be a writer, but I haven't managed to get anything done yet." I thought about saying more but decided I didn't know him well enough to mention I was in the throes of a personal existential funk.

"That's a weird dream," he said.

"Yeah, I need to cut out the late-night snacks."

"Did you read the fine print?"

"The what-what?" I asked.

"On the ticket. Did you read the fine print?"

"Um, it was a dream, so let's see...No."

"Always read the fine print," he warned.

That felt like a loaded statement. "Duly noted."

We came to a stop and stood in front of the old State Capital Publishing building and were silent as we looked up at the three-story structure. It was one of the oldest buildings in town, abandoned now, and slowly losing its former magnificence. We were right in front of the steps leading up to the front door. The door was padlocked shut, and its paint was peeling badly. One pane of glass was cracked. The place was a historical landmark, but it had fallen out of use a few years earlier and there were no plans to spruce it back up anytime soon. If you looked closely, you could still see the former grandeur underneath the dust and flaking paint. It was stately, a reminder of what a thriving town Guthrie had been. But times had changed and people had moved out to bigger cities with more jobs, leaving the old ways behind.

Callan sighed heavily, as if he could relate to the building's state of disrepair and lack of purpose. A melancholy look came over his face as he gazed up at the letters above the door that once had spelled out *THE STATE CAPITAL*. Some of the wooden letters were hanging onto the building for dear life, and a few others had already given up the ghost.

"Poor old building," he said quietly. I couldn't tell if he was feeling sorry for the building, or if its emptiness and dilapidation had reminded him of something else equally as disappointing.

He shifted his weight from one long leg to the other, causing his hips to move slightly. It wasn't a very fancy move, but it was a good one and suddenly I felt very warm under the big coat. We lingered for another beat, then turned to walk back toward our cars.

"So, 'Beverley'—that's kind of an old-fashioned name, isn't it?"

If I had a nickel for every time someone asked me that.

"I guess I'm an old-fashioned girl," I delivered my usual line, hoping I sounded sassy and not too annoyed.

"Is that so?"

"Not really. But what can I say? It's a family name. It was my maternal grandmother's name. My parents didn't give much thought to what it would be like going through junior high with a name like Beverley. And they definitely didn't do me any favors with the unusual spelling. It's got an extra 'e'," I explained.

"Beeverly?"

"So funny," I said dryly.

"I think it's a great name. Unusual, hard to forget. Fitting."

"What kind of name is Callan?" I asked.

"Also a family name," he explained. "I prefer it to Cal, but that's easier for most people, I guess."

"I like Callan. What's it mean?"

"Gaelic for rock."

"Ah," I said, nodding while I looked at the ground. Rock. Steadfast, solid. It was fitting too. "You're kinda different from what I thought," I admitted as we kept walking.

"What do you mean?"

"How can I put this...?" It was turning into another one of those times where I wished I had thought things through more before opening my mouth.

"Whatever you're going to say, you won't be the first person to say it," he said in a very bureaucratic tone.

"It's just that the first time we met, you were less than helpful and probably said ten words the whole time. And you were kind of cryptic about how you smoothed things over with Leona at Christmastime. But tonight, you're more like a real person."

"Gee, thanks."

I ignored his sarcasm and continued, trying for a lighter feel. "And you don't seem like an Oklahoma Sheriff." I turned my head to size him up, looking at the profile of his face way above mine. "Or even a Texas Sheriff. Nope. You don't look like one or sound like one."

"Really."

"Aren't Sheriffs supposed to be kind of fat? And bald, and talk with a thick southern accent? And have corrupt morals?"

"You've watched *Smokey and the Bandit* too many times."

"I don't know..."

"Well, that's just it, you don't know me. It's true I'm a man of few words. I make sure I think before I speak, and often I come to the conclusion that it's best to keep my mouth shut." He shrugged his shoulders. "And I could have very corrupt morals; maybe I'm just good at hiding them."

I thought about this and couldn't find a comeback. That was a first.

"You could turn out to be another obnoxious New Yorker, for all I know," he pointed out.

"True. I could be totally obnoxious!" I wasn't sure why I was so excited about someone thinking I could be irritating.

We stopped walking when we got to my car, which was parked under the lone working streetlight opposite the restaurant. We were alone on the quiet street. He turned to face me, and I could tell without looking up at him that he was studying me intently. "It was nice seeing you again, Beverley Green," he finally said.

I looked him in the eyes and smiled. "It was nice seeing you too, Callan. I'm sorry about the circumstances."

He hesitated for a moment, then spoke again. "I really didn't want to come tonight, but you know the persuasive power of your parents. It's just that, well, I'm not actually looking to meet anyone right now. But I was more than a little scared to say no to your father."

I unlocked the door of my car and opened it, taking off his jacket and handing it to him before getting in. "It's okay," I said. "I'm not looking to meet anyone right now either."

"Okay, that's good then." I could hear relief in his voice.

"Sorry again about my parents. They definitely can be kind of scary. Next time you're in the neighborhood, stop by the bookstore and pick out a Harry Bosch novel, on me."

"That's not necessary, really. It wasn't your fault." He looked down at me, his brown eyes warm and kind.

"I know, but still. Stop by and say hi, then."

"I'll definitely do that. Have a good night now." He closed my car door for me, patted it lightly one time and disappeared into the dark.

5

THE NEXT MORNING, I woke up before the alarm went off and lay in bed for a few minutes before getting up. At least today I hadn't been woken up by Sasquatch's heavy breathing—a real plus. But I did wake up with a sense of restlessness and disappointment. There was only one thing for it: go for a run. And by run, I meant a quick walk.

I got dressed for my run and headed out the door, making my way down the street. It was a beautiful morning and a beautiful time of year. Almost overnight, the redbud and whitebud trees had bloomed and there were explosions of purple and white everywhere. They were my favorite trees and this was my favorite time of year.

As I walked, I thought back to the day before. I thought about Kelly pointing out that I still didn't know what I wanted in life. I thought I had left New York because I wanted a simpler life closer to my parents. But now I wondered if I had left New York simply because I had wanted to get the heck out of New York. I'd read enough self-help books to know that you shouldn't make a decision only because you didn't want the alternative. You shouldn't run away; you should always move toward something. And I thought I had, but when I asked myself about the specifics of what I wanted now, I didn't have much of an answer. Kelly's warning came to mind: *be careful what you wish for*. It sounded so ominous!

A loud bark brought me back to my surroundings. I looked around but didn't see a dog anywhere. I heard the bark again and followed the sound to a big snout that was sticking through a little cut-out square in a wooden fence. I couldn't see what kind of dog it was, but the snout was snarfling at me and letting out barks. I was safe, and I wished the dog would get a life and not worry about someone going for an innocent walk along the street.

Dogs probably didn't have weighty, intellect-challenging questions about the direction their lives were taking. Nope, they were busy sleeping, trying to get belly rubs, and barking at people taking walks. I wasn't a dog person, but I was envious of their dumb-luck *joie de vivre*.

I looked in the front windows of the house. Sitting in one of them was a cat, a big Maine Coon with long hair and regal posture. It was giving me a look like, *Can you believe that guy? I have to deal with this every day*. I felt sorry for the cat and shot it a knowing glance before moving on.

I turned around toward home to get ready for work. I had my cell phone with me, and I thought I might call my parents to chew them out for last night while I walked.

Honestly, they were so exasperating sometimes. They were wonderful people, and of course I loved them dearly, but *still*. I wanted to call them and cuss them out over the phone from a safe distance.

The longer I stayed single, the more they might try to interfere, all in the name of romance. Funny, how everyone who had a partner was always busy trying to match up those of us who didn't. From now on, I vowed to be more on guard against possible blind date ambushes. There was no telling what they might be capable of if they became desperate enough. I would have to be vigilant.

What a disaster last night had been. They'd made me look like a complete and total loser. It was so embarrassing, especially since it happened in front of someone like the Sheriff of Logan County.

Who, on closer inspection, had turned out to be a nice person. He was probably laughing right this minute at what a loser I was. For some reason, I didn't like to imagine him thinking badly of me.

Both of us had been adamant that we weren't looking for any kind of romantic entanglement. So why had it bothered me that he'd been so relieved when I said I didn't want a boyfriend? Was he interested in someone else? Did my spraying breadcrumbs all over the table turn him off? Was he not into women? And again, why did I care?

Yeah, what a disaster of an evening.

On the plus side, we'd ended up having a really nice conversation after my parents left. And he was kind of handsome. Okay, he was pretty good-looking, truth be told. And tall. And that *voice*. But I had told him I wasn't interested, and he had told me the same. So that was that.

I decided not to call my parents just yet. Instead, I got home and got showered and dressed. I had a few minutes to spare, so I sat down in one of the patio chairs on my porch and watched as the girls roamed around their pen looking for errant bits of food. Beryl stood on the roof of the coop and looked at me angrily. You'd think it would be hard to tell if a chicken was staring at you, let alone angrily. But it was different with Beryl. I could feel her eyes boring into me. She was probably willing me to get salmonella from one of the eggs.

Eggs! I let myself into the pen and snuck around to the back of the coop to peek inside. I was eager to see if there were any presents for me. Recently, the ladies hadn't done too well in the egg-laying department, but today I was lucky. Four eggs—jackpot! Enough for a hearty breakfast and then some. As I left the coop, I double-checked that the latch was closed, since Beryl was a professional escape artist. So far, she always made it back home one way or another, but one of these days she'd escape and never return; I just knew it.

I went back in the house and whipped up some sautéed veggies in my cast iron skillet—success! I added a couple of eggs and then toasted up some homemade sourdough wheat bread. Presto! The perfect delicious home-cooked breakfast. It wasn't simply delicious, though; it was also emotionally satisfying. It was like I was a homesteader or a hipster going off the grid. Beverley Green, living off the land. Including wifi and indoor plumbing, natch.

I finished my coffee, freshly ground and hand-poured of course, packed a lunch, and walked to the bookstore since the weather was so nice again. This time though, I wore a heavier jacket.

I used to walk to work in New York too. I would attempt to dodge trash, tourists, taxis, and transients. Most days I was successful. Now, my walk to work was quite different. These days, I didn't have to dodge much, if I caught the streetlights just right.

I passed more redbud trees that were starting to bloom and stopped to look more closely at a particularly beautiful specimen. The tiny buds were magically appearing on the ends of branches that otherwise looked dead. The buds were the most vibrant shade of purple and they made me smile. Spring was beginning to spring, and I couldn't help but feel good, even after last night's disaster. I took in a deep breath, the crisp morning air filling my lungs. It felt better than any deep breath in New York ever had.

When I walked up to the front of my store, I once again imagined I was seeing it for the first time. But again, it felt as if something was missing. I looked the whole storefront over: the door, the windows, the books on display, the name of the shop in the simple, white letters. I stood there a few more seconds before I figured it out. After opening up for business, I made a quick phone call, arranging for some work to be done. Nothing would happen for a week or so, but I couldn't wait. It would be perfect.

I caught up on snail mail and tidied up the cash wrap area. The morning passed quickly, especially since I managed to find plenty of ways to procrastinate. I knew I was going to have to call Leona for an interview for the *Ledger*, and then I was going to have to call the sheriff too. Someday. I didn't feel like calling either of them right now. I'd rather go get my taxes done. And after that embarrassing evening with my parents, I kind of hoped I might never have to see the sheriff again for a long time. Like, ever.

My parents. Ugh. It was about time to call them up to yell at them. But before I could pick up my phone, it started ringing. They were calling me.

"Beverley Green speaking."

"Well?"

"Good morning to you too, Mom," I snapped. I managed to hide my annoyance for about three seconds, pretty good under the circumstances.

"How did it go? What do you think? Did he ask you out on a proper date?" She was totally clueless, my mother. I was going to have to lay it out for her, nice and clear like.

"Mom. If you *ever* do that to me again, I will legally and socially disown you and Dad, then sue you for slander. Or libel. Or for psychological distress, or whatever. And I am totally not kidding."

"What," she moped. "Didn't you like him? He's so *handsome*!"

I rolled my eyes. She couldn't see me, but I knew her mom radar would sense it, nonetheless.

"Stop rolling your eyes at me," she said with more than a little parental warning in her voice. Even though I had known it was coming, it was still scary. "So, I had no idea you two had already met!" she continued. "Maybe he would have asked you out all on his own! Isn't he handsome? You two would make such a cute couple!"

"Uh huh." I looked around for a book to read. I picked up a book on letting things go, written by a Buddhist monk.

"If you would stop dressing like a punk rock chicken farmer, he probably would have asked you out already," she said. "And of course, your attitude leaves a little to be desired sometimes, Beverley Green. You must get that from your father. I swear, both of you are a little hypoglycemic. Have you checked your blood sugar today? I should make you a doctor's appointment..."

I knew I could finish that whole damn book by the Buddhist

monk while my mom kept up her monologue, but I actually was getting a little hungry and I needed to wrap this up. She was probably right about my blood sugar being low, dammit.

"Oh my *god*, mom, you're not getting it. You guys went too far this time. I'm totally happy with my life just the way it is! I don't need, and I definitely don't *want*, you to do anything like this again."

"But we want you to be happy, hon." Her voice did sound sincere and I had no doubt she was. I knew my parents wanted nothing but the best for me. But it was how she went about it all that I had a problem with.

"I *am* happy, mom!"

"You need a man, Beverley! Or is there something you're not telling us? Because if you want to get married to a woman, we are totally okay with that. Well, I am anyway, but I'm sure I can get your father on board. Ooh! Do you and your girlfriend want kids? I want more grandchildren! Maybe you should look for a younger woman..." She sounded like she was excited about the idea I might be gay at this point, since it would at least explain why I didn't have a man in my life.

"No, Mom, I'm not gay. Sorry. I'm just enjoying being single is all."

"No one enjoys being single except for crazy people."

"Well then, I guess I'm crazy."

"Oh, really, Beverley. Now you're just being obstinate."

"Gah! I don't want a boyfriend and I promise you, everything is totally fine. Please forget about trying to set me up."

"Just be careful what you wish for, Beverley Green," she cautioned me.

"Why does everyone keep telling me that? What do you mean by that?"

"Well, it's...you know."

"What? What?"

"Do you want to be all alone? I mean really? No one to watch a movie with? No one to keep your feet warm in bed in the winter? Think it through; that's all I'm saying."

Next she was going tell me I needed to have a plan for my life. "Oh hey, someone just came in the shop, gotta go, bye." I hung up on her. I didn't like doing it; it had been a reaction to what she was saying. Part of me knew she was right.

But this was all too much! It was as if my parents thought that my return to Oklahoma was some kind of admission of defeat on my part. I couldn't get through to them that it was my choice. I was happy, at least for the time being, and I didn't need their help with anything. Hopefully she got the message this time, but somehow, I doubted it. One thing was for sure: Callan might have been a nice guy, but I would *never* give my parents the satisfaction of having picked out the right boyfriend for me. No. Effing. Way.

6

I SPENT most of the afternoon taking care of odds and ends around the store. My work was so glamorous sometimes: ordering paper towels, mopping, cleaning up turtle poop. At least it kept me too busy to do any work for the newspaper, which meant I couldn't call Leona yet. Yeah, that sounded good.

Around four-thirty, I was sitting behind the cash wrap surfing the interwebs when Al and Bill darkened the door to my shop. Mostly it was Bill's stomach that darkened my door, since it blocked out a lot of sunlight. His t-shirt selection today was...interesting. I wanted to laugh and bring legal action against him at the same time. It was a black shirt with *FBI* in gigantic yellow letters on the front. Below that, the smaller letters spelling out *FEMALE BODY INSPECTOR* were just as menacing. He came in and took up a position right inside the front door, standing guard as if he were an actual FBI agent. He was even wearing dark sunglasses, which he kept wearing even though he was indoors. I started to get a little nervous, until he suddenly sneezed, and wiped his nose on the back of his hand and then his pants. Good enough for government work.

"So where can we talk?" Al asked by way of a greeting. He walked up to the counter and looked around the shop like he was expecting a voice-activated doorway to open up that led to my secret meeting room.

What on earth did these two want? I looked around the empty store and held out my hands, palms up. The international symbol for "start talking."

"We want to hire you," he said.

"What exactly do you mean by 'hire'?"

"We have a job for you. We need you to investigate something."

I leaned back and crossed my arms in front of me. I looked up at the ceiling. "Let me think about this for a minute. No."

"But you don't even know what it is yet!" Al pointed out.

"True," I agreed. "But I don't need to know. I'm not an investigator. I'm a bookstore owner. If you have a real problem, go find a real private investigator. Or call the police like a normal person."

"No!" Bill yelled from his spot by the door. "We want you! We want you to be our private investigator. We need something investigated. And it needs to be real private-like."

They didn't want to involve the authorities? What the heck could be going on? I wanted to know, but I wasn't sure knowing would be the best thing for my health. But I couldn't help myself. "Explain," I demanded.

"Okay, so see, it's like this," Al began. "We kind of acquired something and then we lost it. And then we got another one just like the first one, but we lost that too. We need you to do some private detectiving and find them both."

"What on earth are you talking about?" I stood up quickly and walked around the counter to stand in front of Al. "That's exactly the kind of thing the police can help you with. The sheriff seems like a nice guy. Go talk to him. We can call him now if you like."

"Well, see, we can't do that," said Al.

"I'm telling you, I'm not a private detectiving! I mean detective!"

"We don't care. We know you can do it. You wrote that Bigfoot story. That was big-time detectiving work, and that was great! It was a good piece of investigative journalism." Al was trying way too hard to flatter me. Something was definitely wrong.

"Look, guys," I said as I put one arm around Al and started shuffling him slowly toward the door, "I appreciate your confidence in my deductive reasoning skills, I really do. But it's not going to happen." We stopped walking when we got to Bill, who was blocking the entrance and didn't look like he was going anywhere anytime soon.

"We don't want you to deduct anything, dangit. We want you to do some detectiving is all. We can pay; we got some money."

"But I'm telling you, I am not a dang private detective. Go. To. The. Police." Maybe if I spoke slower, it would be more effective.

"We can't exactly do that, Bev. We just can't," said Bill.

"Yeah," continued Al, "we need to keep the law out of this. We want this handled privately."

"Look, will you take the job or not?" Bill asked point-blank.

"No! No, I will not take the job. Now, either buy a book or leave. And either way, go find someone else to help you find your missing stuff."

Unexpectedly, Bill left his post at the door and marched down one of the aisles.

"What are you doing?" I called after him.

"We ain't leaving, so I'm buying a book," he said angrily. Yeah, *that* would teach me!

Al and I had a staring contest until Bill finally came back with a Marvel *Avengers* comic book collection. He tossed it onto the counter where it made a very loud *slap* sound. "I've been wanting this for a long time," he said angrily.

I wasn't sure he knew that even though he was buying a book, it still didn't mean I was taking the job, and that I was still going to kick them out of the store after he paid. But I rang up his purchase anyway. "You want a bag for that?" I asked politely.

"No!"

Al sighed impatiently as I walked back around the counter to usher them to the door. Again.

"We want you. How many times do we have to say it? You aced that Bigfoot thing. We know you're our gal," he said.

"Al, Bill, it's getting late. And you haven't even told me anything about what you're actually wanting. How many times do *I* have to say it? I'm not your gal."

Al and Bill exchanged looks of frustration and they knew they were beat, for the time being at least. "We're not done with you yet, missy. We need your help, and we're gonna get it."

"Yeah? Well, that kind of sounds like a threat, Al." Ooh! Maybe now I had a legitimate excuse to call the sheriff. Well, maybe not quite yet. I felt reasonably confident that I could handle these guys myself, threat or no threat. But still, I didn't like Al's tone. "Okay, time for you guys to skedaddle. If you'll excuse me, I have some work to do. And my phone is ringing, so..."

I opened the door for them. They left silently, but I was sure I hadn't heard the end of it. "Enjoy your book," I called out to Bill.

I paced around the store again, relieved they were gone. Sometimes when I wasn't sure what to do next, I would mill around until inspiration hit. I walked in circles, weaving between aisles. Those damn Turner cousins! It was like they were straight out of a movie, but I wasn't sure if it was a science fiction flick, a comedy, or a mockumentary. Finally, my brain screamed *enough already!* and switched gears. The sheriff popped into my mind once again.

And there went my brain, off on another man-gent, and I didn't bother fighting it. I thought about Callan's warm laugh and dry sense of humor. Dry like toast, just the way I liked it. And I recollected his stubbled, chiseled jaw. I began to wonder...

Oh man. I shouldn't be thinking these things, I admonished myself. I was a grown-up and I should be thinking grown-up things like how I should vote in the next election or researching proper flossing techniques. And then there was the fact that we both told each other we weren't interested. Oh yeah, that. But weren't these thoughts about scratchy beard stubble and warm brown eyes the kind of thoughts that romance novel writers had? I was reasoning hard with myself. I didn't want to stop thinking romance novel thoughts.

If only my parents hadn't blindsided me. I wondered how often people tried to set the sheriff up on blind dates with their daughters or sisters or friends. He was a good-looking man. I'm sure I wasn't the only one who thought so.

Was he still single? If so, why? Was there something wrong with him? Omigod, why did I even care? Nonetheless, I hoped he wasn't thinking the same things about me and wondering what was wrong with me. But if he was, it would have been fair; I was still single too. Not because there was something wrong with me, though. At least, I didn't think there was anything wrong with me. Nope. I was single because I wanted to be single. So, I decided to give him the benefit of the doubt also. He sure was nice. And so very tall.

On top of all the other reasons I gave myself as to why I didn't want a boyfriend was the fact that he wasn't my type. I hadn't ever had a type, but if I did, I couldn't imagine he would wear a cowboy hat and boots and a sheriff's badge. Except maybe on Halloween. I always figured I'd end up with a nerdy, bookish kind of guy, not a frontier swashbuckler. But gosh, Sheriff Branch was so...oh dear.

As I continued to walk through the store, I passed by the romance section and decided it needed some restocking. There were only a few minutes left before the store closed, but I had time to get a few books out, so I pulled down some overstock from the top of the bookshelf and placed it on the floor. It would need to be alphabetized before I could add it to the shelves. I randomly grabbed a book with a half-naked man on the cover. Well no, on closer inspection he was about three-quarters naked. I wondered if I should have a man like that on my romance novel cover, if I ever wrote the damn thing. I didn't think so. Mine would be more... chaste. I started thinking about the sheriff again. So very tall. *Dammit!*

I had almost all the books put up when my not-so-law-abiding reverie was broken by the sound of the front door opening. A customer—yay! I always had time for customers. I put up the last book and walked to the front. I looked down to shake off my t-shirt, which had gotten dusty from pulling down books. When I looked back up again, I had to stop short in order not to run right into something very tall. Wearing a cowboy hat. It was a close call.

"Sheriff!" I exclaimed, balancing on my tiptoes for a second before landing flat-footed again.

"It's Callan, remember?" He had put out his hands to catch me, but when I didn't fall forward, he lowered his arms to his sides again.

"As long as you're not here to arrest me," I said.

"I hadn't planned on it." He stepped back a little, looked at me, then stared at my waist. "But have you broken any laws?"

Was this guy leering at me? Some nerve! I looked down to where his eyes were drawn and realized that I had inadvertently hiked up my t-shirt while I was trying to dust myself off. Oh nice. I just flashed the sheriff.

"No sir," I said, pulling down my shirt. *Someone please help me*, I silently pleaded.

"Well, at least you didn't mistake me for Bigfoot this time," he mused. "Progress."

The lamest nervous fake laugh ever came out of my mouth. Well, at least I was consistent and still making an idiot out of myself in front of good-looking men.

"So, uh, what's new? Need a book?" I asked as neutrally as I could.

When he removed his hat, I could tell he'd been wearing it a while because his hair was smooshed into the shape of the inside of a cowboy hat. He ran his fingers through it to unsmoosh it. Maybe it was because I had been shelving romance books, but I found the act incredibly endearing. No, it was actually downright sexy. *Dammit again!*

"I, uh," he started, but then backed up a few steps toward the door.

"Need a recommendation today? Want to try a new genre?" I

could see he was uncomfortable, but I had no idea why. Maybe he really was there to arrest me. His discomfort was making me uncomfortable and when I got uncomfortable, I started talking too much.

"Are you sure you're not here to arrest me? Did Leona send you over here?" I asked suspiciously.

Being uncomfortable apparently had the opposite effect on him, because he still didn't say anything, so I kept on talking. "Oh man, I bet it *was* Leona. Did she tell you that I—" But before I could incriminate myself, he cut me off.

"No, Leona didn't send me. And I didn't come by for a book either. I came by because, uh..." He shifted his weight from foot to foot and looked down at the ground, his hat in his hands. "I just wanted to tell you that I enjoyed last night. It was...unexpected. It was nice."

"Yes, it was," I smiled. "It's like there was no pressure or anything, since neither of us want any attachments. But I am so, so sorry about my parents. Please, don't you want to pick out a book? Not that it could make up for what they did."

"Well, that's just it," he said, shifting his weight again.

"What, you want *two* books? Okay, that's still fair, but could you make them paperbacks?" I smiled and walked back around the counter to make a note of my 'charitable donation.'

"No, I don't want any books. Not today, anyway."

"Then what?" I had no idea what he was after. He was being vague, and I could tell that I was about to get grumpy.

Right then the shop filled with the sound of rain pounding on the roof. It had come right out of nowhere, like spring storms often did. We both looked up, surprised by the intensity of the noise. It sounded like a rain that knew if it didn't do its damnedest to be the hardest rain ever, it would get fired and never work in this town again. Callan walked to the front of the store and looked outside. "Wow," he said, squinting out the windows. "Toad strangler."

"Toad *what*?"

"Heavy downpour. Drowns frogs."

Well, that was a new one.

"Oh." I couldn't think of what else to say to that, so I just stood next to him and looked out the window too. It was coming down so hard, we couldn't see the other side of the street.

"Well, that's great," I muttered. "I didn't bring an umbrella." Now I was officially grumpy.

"I've got one in the truck. I can walk you to your car," he said over the sound of the rain.

"No, see, I walked to work today. Shoot" I griped. "This is going to suck."

"You walked? All the way from your place?"

"You really remember where I live?"

"I'm the sheriff, Bev. I know everything about the citizens under my protection."

"Everything, huh? I doubt that," I said coyly. His eyebrows floated up in surprise. "Anyway," I continued. "Yes, I walked. I do most nice days. But didn't know today wasn't going to be a nice day."

"Then let me give you a ride home."

I considered this as an option. Truth be told, I felt a little uncomfortable around him. We weren't interested in seeing each other, but I also hadn't been able to stop thinking about him and I didn't know what to do about it. The alternative to an awkward ride home with Callan, however, would be a walk in the cold spring rain, without an umbrella. The awkward car ride won.

"Okay, thanks," I said. "Let me get my stuff."

Callan put his hat back on and went out to his SUV to get his umbrella while I shut down the computer and gathered my things. When I heard the door open again, I didn't look up. "Almost ready," I called out.

"For what?" a woman's voice asked. More specifically, it was Leona's voice. Uh oh. She never visited my store unless she was trying to evict me.

"Oh hi, Leona," I said as I came around the cash wrap. "Was

there something you needed? I've already closed down the computer for the day."

Leona closed her big flowery umbrella and left it by the front door before walking in and straight towards Jimmy Perez's manger. The one thing I had going for me was that she liked my turtle. Other than that, I was on her perpetual shit list.

"Well, I usually buy all my books online, but I needed something to read tonight, so I thought I'd stop by to see what you have." She was wearing a scarf around her head that was also flowery and matched her dress. And purse. And umbrella. Her flowery rain galoshes were dripping onto my floor. Which was her floor.

"Okay..."

Callan came back in, stomping his boots on the floor mat. It was raining even harder now. "Ready to go?" he asked. Then he looked up and saw Leona standing by the manger. "Oh, hello, Leona," he said stoically. I was pretty sure I saw Leona blush. I thought back to Christmas, when Leona had threatened to evict me from the store because of yet another misunderstanding, this one involving a hamster. The sheriff had given me some unsolicited advice and told me to present Leona with a giant bottle of Hendrick's gin as a Christmas gift. Then unbeknownst to me, he proceeded to get her drunk and convince her not to kick me out. Now I wondered what exactly had transpired during that drinking session. On the other hand, I didn't want to know. Besides, she didn't seem like his type. I hoped.

"Leona needs to pick out a book," I explained. "Did you know what you're wanting?" I asked her.

She looked at me with that flat-lipped glare of hers, her eyes narrowing ever so slightly. She was sizing me up, but I didn't know why. "I'll just be one minute," she said. Her gaze turned from me to the sheriff and she sized us both up. Then she moseyed down an aisle, out of view.

The sheriff and I stood there, looking at each other until I couldn't take it anymore and looked away. "It's okay if you have to leave," I said. "I'm sure this rain will let up soon." As if on cue, we heard a big clap of thunder roll across the sky.

"It's not a problem." He walked over to look at Jimmy, who was climbing over baby Jesus to get to some lettuce. I turned the computer back on and waited.

Leona knew that the shop was closed, but she had come in and started to browse anyway. It was a passive-aggressive move, and I was starting to get a might bit mad. But I wanted the sale, and more importantly, I didn't want to piss off my landlady. I was about to go look for her when she reappeared, coming up the aisle that contained the mystery books. She took her sweet time walking over to the cash register.

"This will do," she said, putting the book on the counter.

I can tell a lot about a person by the kind of books they buy. If someone buys just one book from me it's a little harder, but I can still use my bookish sense to get a feel for them. If someone is a regular shopper at my store, I can tell a whole bunch about them because I can look for patterns. This was only the second time Leona had bought a book from me—and my shop had been open for almost a year. However, her choice spoke volumes.

On first glance, the book appeared to be a simple cozy mystery. The covers all looked the same; they were either an oil painting of a bakery still life, or a cartoonish drawing of a round-eyed, buxom beauty standing on a small-town street lined with cute little shops. The titles were all puns, usually about cupcakes or knitting or gardening. Cozy mysteries were stories about cute perky women or matronly sassy women who solved murders that never seemed to involve any blood or gore. This was one of those kinds of books, but I also knew for a fact that it had some pretty racy, steamy bits in it. Like, the kind with naughty words and everything. How did I know? Market research, of course.

The paperback said right on the cover in big letters that it was book two in a four-book series. This meant that Leona had read the first book and was now back for more. She came across so chastely, but perhaps Leona was not who she appeared to be. And we all know I am never wrong.

As I rang up her book and ran her credit card, she turned away from me and looked at the sheriff. "What are you doing here, sheriff?" Her voice was sweet, but her face was unreadable. "Is Beverley in some kind of trouble?" I bet she was hoping I was.

"No, ma'am," said Callan. "I'm giving Beverley a ride home."

"I'll be ready in a minute," I said from behind the register. Leona turned and set her eagle-eye stare on me again.

"Hmph." I heard it come out of her mouth, just barely. Her face hadn't moved, but even with the roar of the storm outside, I'd heard her *hmph* me. She didn't like that I was friends with Callan. Well, that was tough toodles for her.

"Thanks for stopping in, Leona," I smiled. "Let me know how you like that book." I walked around to the front of the cash wrap and started walking her to the door. She came with me but gave Callan a suspicious stare as we passed him by. He just smiled blandly.

Leona left without another word. Whatever! After I picked up my things, Callan and I left too. He held his umbrella over my head as I locked the front door and then escorted me to the passenger side of his SUV. As we walked, I felt his hand on the small of my back again. He placed it there so lightly, it was like it had always been there. And it felt nice. *Dammit dammit dammit.*

The drive to my place wasn't very long, so there wasn't much time to talk. It was a little awkward, but not as bad as I'd feared. We were silent, listening to the wipers on the windshield. The sky was finally starting to clear a little. Of course that would happen, once I got a ride home. It's Oklahoma, after all. To paraphrase Will Rogers, if you didn't like the weather here, just wait fifteen minutes.

Callan pulled into the driveway of my house. We both got out and started walking toward the front door, and I wondered why he was accompanying me. It wasn't raining anymore, and I was pretty sure I could make the twenty steps to the door without getting attacked by a bear or my landlady. I shot him a questioning look, but he was watching the ground as he took long strides up the drive.

He waited silently as I unlocked my front door. "Okay," I said politely, "I think I've got it from here. Thanks so much for the ride. I appreciate it." The door opened and I prepared to say goodbye and go inside. But he kept standing there, looking kind of confused. Or at least I thought it was a confused look. Was it confusion? It could have been a pensive look. Or maybe an angry look. Or... something else? I didn't know him well enough to tell. He just kept standing there, squinting at my lawn.

"Is everything okay?" I asked.

"Yup."

Okay then.

"Did you need something?"

"Nope."

"Well then, thanks again for the ride; maybe I'll see you around." I really needed to work on my cool person dialogue.

"Sounds good," he said, finally turning to look at me. He was still kind of squinty-eyed, still kind of confused looking. Maybe he was hungry. Should I offer him a snack?

But before I could, he smiled, and then silently turned and walked back to his SUV. He got in, backed out of the driveway, and drove on down the street. I wasn't sure what had just happened, and I wasn't sure how I felt about it.

7

Wednesday came and went without incident or excitement, and on Thursday morning I started to think that Al and Bill had given up on trying to hire me, since I hadn't heard or seen them since they'd stopped by on Tuesday. A girl could hope.

However, there was one thing I couldn't put off any longer; it was time to call Leona to schedule an interview. I would have done it the night before, but the last time I called her in the evening, I had interrupted her viewing of *The Bachelor* and she got mad at me. Since I had no idea what was on network television these days, I thought it might be safer to call her during working hours. I could have asked her in person on Monday when she came by for her book, but I was too surprised by her purchase, and too nervous in front of Callan to remember that I'd needed to ask them both.

I opened The Book Store for business and helped a few moms find some required reading for their third graders. When they left, I made the call to Leona, surprised when she actually answered. We set an interview appointment for the following Tuesday at two o'clock. It was the first time slot she had available for me. We would meet at Stacy's, during a thirty-minute window she had in between her hair appointment and a meeting with her attorney.

It was going to be an article about how wonderful she was, so I thought she would be excited about it and eager to get together. But she was making me wait because it was me. When I first leased the space for my bookstore the year before, she'd somehow gotten it into her head that I was running a "porn shop," instead of a book shop. Ironic, considering the book she'd just bought.

She had subsequently vandalized her own property in the hopes of scaring me into breaking the lease. When I discovered the vandal was the property owner, I got Kelly involved, and Leona and I came to a tentative truce. It didn't help when last fall I discovered she was also the owner of the rent house I lived in, and she sort of discovered that I might have illegal chickens in her backyard. It was like she held me to a different set of standards than she did anyone else. It felt like the woman would always think of me as an outsider, and never quite good enough to be anything more.

I wondered if the article about the sheriff would go any better or if he'd agree to it at all. He hadn't sounded all that excited about it when I mentioned it the other night. Maybe I could get him excited about it. Wait, that didn't sound right. The article. I could get him excited about an interview. Excited. Heh. Wait, what was I talking about again?

I tried to forget about the idea of an excited sheriff and moved on to more grown-up pursuits. I figured I should give Mark an update on how my articles were going, so on my way to Hoboken for coffee on my lunch break, I stopped by the *Ledger* offices to pay him a visit.

"What do you mean you don't have an article for me this week?" he asked without looking up from the two computer screens that took up most of his desk. All I could see was the top of his head over the screens and a half-eaten sandwich lying on the desk.

"When you assigned me the stories, you didn't say which should come first, and technically you didn't give me a deadline for either." I knew he was a busy guy, but I was getting tired of talking to the back of his computer screens, so I moved to stand next to his desk. Now I could see what was on the screens. He was playing some kind of computer game involving cats. I tried not to laugh out loud, but it didn't work so well.

He quickly tabbed over to another application and stood up to draw my attention away from what he'd been doing. "God dammit, don't sneak up on me like that."

"Sorry," I said a bit gleefully, "I didn't realize I was all that stealthy."

"Look, Bev. I've got stuff to do, so you'd best be on your way. Or is there anything else you want to bug the shit out of me about?"

I stopped laughing and faked a ponder. "Nope, I think that was it. Listen, you can throw me another story this week if you want. Let me know if you need some help with anything." I thought this might make up for me laughing at his lunchtime cat gaming.

"Well, as a matter of fact, I *do* have something for you." He sounded a little too happy, and my stomach started to feel jittery.

"Oh yeah?"

"Yeah," he said, picking up a notepad and thumbing through it. "Ah, here it is. Al and Bill Turner."

My good mood vanished. "What about them?"

"Apparently, they've seen Bigfoot again. I want you to talk to them, get the scoop and put together another article. Let's see where this thing goes." He tore out a page from the notebook and handed it to me.

"They didn't happen to specifically request me, did they?" I asked tentatively, taking the paper and folding it as small as I could, without looking at what was written on it.

"How did you know?"

"Just a hunch." I sighed. "You don't seriously expect me to do this again, do you?"

"I'm as serious this time as I was last time." That was pretty serious.

"Mark, for reals, you can't do this to me. I'm already known as the Bigfoot Lady around town. I'll never live it down as it is."

"You offered to help..." He tried to hold back a smile.

"You're loving this, aren't you?"

He didn't say anything, just kept trying not to smile. He was pretty cute when he was trying not to smile. I knew I was beat. He was my boss and he was cute.

"Okay, fine. But for the record, I'm not happy about this."

"See you later, Bev." He sat back down and took another bite of his sandwich. I left, feeling a lot grumpier than I did when I'd walked in the building.

I walked over to Hoboken and chatted with Seth as he made my flat white. I liked to talk to him when we had time; he had his finger on the pulse of the Guthrie hipster population. Seth had moved here a few years ago to open the coffee shop. He roasted coffee beans after the morning rush died down and was doing well selling wholesale to local restaurants. He'd even gotten some national recognition once he set up an online ordering system. His was a great example of a new type of small-town life. Today, he informed me of a photography exhibit that was opening the following month over at Monty's Art N Frames. It sounded interesting, and I made a note to talk to Mark about writing a story on it.

I decided to drink my coffee there, so I sat down at one of the small tables. I wanted to read my book, but instead my mind wandered to all those important thoughts I should be having but wasn't. Like coming up with a plot for a romance novel. And there was that small question of what the hell was I doing with my life. And the part about whether I was successful enough by whoever's standards I was supposed to be measuring myself by. How was I supposed to know where I was supposed to be right now? These were big questions. I didn't feel much like reading anymore, and now I needed an Emergency Beer instead of a flat white. I was starting to feel angsty. But before I could swing into full panic mode, I was rudely interrupted.

"We brought you a present," someone said behind me. I spun around to see Bill and Al. I didn't care about no stinkin' present right now, especially from them. They could bring me a new car and I'd still be grumpy about how they'd roped me into their mystery mess.

"Humph."

Bill tossed a plastic Walmart grocery bag onto the table in front of me, almost knocking over my coffee. "Hey!" I yelped.

"Sorry about the gift wrapping, but we're supposed to reuse or recycle, so that there's your gift bag. See how I tied the straps? That's the bow!" he said proudly, sitting down next to me. His t-shirt today was the best yet. It was yellow and displayed a caricature drawing of a slice of Swiss cheese with a smiling face. *I CUT THE CHEESE,* it said under the drawing. I made a mental note to ask him where he got these gems. Later. When I wasn't mad at him.

Al took the seat across from me, setting down his iced coffee.

"You guys aren't playing fair, going to the paper," I complained.

"Open the damn bag," said Al. He sure was getting me excited about this mystery gift.

I sighed and reached for the bag. I had to tear it apart because Bill had tied the handles together too tightly. I pulled out a dark grey t-shirt. Was Bill giving me a prized item from his t-shirt stash? I unfolded it to see what was on it. On the front of the t-shirt was a hand-drawn Bigfoot, half monster, half hipster, and under it were the words, *GUTHRIE SASQUATCH APPRECIATION CLUB.*

"You're the president!" Bill said proudly, pointing to the shirt.

I had to admit it was a good-looking shirt. I started to get a little emotional. Me, president of something! Bill looked proud.

I was about to thank him but remembered I was supposed to be mad. They wanted me to forget what they'd done, but it wasn't going to work today, no sirree. I put the shirt in my bag.

"So I refused your offer. Then you go behind my back and get the *Ledger* involved, and you try to sweeten it all with a t-shirt?" I asked.

Seth came over and brought Bill his drinks, a cortado and a glass of mineral water. He had surprisingly refined taste in coffee drinks. "Yeah! And it worked, right?" he asked.

I glared at him.

“We could still pay you, like for the detectiving,” Al added.

“I haven’t told you how much I charge.”

“We don’t care.”

“You might not like what I uncover.”

They looked at each other, a little worried now. Maybe they hadn’t thought about that. Maybe they had some deep dark secrets they were hiding. If so, I for one didn’t want to know about them.

“We don’t care about that, either,” Al finally said. He leaned forward in his chair, one hawk eye trained on me carefully.

Right then my butt buzzed, informing me I had a new text. I pulled my phone out of my back pocket to read it.

405-555-5555: *YOu look nice tofay.*

I looked around the coffee shop for someone who might have sent me this text. All I saw were Al and Bill staring at me expectantly. My gaze swept to the windows, and right outside I saw a tall figure in a cowboy hat talking to a portly older gentleman. They were in an intense conversation, but the man in the hat glanced inside the coffee shop, right at me, and nodded ever so slightly. The sheriff had texted me. I hoped he had used his personal cell phone; I didn’t want to be accused of any kind of unlawful flirting on the taxpayer’s dime.

Based on the typos, I guessed he didn’t send too many texts. Maybe it was hard for him to type on a little keyboard with those long fingers. He’d looked away again, but I smiled anyway as I put my phone back in my pocket. I didn’t even care that I’d never given him my phone number.

“Ahem,” Al cleared his throat pointedly. Oh, right. Detectiving.

“Look, I’m not going to find Bigfoot for you.”

“Yeah, but finding Bigfoot might be an internal part of the mystery,” Bill said. I was pretty sure he’d meant *integral*. But perhaps it was internal too.

I was stuck here, and they knew it. Shit. “Okay then,” I started.

"This next statement does not in any way mean that I am working for you, but start explaining." I pulled out my notepad and pencil. Usually the two of them never said anything worth writing down, but it wouldn't hurt to be ready in case this time was an exception.

They looked at each other triumphantly. Al scooted his chair in a little closer and began explaining in a low voice. "It started a couple months ago. I got this sheep, see, and then it disappeared."

I almost dropped my pencil. This was going to go about as well as when I interviewed him about his Bigfoot sighting last year.

"You got just one sheep?" I asked.

"That was all I needed." Of course it was.

I tried to write something in my reporter's notebook, but my pencil lead broke. I didn't think it would matter much.

"Then the first sheep went missing, so I got another one. And it up and disappeared too."

"Okay, two missing sheep."

"Now, this is where it gets tricky," said Al in an even lower voice. He leaned forward, over the table. "I sort of borrowed the sheep, see."

"You...borrowed two sheep." I couldn't believe I was saying these words together in a sentence. "I'm not following, Al. Start from the top."

"It's like this," said Bill, but he didn't get any further because Al reached out and punched him in the arm to get him to shut up.

"I'll tell the story, thank you very much," Al told his cousin. He turned back to me. "It's like this. Our church has a living nativity scene every year for Christmas. Biggest one in town. It's world famous even! Every January, we pick the person who's gonna produce the next year's show. So, they got plenty of time to put together a good one. I got picked, see, so I'm gonna be putting on the nativity scene this year. And ya know, I want to be *in* the show, not just produce it. It's real important, you know!"

"Yeah," Bill added. "Getting picked to produce the show is a big deal!"

This part made sense; I knew that Christmas was a Really Big

Deal in Guthrie, which had been the first territorial capital of Oklahoma before it became a state. Oklahoma City stole the title in 1910, but up till then, Guthrie was number one and the town's Territorial Christmas celebration was a huge production. Downtown was decorated with lights and garland, and people dressed up in old-fashioned clothes and walked around singing carols and drinking cider. It was kind of like Christmas in New York. Rockefeller Center maybe. Only with less cultural diversity and more horse poop.

I realized Al was waiting for some acknowledgement on my part. "I'll bet!" I exclaimed.

He seemed satisfied with that because he continued his story. "I got some problems with sheep," he said with sadness in his voice. "Some kind of traumatic childhood experience that my therapist says I've blocked out, but we're working through it."

My jaw dropped. A traumatic childhood experience? With a sheep? This was the stuff that people turned into horrendously inappropriate jokes. I prayed that Al wouldn't elaborate any further.

"Anyways," he continued, "I wanted to get a sheep so I could start practicing for Christmas. Only I didn't want to spend the money buying one because I didn't have no need to keep it very long. So, I decided to borrow one." Here he stopped and motioned for Bill to bring him some water. I couldn't bring myself to write any of this down, so I sipped my coffee and we waited in silence. After Bill came back with a glass of water and he'd had a few sips, Al continued.

"Anyways, Bill here found a good sheep source and we planned to give it back before it was ever missed. So, there I was, with my borrowed sheep. I thought I'd just practice a bit, you know, spend some time with it, get used to being around it. My therapist said it would be okay if I tried it. The first day went fine; I went out in the afternoon and had a few beers with it. The little fella was nice enough. I made sure he was safe in the backyard that night, but when I went out the next morning, he was gone. Just up and disappeared, he did."

"That explains one sheep, but how did you lose two sheep?"

"Well, I kept hoping the little guy would show back up. I waited a few weeks, but he never came back. But I still wanted to practice, so I went and got me a second sheep. I figured I'd hang onto the second one and when the first one came back, I'd return 'em both. But then after one night, that second sheep vanished too!"

"And *now* you want to try to find them?" I asked. "When did the second one go missing?"

"Just last week. Now we need your help. I gotta find those sheep so's I can give them back to their owner."

"Whose sheep are they, Al?"

"Oh, that's not really important." He waved his hand nonchalantly. "You just find 'em, and I'll return 'em."

"So the thing about the Bigfoot sighting..."

Bill looked down and cleared his throat but said nothing.

"Yeah, well," said Al, "You weren't gonna talk to us no more, so we had to take desperate measures."

"We weren't fibbing," said Bill. "I mean, okay, we were kinda fibbing, but we do think that Bigfoot could be involved. It makes sense, doesn't it?" His voice rose in pitch as he got more excited about the possibilities.

There was so much *nope* going through my head. I should have known it would be something weird like this. I could kick myself. How on earth had I managed to get tangled up in this nonsense? But maybe they were right and maybe Sasquatch actually was involved. I couldn't rule it out anymore, not after last year, even though I thought it was all certifiably stupid.

"So, where d'you think you'll start?" asked Bill.

"I'll start by heading back to the bookstore," I said, standing up and gathering my things.

"Oh, no you don't. We've hired you already," Al countered.

"We got that patient-doctor confidential thing. We told you our story and now you have to help."

It wasn't even worth my time to point out the four hundred things that were wrong with what he'd just said. The two of them were beating me down, plain and simple. They were winning. In a way, I felt bad for Al and Bill; they were probably under a lot of mental anguish from having misplaced two sheep. Besides, even though it was all ridiculous, it couldn't be all that hard to find out what really happened, right?

"I can't believe I'm doing this," I sighed. Al gasped with anticipation. "Tell you what, I'll stop by your place on Saturday afternoon to check things out. Say around two."

"Can't you start today?" Al asked, wringing his hands. "I gotta find those sheep."

"Yeah, but how long have they been missing, and how long did it take you to ask for help? I think it can wait a few more days."

"Yeah, but—"

"I've got a bookstore to run guys," I insisted. I raised my hands, palms up. "Plus, some other work to do for the *Ledger*."

Al and Bill exchanged a look. "Dangit, you drive a hard bargain, missy," said Al. "Just you remember though, not a word about the missing, uh, artifacts to anyone." He shot me a knowing glance, and they filed out of the coffee shop. I didn't have a chance to explain that sheep weren't artifacts, but it wouldn't have made a difference anyway.

When I was sure they were gone, I bussed my empty cup. On my way out, I started laughing. I didn't care that the other customers were staring at me like I had just landed on this planet. This was the funniest thing that had happened to me in Guthrie so far. These guys wanted me to find two sheep! That had been missing for weeks! And I was being forced into it! But then again, I didn't mind helping. Al and Bill were a little strange sometimes, but if they were in some kind of trouble, maybe I could help. And maybe I was the tiniest bit curious.

I walked out the front door of Hoboken, still smiling at the ridiculousness of my situation. I needed to come up with a way to find two missing sheep. Maybe this was the moment that I'd been reading all those mystery novels for. I was lost in thought when a voice to my left made me jump.

"Hello."

The voice was smooth and deep and gave me goose bumps. I turned to see the sheriff leaning against the wall, his arms folded across his chest and his long legs crossed at the ankles. The phrase *tall drink of water* floated into my mind.

"Have you been waiting for me?"

"Doing surveillance. Some shady characters hang around these places. Can't trust people who drink coffee in the middle of the day." He shifted his weight and pushed off the wall.

"I got your text," I said, starting to blush. "But I couldn't text you back, I was in a meeting. I mean interview."

"Glad it went through. I don't text much."

"It went through fine. I guess I don't have to give you my phone number, huh?"

He let out a small laugh that was so sweet, it dripped honey all over my shoes. "I've got your number."

Yeah, he probably did.

He fell into step next to me. "Need a ride anywhere?"

"No, I'm fine, thanks. I'm just heading back to the bookstore."

"I'll walk with you. Can I still take you up on your offer of a free book?"

"Sure!"

We walked side by side in the sunshine, exchanging a few pleasantries about the weather before falling into an easy silence. It hit me how different he was from most people I knew. So many people were parodies of themselves, trying to be something they weren't. But Callan seemed genuine, straightforward, and honest with no pretense or guile. He seemed like the real deal.

As we turned off of Division Street, we passed by Barb's Salon, the place where Leona and her floral-clad lady gang hung out. I turned to look at the sheriff and was about to say something, when we literally ran into Leona. She had been hurrying into the shop from her car and hadn't seen us on the sidewalk.

"Whoa!" Callan extended a long arm to steady her as she came to an abrupt stop, two inches from my face.

"We're going to have to stop running into each other like this," I said, trying to keep the mood light, but feeling fear in my guts.

"Yes, we are," she said curtly. She turned to Callan and smiled. "Hello, Sheriff."

"Leona."

"Did you get the complaint I filed?" she asked him.

"Yup."

"And?"

"And it's been filed."

She waited for more of a reply, but he didn't give one. It looked like they were going to have a staring contest. If it came to it, I would put my money on him any day.

Finally, Leona broke. "Okay then," she said, and turned to look at me. Then she walked into the beauty shop.

"What complaint?" I asked as we continued our walk.

"Nothing," he mumbled. "She files a lot of complaints."

"Did it involve me?"

"No comment," he said, and I could tell he was trying not to smile.

"Well, if it's something that goes on my permanent record, let me know, okay?"

"This isn't elementary school, Bev. She can't lower your grade."

"No, but she might prevent me from getting into a good college."

He made a quiet sound that must have been a laugh, and we kept walking.

When we got to the store, I gathered a few books for him to look at. "You might like these," I said as I put them down on the counter. I stood next to him as he looked at his choices. He picked one up and read the back cover. He moved a little closer to me and picked up a second book. His arm brushed up against mine, and I didn't move out of the way.

"I don't know," he finally sighed, lifting one shoulder as a sign of resignation. "How about you pick one for me? They all look good."

"Okay, try this one then." I handed him *The Cuckoo's Calling* by Robert Galbraith. "It's really good. I'm reading the second book in this series right now, so when you finish this one, we could talk about it."

"Perfect," he said, taking the book from me and tucking it under his arm. "Thanks."

"You're welcome." I waited for him to make a move for the door, but he just stood there. I was beginning to understand his silences. He was thinking about something he wanted to say. I decided to wait it out, so I stood my ground and watched him.

"So..." His voice trailed off and I had a feeling that this might take a while. I moved back around the counter and sat down on my stool, waiting for him to continue. I hoped whatever it was wasn't bad news.

"So," he started again. "What are you doing this weekend?"

Well, I'll be a monkey's bookseller. I hadn't expected *that*. "Not much," I answered lightly, "probably re-alphabetizing books here at the store; it's a never-ending battle. And maybe some reading. Oh, and Al Turner invited me out to his place."

"What for?"

"Well, I guess he wants me to take a look at something," I said. I couldn't tell him any more than that without giving away that Al had stolen something, so I tried another tack. "I'm supposed to write an article about...about..." I couldn't bring myself to say it out loud. This new tack was no better than the old tack. "...About some stuff. I guess I have to interview him." It would have to do.

"Oh."

"How about you?" I asked. I figured that we were making small talk because he was trying to avoid going to do something he didn't want to do and chatting with me was a way to procrastinate. It's what I would have done, anyway.

"I'm on call this weekend."

"Like you have to be on standby to go catch bad guys?" I marveled at my spectacular lack of eloquence.

"Something like that, yeah." He strolled over to the display table full of new releases and casually looked at the stacks of books. "Do you eat breakfast?"

This gave me pause. "Are there people out there who don't?"

"I guess so."

"Well, that's just crazy. Of course I eat breakfast! It's my favorite meal of the day." I loved making breakfast and I was good at making breakfast, unlike dinners, which could be hit or miss.

Callan nodded silently and moved on to the next table. I waited for him to say something else breakfast-related, but he remained quiet, just looking at books. Then, I did it. It wasn't like anyone used mind control on me or anything. I knew I was doing it, and decided to do it anyway, despite my parents. I didn't do it sheepishly; I didn't do it meekly. I did it assertively, with an air of confidence and bravery. I did it as a gut reaction, without using too much logic. And then I made a mental note to remember all this because it would be great copy for a romance novel.

"Would you like to come over for breakfast on Sunday?" Breakfast didn't count as a *date*, right? So, we were both still keeping with our stated desire to not get involved with anyone. I mean, what could happen at *breakfast,* right?

"Okay," he answered, practically before I'd finished asking. "Can I bring anything?"

I was no dummy. I knew how to play this. "Chocolate donuts," I told him.

8

Friday morning, I woke up with a start, and for a few seconds I couldn't remember what day it was, and I immediately went into a panic that I was late for something. After a few deep breaths, I remembered it was Friday and I only had to work a half day today. Yay! But after a few more deep breaths, I realized I *was* running late.

I got up and got going, trying to move a little faster than usual, but still not hurrying. There is nothing worse than hurrying your way through breakfast. I used to do it on a regular basis when I lived in New York. Finally, I'd caught on that breakfast should be three things: packed with protein, large, and never hurried. Today I tried my best, but I did end up having to take some of my breakfast with me to finish at the store.

The chickens had picked up on the fact I was a bit stressed; there were no eggs waiting for me and Beryl tried to fly the coop twice while I gave them food and water. She knew I didn't have time for her bitchy antics, the ungrateful hen. One day she would be sorry. She made me sorry most days, but someday the tables would be turned. I was carefully biding my time.

To save time, I drove to work instead of walking, but still accidentally ended up at Missy's for a chocolate old-fashioned donut. I swear, I had no idea how this kept happening.

Once I got to work, I finished my breakfast and donut and kept busy by checking stock levels, before I spent a little time working on marketing. The Book Store didn't rely on social media much, but we had a presence, nonetheless. You pretty much had to these days. Plus, it was easy to take photos of books with pretty covers, paired with a vase of flowers or a pair of reading glasses, or simply placed in front of the exposed brick wall that ran down one side of my shop. Last Christmas, the shop became semi-famous on Instagram when people started posting photos of themselves with the shop turtle. Jimmy was all over Insta now, and people would message me, asking how he was. So, I posted regular Jimmy updates too. Today I took a picture of him sitting in his water dish.

I did a little print advertising in the *Ledger* from time to time, and in the school football programs, but not all that much. I hoped I could rely on simply on good service, a good selection, and good luck. So far it was working.

The longer I was in business, the more I got a feel for what the locals liked to read, what the tourists wanted to buy, and what the schools needed. I was slowly learning to tailor my inventory to fit the needs of the town, and it was helping me increase my sales. I didn't have an overarching plan, per se. Did I need one?

Oh dear, not only was I lacking a life plan and a novel plan, I also didn't have a bookstore plan. All the business coaches trying to get my attention on social media were telling me I needed a business plan. And the life coaches wanted to help me with my life plan. I needed a coaching coach to help me with my coaching plan.

I had to get up and walk around to take a few deep breaths before sitting back down to finish up my work. By the time I was done, I had avoided any further mental breakdowns or yelling fits. I gave myself a high five.

Around noon, the door opened, and I looked up in time to see Julie walking in. With blue hair. Her hair had previously been long and dark brown. But now she had cut most of it off, and what was left was dyed the brightest shade of electric blue I'd ever seen. "Wha...?"

"I know, right? Don't you love it?" She swished her hair around and it practically glowed.

This was so far out of character that I wasn't sure it was really her. "Are you—is that—wha—?" I just couldn't.

"My new boyfriend Yurt said I should try it. Isn't it great?"

Yurt? "Your boyfriend is named after a tent?" This was a new development. Since I'd met her, she'd always been straitlaced and single. A boyfriend named after a tent was new. And the hair...was blue hair a gateway to other strange things? I wondered what people like Justin and Myrna would think. Or Leona...

She rolled her eyes at me. "Look," she said pointedly. "There's nothing you can say to me that my mom didn't already tell me last night. I know it's blue. I'm still an honor student. I'm not getting into trouble, and I'll still do a great job for you here at the store."

She sounded so confident. But that blue...

"*You* wear Vans," she pointed out. "Not exactly age-appropriate, you know?"

I put one hand on my hip. "Listen, honey, I've been wearing Vans since before you were born. I'm Old School, OG, whatever you kids call it."

"Someone's a little defensive," she mocked my indignation. Point taken. She could dye her hair whatever color she wanted because I sure as heck wasn't getting rid of my shoes.

"We can be the awesomest bookstore around," she suggested.

"Deal!" Still. That blue hair. I hadn't pegged her for the type, but that would teach me to judge a book by its cover.

Julie walked through the store to put her school bag in the back room and then came up front, ready for duty. Fortunately, she was nerdy enough to know a fair amount about books, cool enough to be social with the customers, and popular enough to be known by everyone. She was a great asset to the shop, whatever color her hair was, and I told her so as I gave her a list of things she could work on if the store was quiet. Then I said goodbye and went on my way.

I had eaten lunch in the store and now I was craving a coffee, so off to Hoboken I went. I kept telling myself I shouldn't go there every day, but I was a master rationalizer and could always think of a good reason to go. Today was Friday and that was cause for celebration! With coffee!

After getting my flat white to go, I wandered over to the *Ledger* offices to see how everyone was doing. I walked around the first floor and ended up in Mark's office. I plopped down in the chair in front of his desk.

"Are you lost?" asked a voice behind the computer screens.

"No more than usual," I sighed.

Mark slowly peered around the corner of the screens, as if he were afraid of what he might see when he did. When he saw that I looked fairly relaxed and not too crazy, he slowly slid back behind his screens. "I need to remember to get rid of that chair."

He asked if I'd made any more progress with my articles about Leona and Sheriff Branch. I told him no, I had been much too busy with Bigfoot articles to do any real journalism, hoping he'd get the hint. Instead he mumbled "that's fine," without even poking his head out from behind his computer screens. I told him about the upcoming photography exhibit at Monty's the following month and offered to write an article about it. He said that would be great.

"One more thing," I said as I stood up and moved toward the door.

"Hmm?" the screens asked.

"You haven't heard anything about any missing or disappearing farm animals around town, have you?" I tried to keep my voice sounding casual, but Mark's head peered around the side of his screens a little quicker this time.

"What was that now?"

"You heard me. Has anyone reported any missing farm animals?"

He let a big puff of air out of his lungs. "Hell, Beverley, that's a weird question to ask. No, I have not heard of anyone reporting any missing farm animals. What kind of animals? Why on earth are you asking?"

"Oh, nothing, no reason," I replied. "Thanks, though!" And with that, I floated out of his office and back to my car where it was parked at the bookstore.

The rest of the day passed uneventfully. I spent the afternoon taking care of things around the house and definitely not writing a novel. I never minded being by myself; in fact, I really enjoyed it. It was easy for me to be around people, and I did enjoy the social aspects of working for the paper and owning a retail store. But I also loved evenings at home, sitting out in the backyard if it was warm or curled up in front of the fireplace if it was cold. I'd hang out and read or watch a little Netflix. Basically, I'd do anything but write a novel.

This Friday evening, I finished the second Robert Galbraith novel. It was quite good, and I was looking forward to starting the third one. That counted as a life plan, right?

I wondered what the sheriff would think of the first book in the series. I was thinking those romance novel thoughts again. But before I could obsess any further, I heard my phone buzz on the coffee table. A text! Maybe it was him. Great timing! I reached for my phone and checked it.

Mom: ***Are you coming to dinner Sunday? Fixing your favorite :)***

Not quite what I'd been hoping for.

My mom thought she could bribe me with food. Which would normally work, but right now I was still hopping mad about the other night. I couldn't help but notice she didn't mention what she was fixing for dinner; she was hoping I'd fall for the word "favorite" and drive down with my stomach leading the way. Well, not this weekend, lady.

Me: ***No, sorry. Stomach flu. Can't eat.***

I figured this would buy me another week. Right after I sent the text, I got another one.

Callan: ***HEy there***

Huh.

Me: ***Hiya. What're you up to?***

I wondered what he was doing and where he was. I was overwhelmed with embarrassment; it was like I was one step away from asking him what he was wearing. I'd hit send before I'd thought it through and now I worried I sounded nosy. Or like I cared. I wasn't supposed to care, right? I got an immediate response.

Callan: ***Working.***
Me: ***On a Friday night? Everything OK?***
Callan: ***Can't talk about it.b***
Me: ***I should have known...***
Callan: ***Just wanted to say hi.***
Me: ***Hi!***
Callan: ***Gotta run.Have a good night : |***
Me: ***Thanks! You too :)***

Wow! What did it all mean? I was a smart woman, but I had to admit I was clueless when it came to stuff like this. I didn't want a romance. Neither did he. So, did this mean we were friends? Should I text first next time? Was that too forward? Was it okay for a woman to text first? And he had sent a *meh* emoji face. What was up with that? Was it supposed to be a smiley face? Or was he really just feeling *meh?* I needed to consult the internet. Oh, for crying out loud. I was a grownup. Screw it.

Another text came in, and for a split second my heart rate went up. But it was from my mom again.

Mom: ***Sorry to hear that honey! I will come up for a visit tomorrow and bring u soup. Xo***

Uh oh. I didn't want to see them just yet.

Me: ***No! Stay home. Too sick. Off to bed now.***
Mom: ***Oh. OK. I'll call you tomorrow to check on you...Feel better :)***

I felt guilty for telling her I had the flu. I promised myself I'd call her soon and patch it all up once and for all, and I'd tell her I'd come down next weekend for sure.

I went to bed and dreamt that I was in an episode of *Longmire.*

9

Apparently, lots of people don't like chickens. They think chickens are loud, mean, dirty, and make ridiculous pets. I didn't have room for people like that in my life.

It's not like I knew ever since I was five years old that I wanted to be a chicken farmer or anything. It just kind of popped into my head one day, shortly after I'd decided to move back to Oklahoma, that I was going to get me some. They'd proven to be a lot more work than I anticipated, but so far, it had all been worth it. Except for Beryl. It was like she was some kind of evil super chicken. How could a normal chicken be that smart, that mean, and that hell-bent on escape?

On Saturday morning, I cleaned out the chicken coop from top to bottom. I made sure the nesting boxes and floor inside were tidied up; then I raked the ground around the coop. The week before, I'd gotten some fresh straw, and today I put it in the pen.

Everyone was happy, clucking and checking out their new stuff. Everyone except for Beryl. She didn't even attempt to flee, which was somehow worse than if she had tried something. It was darkly foreboding, and the fact that she was quiet and docile worried me even more. It was like the calm before the storm. I would have to be extra vigilant. The last time this happened, she ended up hanging out with Bigfoot. The logical assumption would be that Bigfoot came and snatched my chicken but knowing Beryl, I wasn't so sure. It was probably the other way around. I was on high alert, whatever good *that* would do.

I had the whole day off, which was unusual for a Saturday, and I'd decided to splurge. Julie and Chuck would be fine minding the shop; they could always call me if they needed anything. I was kind of a control freak when it came to my bookstore, but I was learning to let things go. A tiny bit.

In the afternoon I gathered my Private Investigating Gear—my PIG, if you will—and drove to Al's place. The sun was shining brightly this afternoon, like the whole universe was excited that an Oklahoma spring was on its way. I felt some kind of new emotion, or feeling, or some junk like that. What was it? It felt warm, but not too hot. It made me smile, and I felt kind of like a unicorn. Oh. Now I could identify it. It was something between "calm" and "peaceful." I was having a perfect moment in the car and I felt satisfied with, well, everything. Weird! Did this mean I was on the right track with life and everything?

Before I had a chance to overanalyze myself out of my good mood, I got to Al's place. There were a few cars next to the house, but I parked along the dirt driveway and then walked in the direction of the front porch. I was still a little ways off when the front door popped open and Leona Tisdale popped out.

Immediately I could tell something was off. She didn't seem to have her regular air of grouchy diplomacy about her. She was also a little out of breath. Her perfectly coiffed head looked a little rumpled, and one side of her hair was flattened like she'd slept on it. Either that or her head had actually been flattened on one side. That was almost more believable than her running around in public with messy hair. And if I didn't know better, I'd say the front of her dress wasn't buttoned up straight, based on how it was hiked up on one side. On closer inspection, it appeared to be hitched up, maybe tucked into...her pantyhose? She was definitely revealing a little more leg than I imagined she'd want me to see.

Holy cheese on a cracker. What on earth had she been doing in there?

At first she didn't see me; she must have been in too much of a rush. But when she did notice me standing there, she let out a little "Oh!" and her face turned bright red. I smiled at her calmly. I was surprised I was able to keep my cool because this shit was truly weird.

"Hello, Leona. How are you? Beautiful day, isn't it?" I asked.

She opened her mouth as if to say something, but then quickly closed it again, apparently changing her mind. She didn't seem to want to look me in the eye. Her gaze remained toward the ground as she walked quickly to her car. "Yes, hi. How...yes, nice day," she finally managed. Her voice trailed off as she got in her car and drove off in a big ol' rush, leaving a trail of dust behind.

I didn't know whether to laugh or call the police. What on earth was that about? Did I just see my landlady come tearing out of Al's house looking like she had just...? Oh my. I shook my head at the thought of what I might have interrupted. I shook my head again, more vigorously, still trying to get the picture out of my mind.

I kept walking and almost made it to the front door before it opened up a second time. This time, out popped Bill Turner who waddled straight past me in a similar state of dishevelment and embarrassment. He walked so fast I didn't even get a chance to see what his t-shirt said on it. He didn't look at me. He got right into his car and drove away, setting off a fresh dust storm that added to the cloud that hadn't quite settled from Leona's dramatic exit.

Oh. My. Goodness. I had to admit that now I really wanted to know what the hell had been going on in there. Then again, I did *not* want to know what had been going on in there. What was I getting ready to walk into? A rave? A senior citizen orgy? An intense game of Death Scrabble? I wished I had put my can of mace in my bag like my dad told me to when I first moved to New York. "You never know," he'd always say. Today I was going to have to take my chances without a weapon. I took a deep breath and walked the rest of the way up to the door, knocking on it gently.

After about half a minute, the front door opened and there stood Al. He was in a slightly lesser state of dishevelment than his cohorts, but he still looked a little rough around the edges.

"Hi, Al. We were supposed to meet at two, right?" I tried to keep my voice steady and upbeat. I looked at my phone. It was five after.

"Uh, hi, missy. Yeah, two o'clock, right. Sorry, I was taking a nap. Come on in." He opened the screen door for me, and I walked into the foyer. A nap? With his cousin and Leona? What kind of nap was *that?*

"I hope I didn't disturb you," I said, my voice betraying my nervousness.

"Oh no, not at all. We were just, uh, having a meeting, and it went a little long. I mean late." He tried to smooth out his Hawaiian print shirt.

"I thought you said you were taking a nap?" Oh, why do I ask these things.

"We had a meeting and I fell asleep in it."

I nodded my head at that. The kind of meeting they were having might actually be illegal in some places. But who was I to judge? If the three of them wanted to fly their freak flags together, go for it, y'all.

"Alrighty then." I wanted to get this over with so I could get the hell out of there. "Let's just get down to business, shall we?" I pulled out my reporter-detective notebook and pen. "Show me where you were keeping the alleged sheep."

"What do you mean alleged? It was a real sheep. Cute and furry. A little smelly, though." Al wrinkled his nose and looked around the room like he had lost something. Maybe he was looking for the alleged sheep. In any case, he didn't have his glasses on again, so he wouldn't have seen a sheep if it had been standing right next to him.

"Yes, but I haven't personally seen the sheep. In the context of this investigation, if I haven't seen it, it may not have existed. My boss said I have to be here, but that doesn't mean I have to believe one single word you say."

"Oh." He looked around a little more, then gave up. "Whatever. I gotta go find my sweater. I'll be right back." He walked down the hallway toward the back of the house, trying to smooth out his hair which was standing up on one side, just like Leona's had been.

As I waited for Al to return, I looked around the living room. It was pretty much what you'd expect as far as retired bachelor pad ambience goes. The curtain style and pattern were outdated and the couch fabric was even worse. The ruffles on both indicated there had been a woman involved in the decision-making process at some point. A bunch of TV remotes and a few beer cans sat on a 1970s-era TV tray next to a worn-looking Naugahyde recliner. There were knick-knacks on the mantle along with a few faded photographs and a very dusty, very old candle.

I noticed a larger photograph hanging in a frame on the wall next to the fireplace, but from my vantage point I couldn't figure out what the subject of the photo was. I walked over to get a better look and discovered it was a photo of a musician taken at a concert. The photo background was black except for a bank of colored lights along the top, shining down on a bare-chested, long-haired guy sitting behind a drum kit. One arm was raised above his head, drumstick in hand, like he was about to beat the living daylights out of his cymbal. Sweat was flying off his face and his mouth was open like he was uttering a rock and roll war cry. The man sported a cheesy mustache that went perfectly with his long stringy hair. I guessed the photo to be from sometime in the mid-seventies, and closer inspection revealed that the dude was Al. My jaw dropped all the way down to my Vans.

I wanted to investigate the room further, but by this time the present-day, sixty-something Al had reentered the room and was looking at me expectantly. "Okay then, let's go," he said cheerily.

I had to tear my eyes away from the picture on the wall,

wishing like hell I knew what the story behind *that* was. I studied the Al in front of me with renewed curiosity. His old-timey demeanor and bachelor frump were now bundled up in a big sweater and he was watching me expectantly, oblivious to my having discovered his rock star photo, and also oblivious to the fact that I was completely floored by said discovery. If I looked at him closely, I could see a tiny little semblance of that former rock star and his faded youthful vigor. To quote Iggy Pop, he'd had a lust for life. But now that rock star life was buried in aging country bachelor life. But maybe not entirely. Respect.

Al turned on his heel and we headed through the house to the back door, then out onto a small concrete slab of a patio. His backyard was very big and enclosed by chain link fencing on three sides with the house on the fourth. The fence was at least six feet high. On one side of the yard, there was a pen with a fairly large chicken coop in it, and along the back fence in one corner stood a small structure that must have functioned as a barn. He pointed to the little barn.

"That's where I had them, in there."

I stood still, looking at the barn but trying to take in the whole yard to get a feel for the place.

"So, what do *you* think happened back here, Al?"

"Isn't that what you're here to figure out?" he asked me, like I was a little slow on the uptake.

"Yes, but I'm curious to know what your theory is."

"Well," he said, "you already know what I think." He took a step toward me, looking first to his left and then to his right. I was giddy with anticipation. "I think that Bigfoot took 'em," he finally whispered. "Climbed right over that there fence and took himself some free lamb chops."

"Ah," I said calmly.

"No other explanation."

"No other explanation? Like, none?"

"Nope!"

"Show me your proof," I politely suggested.

"*You* find the proof. That's what you're here for."

"Al, I can't...that's not how..." Aw, to heck with it. Why bother trying to explain how this was supposed to work? Once again, I mentally kicked myself for getting hornswoggled into this mess.

"Okay, Al," I said slowly, trying not to burst into tears. "Let me look around a little bit." I started to walk toward the chicken coop. Al followed, one very small step behind me.

"Why are you gonna check the coop?" he asked.

It felt like he was breathing down my neck. I wasn't in the mood to have my nonexistent, make-believe investigative skills questioned, so I gave Al something else to work on. "Hey, Al, I'm really thirsty. Would you mind going inside and getting me a glass of water?"

"Sure thing, missy," he said, turning to walk back into the house.

"Oh, and Al, could you make sure the water temperature is exactly seventy-three degrees? I have a very sensitive stomach; it has to be seventy-three-degree water." Al stopped walking and stood stock still. One hand reached up and scratched the back of his head. I could see the hamster wheel turning slowly up there.

"Um, okay..." He ambled off. And I was free.

I decided to look around the barn before he came back. I didn't think he'd be back for at least an hour, but I had better hurry just to be sure. I walked toward the barn, checking the ground as I went; I didn't want to step on any possible evidence. When I got inside, I saw a few hay bales and it looked like one corner had been made into a sleeping area for an animal of some kind. Hay was spread out over the ground and there were all kinds of scuffle marks in the dirt around the hay. I had no idea what this could mean. Maybe it would be helpful to learn some tracking skills. Some other time.

I was kind of curious though, so I examined the bed of hay carefully. I noticed a small fluffy ball of grayish-white fiber in the hay and maybe some kind of animal poop. I had no idea what sheep poop looked like.

I got my phone out of my back pocket and took a picture of the poop. I hoped that this would be the weirdest picture that I would have to take for this project, but I was only about forty percent confident it would be. Then I took a snack-sized plastic bag out of my PIG kit and put the little ball of grayish-white fiber in it. I felt so professional! Except for the photo of poop that was now on my phone's camera roll.

It was hard to do, but I tried to take this seriously. I mean, who borrows a sheep and then manages to lose it? Two times in a row? Based on my experience last fall on my Bigfoot stakeout, I couldn't rule out the possibility that Sasquatch had enjoyed a couple of sheep snacks at Al's expense. But there had to be another explanation. Sheep didn't just up and walk away, right?

I turned to leave the barn but stopped for one last look around. I didn't see anything that looked like it could have been a Sasquatch footprint, but something did catch my eye on the ground to the right of the doors. I walked over and bent down to discover a wispy clump of brown hair. There wasn't much of it, but it was quite long. I supposed it could have been Bigfoot hair. I almost laughed out loud at the thought. I picked up the hair and considered smelling it, but then decided I wasn't quite that desperate yet. Instead I pulled out another baggie and dropped the fur ball in. Maybe I should go back and put the poop into a bag, but that was taking things too far and I wasn't getting paid enough for that level of investigation.

I walked around to the back of the barn, but there was nothing there of interest. Just a plastic water bowl that looked like it had been chewed on by a dinosaur and then abandoned. I was starting to wonder if someone simply broke in one night and took the sheep. But twice?

Al walked up, startling me. He didn't have my glass of water.

"Who knew you had the sheep here?" I asked him.

"Well, Bill knew, 'cause he helped me borrow them. But I think that's it. As you can see, ain't no other neighbors around who can get a good look back here."

This was true. I turned around to look out past Al's back fence.

"Whatcha lookin' for?" Al said from right behind me. I jumped a few inches.

"Al, I appreciate your interest, but would you mind giving me a little space here?" I drew a big circle in the air, encompassing the entire backyard.

"Oh, sorry. Sure. I'll go wait over on the veranda."

Veranda? I hadn't realized *veranda* was synonymous with *cement slab,* but then again, Al did do things a little differently as a general rule. As he walked back toward the house, I began to walk the perimeter of the fence. I passed the house and then started toward the other side of the yard. About twenty feet away from the house, I got to a spot that looked interesting. I crouched down and sat back on my heels for a better look. There was a break in the chain link fence, creating a small opening. The bottom of the fence was bent upwards, and it seemed to me that something larger than the actual opening could easily fit through it by pushing the fencing aside. I looked even more closely and hanging from a sharp piece of chain link was something kind of wispy, the color of cream. I took it off the fence to inspect it. It looked similar to the fluff I'd found outside the barn. On the other side of the fence, stuck in the grass, were two white feathers.

I placed the wispy wool in another PIG evidence bag and kept on walking.

When I got to the chicken coop, I let myself in the pen. Not because I was looking for clues; I just wanted to sneak a peek at Al's chickens to see how many he had. It was a nicely built coop, very solid and tidy. There were no signs of any chickens anywhere, so I peeked in the back door of the coop and still didn't see or hear any birds. I guess they had all flown the coop. I looked down at the ground and spotted another wisp of brownish hair.

I let myself back out of the pen and walked the remainder of the fence but didn't see anything else of interest. I took one last look around and walked back toward Al's veranda, stuffing my PIG bags into my purse. Al was watching me expectantly.

"Well, I will need to review my notes and the evidence that I collected," I said, hoping I sounded like an FBI agent. I shoved my notebook back in my bag and fished around for my car keys.

"That's it?" He pushed himself up out of the lawn chair he'd been sitting in. "Do you know what happened? When can I get my sheep back?"

"*Your* sheep?"

"Dammit, you know what I mean. When can I get the sheep back?"

I almost went ahead and told him that Bigfoot had eaten the sheep and he would never see them again.

"You do know that I have to write about this for the paper now, right?"

"I *know,*" he said proudly.

"And you know I could mention in the article that you stole some sheep."

Al deflated before my eyes. Clearly, he hadn't thought things through. I immediately felt bad about having brought it up, but I was not happy about being forced into getting involved, and really not happy about being forced into it by means of a fake Bigfoot sighting. Al said nothing but lowered his gaze to the grass.

"Look," I went on, "I'm not going to tell anyone about what you did. In fact, I want to help you straighten it all out, okay?"

Al nodded solemnly.

"But you have to promise me two things," I said sternly.

"What's that?"

"First, promise me you're not going to hound me day and night to get this figured out. Second..." I had one more chance to ask for something good, but nothing came to mind. Well, maybe I could buy myself some insurance. "Well, I'll get back to you on the second thing. But it will be important, and you will promise."

"All right, that sounds reasonable," agreed Al. I held out my hand and we shook on it. "So—"

"What did I just say? No hounding! Patience! I need to run a few tests, make a few calls." I wanted to work the words *particulate* or *tox screen* or maybe even *biological evidence* into the conversation, but it was too much effort. "Don't worry, the sheep aren't going anywhere." I smiled broadly. "I'll be in touch soon."

I turned to leave, but then had another thought. "Say, Al, where are all your chickens?"

He scratched the side of his head thoughtfully. "Well, it's the darndest thing," he said slowly. "They kind of disappeared, too. One by one, they just vanished—poof!" He spread his arms wide.

"I see." I nodded my head. "How peculiar. Okay. Well, talk to you soon!" And with that, I excused myself to my car via the backyard gate.

When I got home, I put my evidence bags on the desk in my office and scribbled a few notes while things were still fresh in my mind. What *did* happen to those sheep? I was reminded of when I was a little girl and I would watch *In Search Of* on TV with my grandma waaaaay back when. One episode, narrated by Leonard Nimoy, was about the Bermuda Triangle and it had freaked me out. Maybe the sheep were in the Bermuda Triangle with Leonard Nimoy? If I wasn't mistaken, there was also an episode about Bigfoot. Of course! Bigfoot took the sheep to the Bermuda Triangle to party with Leonard Nimoy. Case closed.

I supposed I was going to have to approach this as an investigative journalist for the paper and as a private detective for Al and Bill. The two titles weren't all that different; I could do both at the same time pretty easily. I found myself feeling curious and oddly inspired. Dammit! They'd sucked me in and now I was invested in finding an answer.

Did Bigfoot take them? Could be. Or was it some other kind of animal? Or a person? Could I even figure this out? I knew what Al and Bill wanted me to come up with. And I knew what kind of article would sell copies of the *Ledger*. It would be the easy way out to point the finger at Bigfoot. For now, I decided to follow in the footsteps of all the brilliant thinkers who came before me and solve the mystery by completely forgetting about it for a while and doing something else.

One thing I couldn't forget, however, was the spectacle of Bill and Leona leaving Al's place. It was burned into my memory now. What the heck was up with that? I might have disturbed some kind of senior love triangle. I might never know the real answer, but even the possibility of the existence of senior love triangles in Guthrie went a long way toward changing my opinion that this town was boring. What else was going on around here that I had no idea about? More love triangles? Love octagons? Political scandals? Intrigue involving something more interesting than sheep? The possibilities! My stomach grumbled. The possibilities could wait until I'd had a snack.

I made myself a peanut butter, jelly, and potato chip sandwich, then took it and an apple out to the backyard to multitask; eat a snack while checking on the chickens. I set my plate down on the picnic table and noticed the package of Hostess Cupcakes Danny had given me the other day was still sitting there. I'd have to do something about that.

I took a loud bite of my sandwich and it was like the hens had supersonic hearing; they all came over to the fence and watched me eat. It made me uncomfortable to be watched by so many eyes, even if they were just chicken eyes. For some reason, I wasn't as uncomfortable as I should have been, though. I felt self-conscious, but I didn't feel like anyone was glaring at me or plotting my untimely demise. Uh oh. This was a bad sign. I should have been feeling glowered at by Beryl. But I wasn't.

I put my sandwich down and went over to the pen. I counted the hens; one was missing. And I knew exactly which one. After a quick look around, I pronounced it official. Beryl had escaped again.

The gate to the pen had been shut tight; there were no signs of a kerfluffle and no Sasquatch footprints. There were no clues as to how she'd done it.

Normally you might simply pronounce your ordinary chicken

lost forever, but this was Beryl. All bets were off as to what was going on or what would happen next. What should I do now? I could go look for her. Or I could let fate take its course. I chose the latter. I said a little prayer for her, hoping I'd see her again someday and hoping that nothing too violent or painful—like being barbecued by one of my neighbors or getting picked up by a roving Tyson Chicken semi bound for a very scary place—would befall her. I ate the rest of my sandwich with a little less gusto, fed and watered my remaining hens, and made sure they were locked up tight.

I spent the rest of the day at home and in the evening made myself a simple dinner, after which I went back into my office and looked at all the little baggies of weird, wispy hair sitting there. I didn't know why I had bothered taking any of it. I had no idea what to do with it. I sighed, gathered them up, and put them in a drawer. Brown hair, cream-colored hair, wispy woolly hair. Got it.

I called my mom. I came clean about not having the flu, but I also told her I was still mad that she and my dad had set me up with the sheriff.

"How is he doing?" she asked me.

The question caught me off guard, but I collected myself quickly. "How the hell would I know?"

"Beverley. Watch your language." I started to roll my eyes but thought better of it. "I just thought that maybe you and he—" she went on.

"No, mom. Hell no. No...nope."

"You sound a little too insistent, sweetie."

There was a saying or an axiom or hypothesis or something like that, about how you can never lie to your mom because she always *knows*. I tried to convince myself that she was simply guessing or hoping. In any case, there was no way I was going to say anything about anything. Nope. She didn't need to know I had invited him over the following day for a non-date breakfast.

"Mom, give it a rest, please. And for Pete's sake, don't ever do that to me again. Let's just drop it, okay? I'll come over for dinner next Sunday. Maybe I will even have some eggs to bring you; the chickens have been busy!" My subject change worked, and we talked about chickens and eggs and what she should make for dinner next Sunday. When we hung up, everything was good, and she didn't even ask me about the sheriff again.

I wondered what I should make for breakfast the following morning. For my non-date. I probably should have thought of it earlier, in case I needed to go to the store for anything. But at this time of day, the only thing that would get me out of the house would be a real food emergency, something along the lines of running out of chocolate or peanut butter. Whatever I had in the house would have to do.

Had I been too forward by inviting him over? I hoped it wasn't sending the wrong message. But I wasn't sure what the right message was. I was gearing up for a really productive bout of second-guessing myself when I heard my phone buzz on the table in the kitchen. I got up to check my messages.

Callan: ***Looking forward to breakfast.***
Me: ***Me too!***

Maybe I should have left that exclamation mark off.

Callan: ***What time?***

We settled on nine o'clock, since it turned out both of us were early risers. The texting ended with me reminding him to bring donuts and him asking if he should bring anything besides donuts. I assured him I'd have everything else taken care of. I was thinking that it was starting to sound a little like a date, when I got another text from him.

Callan: ***breakfast doesn't count as a date, right?***
Me: ***Of course not!***
Callan: ***What a relief. sleep well.***

Me: ***you too.***

I found myself wanting to text something suggestive back to him. What did he wear when he slept? Yeah, that would have blown us right out of non-date territory, so I just left it. Must have been all those romance novels again. I went to bed with a mug of tea and a new book, some kind of romance called *Throb*. Sounded promising.

10

I'd been dreaming about lumberjacks when my alarm went off Sunday morning. Big, strong lumberjacks wearing steel-toed boots and suspenders, little wood chips stuck in their beards. They were cutting down trees with giant axes, clearing a space in the woods way up in the mountains. I was watching them from behind a tree when I looked over to the tree line across the clearing and there was Bigfoot, also peeking around the side of a tree. He was looking right at me. Why couldn't I have nice dreams about fluffy clouds or rainbows and unicorns? Or just lumberjacks?

Then I remembered—breakfast! With the sheriff! I shot out of bed as if my croissants were on fire. What to do first? I probably should have started preparing the night before if this were a date. But since it wasn't, I was going to act all cool and throw together a delicious breakfast with very little forethought. Also, I was going to go ahead and assume that my bathroom was clean enough for a non-date. And if it wasn't, who cared, right?

I put myself together, taking a quick shower and adding about ten percent more than the minimal effort to try to fix my hair. It was curly today, but it was doing me a favor by keeping the frizz at bay. My lucky day! I put on jeans and a white t-shirt under a goldenrod cardigan. Then I made sure my bathroom was clean. This might not be a date, and I might not care, but I also wasn't a philistine.

Breakfast would be sautéed veggies and cheese omelets, home-baked bread, and fresh fruit. And hopefully Callan would remember the donuts, if he knew what was good for him. I had everything ready to go save for making the omelets, and at one minute after nine, there was a knock on my front door. The brim of a cowboy hat was all I could see through the peephole.

I opened the door and there stood Callan, definitely not looking like Bigfoot today. His wardrobe almost looked similar to mine with his worn jeans and white cotton oxford shirt. Only he had a few extra accessories: hat, cowboy boots, and a holstered gun under his dark coat. And most importantly, a white bakery bag.

"Hi, Sher—Callan," I said. He nodded at me, and I moved aside to let him into the house.

He walked in and handed me the bag. "I hope these are the right ones."

"If they are chocolate and donut-shaped, they are the right ones," I said, peering in the bag. This was a half-lie because in order to be "the right ones," the donuts had to be old-fashioned and from Missy's. They appeared to be the real deal. The sheriff had just scored some major points. Not that I was keeping score.

Callan laid his hat, coat, and holster on the couch. I was relieved to know that the gun wouldn't be joining us for breakfast. "Sorry about the gun," he explained, seeing the look on my face. "I'm working later today, and I didn't want to leave it in the truck."

"No problem," I said. I didn't think I'd ever had a gun in my house before; it felt kind of weird knowing it was there. Normally I wasn't a fan of guns, but he was The Law so maybe it was okay. It actually was kind of cool. The sheriff was a badass. I bet he knew how to use that gun. This had romance novel written all over it.

I led him back to the kitchen where I had already set the table. I'd made a double batch of coffee in my Chemex coffee maker and I offered him some. He took it black. Of course.

"I hope you didn't go to too much trouble," he said, smelling the steaming coffee in his mug. The look on his face seemed to indicate approval.

"No trouble," I said. "My favorite meal is breakfast and it's the only one I do well." I motioned for him to sit at the table and I started to make the omelets. "Hope you like omelets."

"Love them."

We chatted about nothing in particular while I prepared the eggs and toasted the bread. When everything was done, I placed two plates heaping with food onto the table. The donuts sat on a platter in the middle of the table, arranged carefully in a pyramid shape. A deep-fried centerpiece. He'd brought enough for a small office meeting.

I sat down and we started eating, neither of us speaking for a while as we enjoyed the food and the easy company.

"So whatcha got going on in the Sheriff's Department this week?" I asked, hoping whatever it was would be suitable breakfast conversation.

"Oh, you know, the usual," he said offhandedly.

"No, I don't know," I admitted. In the few times we'd spoken, we hadn't talked much about his work as the sheriff. He hadn't volunteered any information and I hadn't asked. I wasn't sure what made me ask today, but there it was. "I mean, you must see some weird stuff, right?"

Callan put down his fork and sighed. "You wouldn't believe it."

"Probably not!" I laughed. "How do you manage the stress?"

"Meditation," he answered without missing a beat.

"Mediwhat?"

"You know, that thing where you sit still and breathe." He picked his fork back up and finished off his omelet. "You should try it."

I could not quite comprehend what he'd said. A meditating sheriff? Nah, couldn't be. And was the suggestion to a give it a try some kind of not-so-subtle hint? "Excuse me?" I asked.

"Meditation?" He was being kind, but I could tell he thought I was a little slow on the uptake. I couldn't blame him. "I meditate every morning and every evening for twenty minutes. Been doing it for fifteen years."

"I know what meditation is." I tried to sound cool. "You don't strike me as the meditate-y, yoga-y type. You're from *Texas*, for cripes' sake."

"How did you know I also do yoga?" His face was expressionless, but I could tell he was enjoying this.

"Don't they go together?"

He shrugged. "Many people who meditate don't practice yoga. And vice versa."

"You are weird," I marveled, placing my elbow on the table and my chin in my palm. I mooned over him from across the table. His left eyebrow shot up.

"Excuse me?"

"I mean, you're just not what I expected. You're always surprising me."

"You're welcome," he said, lowering his eyebrow.

"So, *is* there anything interesting going on in Sheriff World this week?"

"We do have a weird one," he said as he picked up a donut. "Someone lost two sheep."

My stomach dropped to the floor, but I tried to act casual. "What's so weird about that? Don't people lose sheep all the time?" I hadn't thought it through all the way; that on the other side of Al's missing sheep equation was someone who had lost the sheep. And I hadn't considered that they would involve the Sheriff's Department over it.

"It's weird because only two sheep were taken. And they weren't taken at the same time. Usually if someone's going to steal sheep, they take a bunch."

"Oh." I started to feel a little weird. "I'd think it would be hard to notice when only one or two animals go missing from a whole herd of sheep," I thought out loud. "Who reported them missing?" I hoped I didn't sound like I knew anything about it.

He leaned back in his chair and squinted at me. "Why? Do you know something?"

"About missing sheep? What? *Pffft!* Of course not! That's silly."

His eyebrow only went halfway up this time. "It was your pal, Danny. So far, there are no leads and there's probably not much we can do at this point. I think he just wanted to let us know in case it happens again. But I'll run over to his place later and check it out."

"Oh. Well, good luck with the case," I said. Although I wasn't sure I wanted him to solve the mystery. Al and Bill weren't the sharpest knives in the drawer, but I didn't want to see them get busted by the law, either. I felt conflicted.

"There's an old law on the books in Guthrie," Callan said. "We still shoot sheep rustlers here."

My eyes went wide, and I might have gasped. I started to panic, until I saw the look on his face. He usually stayed pretty stoic, but now he was laughing. I started laughing too.

"You have a nice laugh," he said as he got up from the table and picked up our plates. He walked to the sink and set the dishes on the counter top. "You know you're not supposed to have chickens, right?"

Oh my gosh, how could he tell that the eggs I'd served him hadn't been from the store? Wow, he was *good!* Was he reading my mind? I hoped not, due to all the times I'd thought about his stubbled jaw and kind eyes and...

But he magically knew I had chickens! Oh, hold up. He must have spotted my avian contraband out the kitchen window. Oops.

"Sheriff, are you accusing me of knowingly breaking the law?" I asked innocently.

"No," he said, turning around and leaning against the counter. "Not today, anyway."

I watched him standing there, looking so at ease. If I hadn't been distracted by his long, tall form, I might have been worried about breaking the law. Instead, I started worrying about something else. He looked mighty fine, standing in my kitchen like that.

"Well, in any case," I finally said, "you just ate all the evidence."

"It was damn tasty evidence."

I got up and reached for the Chemex. "Maybe I can bribe your silence with more coffee."

"It's worth trying," he said, picking up his mug and holding it out for a refill. I took a step but before I knew what was happening, I tripped and began sliding toward him, my feet not finding any purchase on the kitchen floor. I slid his way, he caught me, and the coffee sloshed out of the Chemex and onto his nice white shirt.

I pulled away and we both stood there, looking at his shirt. He must have been surprised—I was mortified. At least the coffee hadn't been hot; it had been sitting on the table for a while. Yes, at least I didn't give him second-degree coffee burns as well as ruin his shirt. Why, oh why, did I have this knack for being such a doofus?

"Oh my god," I finally said, still not able to move. *Hey, Beverley, you idiot,* my brain finally said, *why don't you try to clean that up?*

Callan turned toward the sink, looking for a towel. "Here, let me help," I said, rushing to his side and picking up a clean towel off the counter. I began to wipe the front of his shirt. Which did absolutely nothing. But he let me continue anyway, just to be nice.

"Oh my god," I said again.

"You already said that."

"I am so sorry. I think I may have ruined your shirt."

"It wasn't a family heirloom."

"Still. I'm so sorry! Here, let me see if I can clean it up a little more..." I reached out both hands to his shirt but then stopped short. It looked like I was trying to grab him. Great, spill coffee on him, then accost him.

"It's okay," he insisted.

"Please, let me try to clean it. Maybe you could like, you know..." My voice trailed off.

"What?"

"Take off your shirt? I mean, so I can clean it?"

A teeny tiny smile showed on one side of his mouth.

I turned a very dark shade of red, and my face felt so hot I thought it might catch fire. I cleared my throat. "Yeah, I mean, so I can clean it. Before the stain sets." I could hear words coming out of my mouth but none of them sounded right.

He stood up tall, looked down at me, took a deep breath, and started unbuttoning his shirt. I thought I might faint, but I kept trying to take slow, full breaths. It wasn't helping. The buttons were pearl snap buttons, and suddenly I had the urge to reach over, take hold of each side of his shirt, and start ripping it wide open. I realized I was staring at him, and I tried to think of someplace else to look instead. Probably anywhere else would be fine. I coughed and started clearing the table.

A hand appeared in my line of sight, holding a coffee-stained white shirt out to me. Which meant the sheriff was shirtless in my kitchen. I had said I wasn't interested in dating anyone, but that didn't mean I wouldn't still swoon when a good-looking man took off his clothes in front of my stove.

I took the shirt from his hand and turned to face him. I tried not to do that once-over, up-and-down look—I hated it when men did it to me—but it was really hard not to. His bare chest took up most of my kitchen. It was slightly tanned, quite muscular, and extremely impressive. It was so broad that it needed its own zip code. I could have landed a small plane on it. And the landing strip...*gah.* I may have swayed where I stood. I found myself staring at his belt buckle.

"Thanks, uh, um..."

"Callan."

"Yes, right."

"Are you okay?" he asked.

"I'm not sure..." I tried to tear my eyes away from the spectacular sight before me, and I finally did, but not before it was painfully obvious that I was ogling. "Let me just something on put go this," I said, holding up his shirt. "I mean, let something...I go..."

"Okay."

"Okay." I finally turned and walked down the hallway to get some stain remover from my laundry room. My legs felt like Jell-O and I was very warm. I might not be able to be trusted to go back into the kitchen. I considered locking myself in the garage until he left.

I stood for a moment holding his shirt. I wanted to hold it up to my face and take a deep breath. And I would have, but I didn't want to get caught. I'd never be able to explain why I was inhaling his clothes. I almost did it anyway, but *nope nope nope!* I started spraying cleaner on the shirt instead. I was unsure if I could ever get it back to a wearable state. I was still standing there debating what to do when he called to me from the front of the house.

"Hey, Bev, I have a uniform shirt in my truck—I'll run out and get it."

"Okie dokie," I called back. I made an executive decision and threw his shirt into the washer and turned it on.

As I started walking back toward the kitchen, I heard voices. What the what? I turned the corner and there was Callan, shirtless. Talking to my parents. In my living room. Oh, for the love of Mike.

"Hi, hi, Sweetie Pie!" my dad said, sounding a little more upbeat than usual. He looked from me to Callan, a huge grin on his face.

"Good morning, Bev, honey! We were just in your living room, visiting with the sheriff here," my mom said, gazing longingly at Callan's bare chest. "In your living room."

Callan looked at me helplessly. He didn't seem like someone who flustered easily, but this particular situation was getting the better of him. Taking down bad guys was one thing but being caught in what appeared to be a compromising position by Steve and Bob Green was quite another.

"I'll just, I mean, let me—" he started.

"Yes, just...fine, and—" I didn't do much better than him. I waved at the front door and he practically ran out of the house to his truck. If I had been embarrassed before, I was completely mortified now.

"What the hell are you guys doing here?" I asked. My parents had never visited me unannounced.

"Don't use the 'H' word," my mom scolded, glancing around the room. She was probably looking for more discarded articles of clothing. Like my bra hanging from the lampshade or something.

"Are we interrupting?" my dad asked hopefully, jerking his head toward the door.

This was where I should have said something like "it's not what it looks like," or "we had a random coffee accident," but what was the point? They were going to believe whatever they wanted to and if I protested, it would make me look guilty. Guilty? Guilty of what? Coffee spillage? I had nothing to feel guilty about. I still felt guilty.

"Yes," I said. "For reals, what are you doing here?"

Callan came back in, wearing an untucked uniform shirt, a shiny badge above the breast pocket. He cut quite a figure and I think I heard my mom gasp. We all stood there and watched him.

We stood there. He stood there. Still, no one said anything. I could tell he was uncomfortable with us all looking at him. I looked at my mom looking at Callan. My mom then looked at my dad, who looked at Callan and then me. Everyone wanted someone else to go first. Finally, Callan pointed to the door behind him. "So I'll just..."

"Yes, okay," I said. I walked to the door with him. "Thanks for stopping by."

"Right," he said, looking at me for a second before picking up his coat and hat and gun. "Steve, Bob." He put on his hat and tipped it at them before slinking out the door. I closed it behind him. I was supposed to feel more grown up than this.

Before I could even get the door closed all the way, my mom started in. "So, what was *that* all about?" she asked excitedly. He probably heard her, and I cringed.

"Nothing," I said, using the same tone I used all through high school every time she would ask me what I'd been up to the night before. She hadn't believed me then and she probably wouldn't believe me now either. Except *this* time, she was wrong.

"So, it worked, huh?" she asked.

"What worked?"

"Why, the blind date of course!" She walked to my bookshelves and started rearranging the books. "I told you, Steve. They're perfect for each other!"

My dad, who had been wandering around the living room, finally stopped in front of the wall right outside the kitchen and pretended to inspect a very small crack at very close range. He didn't have his glasses on, so there was no telling what he was actually trying to do, other than pretend not to hear what we were saying so he wouldn't have to get involved.

I walked over to where my mom was standing and started unrearranging the books she had just rearranged. "Mom," I said calmly, trying to guide her away from my bookshelves, "we are not perfect for each other. He came by to tell me something, and he surprised me at the door and I spilled coffee on his shirt, okay?"

"Sure, honey, sure," my mom said, trying to give a knowing look to my dad, who was still busy pretending to look at the wall. "So, how was he?" she asked me.

"You didn't just ask me that," I said, standing with my hands on my hips.

"Well, he looks like he'd be a real *dynamo*." She giggled like a teenager.

I was about to pass out from shock and embarrassment. "Seriously, what are you doing here?"

"We were on our way up to Wichita for the day and wanted to stop in to make sure you were feeling better," my dad said, still inspecting the wall.

"And to bring you donuts!" My mom held out a white paper bag that I hadn't noticed before.

"Okay, thanks," I said. I wondered why she wanted to know if I was feeling better, since I'd already admitted that I never had the flu. Of course—they had needed an excuse to stop by to check up on me. And boy, had it paid off for them.

"You're welcome, dear. We'll try to give you more notice next time, I promise. So we don't surprise you and your friend," my mom said with a nod. "Just be sure to...*you know*."

I didn't want to *know,* but I took the bait anyway. "To what?"

She leaned in close to me, then looked at my dad, making sure he was still pretending not to listen. Then she turned back to me. "Well," she stage whispered, "just be sure to use protection. You never know these days."

"Oh goodness, look at the time. You're going to be late for something important." I took my mom by her arm, and gently ushered her toward the door. My dad followed obligingly. I had to hand it to him—he knew when to take the conversational lead, and he knew when to hang back and not get involved. It was like having relationship sixth sense. I wondered if that was a common thing to develop, when two people were married for a long time. I hadn't been able to find out yet myself, but I did have two pretty good role models. When they weren't dropping by and finding me in *breakfast interruptus*, that is.

11

It took me the rest of Sunday and two Emergency Beers to recover from the morning's events. My mom had seemed pretty darn happy to think she'd walked in on a boy-girl sleepover party. Ugh! I was conflicted. I didn't want my parents to think I was dating the sheriff, let alone sleeping with him. Because I wasn't! Regardless, you weren't supposed to get caught by your parents. On the other hand, who cares! It was absolutely none of their beeswax.

But now it might get out that we were seeing each other. Because if there was one thing my mom could do, it was talk. Now there might be rumors about us, and I felt bad for the sheriff. Don't get me wrong, he could definitely do worse, but I didn't want to be the one to put him in a compromising position.

I hadn't heard from him since he'd left my house, and I wondered if he was mad or embarrassed or feeling some other dude emotion I wasn't familiar with that may not be covered in the Manspeak Dictionary. I felt bad and hadn't wanted to bother him, so I didn't call or text first.

But as I walked to work on Monday morning, I thought about texting him that afternoon to say hi and test the waters. Yes, that sounded like a good idea.

It had been a weird weekend, between my chicken disappearing again, looking for lost sheep, discovering a love triangle, having breakfast with the sheriff and having my parents think I slept with said sheriff. After all that, I was looking forward to a nice, quiet Monday at The Book Store. I had, however, washed, dried, *and* ironed Callan's white shirt. And I never iron. It's one of my cardinal rules. Never iron, tie your shoelaces, or use excessive cutlery whenever you can avoid it.

I made sure his shirt was tucked neatly into my bag when I left for work, so I'd have it with me, just in case. In case of what? In case...in case I happened to run into him somewhere. I hoped I would.

When I got to work, I opened up the store and settled in to check email, and stock levels, and catch up on my bookkeeping. I told myself this stuff was more important than looking at sheep poop photos on the internet. But when Al and Bill walked into the store a little before lunch time, I wished I'd had spent a little time on what I now referred to as the Sheep Problem.

"What's cookin', Bev?" asked Al as he walked over to look at the turtle, who was enjoying a Monday morning snack. "Aw, what's your little turtle eating?" He looked closer and discovered Jimmy's snack was a pile of dried crickets. He scrunched up his face and stepped back.

"Hi guys," I said jauntily. "Say, Bill, that's a swell t-shirt you've got on today!"

Bill had walked in behind his cousin and looked down at his shirt after I'd complimented him. "What, this ol' thing?" he asked, obviously proud. Today's selection was chosen specifically for his visit to my shop, I was sure: it was a heathered grey shirt with simple black, italic lettering that said *BOOKISH AF*.

"Are you really bookish A-F?" I asked. I was pretty sure I knew the answer.

"Oh, heck yeah!" he exclaimed loudly. "I read all the dang time. I finished that comic book pretty quick, and now I'm reading an old Louis L'Amour western."

"Well, let me know if you need any recommendations, or if I can special-order anything for you."

"I will! Julie helped me pick the L'Amour novel out. She's real smart with the book stuff."

I couldn't argue with that. "So where do you get all these t-shirts, anyway?" I asked, pointing to his belly. I knew that wasn't a polite thing to do. But this was Bill we were talking about.

"You know how it goes with collections," he said, rolling his eyes. "You start out collectin' a few things, then everybody thinks you need more, then *they* start collectin' for you, and before you know it, you've got a billion of whatever it is."

"That's for sure," seconded Al. "I got way more dishtowels with ducks on 'em than any one man should own."

I could also relate, with my collection of Bigfoot tchotchkes growing at an alarming rate. The latest item was the t-shirt that Bill had just given me. "Word," I said, nodding my head slowly.

"Anyway," Al continued, "we're not here to talk about t-shirts 'n' stuff. We wanna know what's up with the sheep."

My attempt at stalling was over, but still I tried another tactic.

"I haven't received a comprehensive full-spectrum particulate analysis yet. However, preliminary findings are encouraging, and I'm running some additional visual structural comparisons which should give us more information on possible inter-species collaboration and geographic origination." I finished by flipping my hair out of my face. Both of their jaws dropped, and they didn't say a word. Perfect.

"So...you'll call us?" Al asked slowly.

"As soon as I hear back from the lab."

They stood there looking at me. It was almost too easy, and I felt a tiny bit bad. Then I got over it.

"Great!" I said, clapping my hands together loudly. "Okay, I have to get back to work now, but I'll be in touch." I started walking them toward the door.

They left the store and as the door closed behind them, I heard Al say, "Wow, that little lady is *smart!*"

"Yeah," said Bill, as they walked out of range. "She's smart as f—!"

I had placated them for now, but I had to admit, I didn't know what to do about the Sheep Problem. It was time to pace around the store again. Pacing around the store not only helped me think, it also helped me see what tasks needed to be done. As I walked, I noticed that I needed to dust a few of the display tables so I made my way to the back room to get the duster. I was still going to have to do something about the damn sheep though. Was I really going to have to do a *particulate analysis?* Was *visual structural comparison* code for looking at photos of sheep poop on the internet? This was getting out of hand. It felt like everything was getting out of hand.

Before I could make another pass through the store, I ran smack into something that wasn't there the last time I'd looped through. It was hard, but also soft. Its arms were wrapped around me. And it was warm, and it was laughing at me.

"Danny!" I gasped. I was so lost in thought, I hadn't heard him come in the door. Even though I was surprised, I made no attempt to pull away.

"Hiya, Bev." He made no attempt to pull away either. "What's new?"

It seemed like an all right place to be, wrapped in his arms, and neither of us appeared to be in a rush to be anywhere else. He was so close that I could hear him breathing lightly.

"Not much," I finally answered, still not moving. His face was *right there*, and my lips informed my brain that, sheriff or no sheriff, they wanted to head over and give Danny's lips a sexy fist bump.

Just then I heard a cough. It hadn't come from Danny. Someone else was in the store.

Still in Danny's arms, I slowly peered around his head and saw the sheriff standing by the door, hat in hand. "Sheriff!" *Uh oh,* my lips thought. Busted.

Danny released me from his arms, and we both turned to face the sheriff. He was watching me, and I felt self-conscious. My hand instinctively went up to my head, to check that my hair wasn't messed up. I started to feel guilty and I wasn't liking how often I was getting caught in awkward situations that weren't what they looked like.

I watched as the sheriff's gaze traveled next to Danny, and his eyes squinted ever so slightly. "Hi, Beverley," he said, still watching Danny. "Hello, Danny." He moved toward Danny with an outstretched hand.

"Hi, Sheriff Branch," Danny said as they shook hands. "I came by to grab a book and ran right into Bev here!" He stood back, hands on hips, and they both looked at me. It was like they were waiting for me to start tap dancing.

"Yes, well," I started. And then stopped. I didn't know any tap dance steps.

"I'll just go look to see if you have it," Danny said, walking off down one of the aisles and leaving the sheriff and me to stand there looking at each other.

"Hi," I said.

"Hi."

I couldn't think of what to say next and I was starting to panic. Fortunately, Danny made his way back up to the front of the store, holding a book. "Found it!" he said happily. He didn't seem to notice that he was walking into an awkward moment.

I moved to the cash wrap and rang up Danny's book: a field guide to trees of the Eastern United States. "A present for my niece," he explained. We completed the rest of the transaction in silence; I didn't know what to say. And Callan was making me nervous and I felt guilty. I was getting tired of feeling guilty. But why would I feel guilty? Was I feeling guilty because I liked Callan more than I cared to admit?

I handed Danny his receipt, and he headed for the door with his purchase. He looked at me, and then at the sheriff; we were both watching him. "Well, okay then," he said, sounding a little confused. "See you later, Beverley. Sheriff, let me know if you hear anything about that, um, thing."

"Will do. Take care," called out Callan.

"Bye, Danny, see ya." I held up my arm and started to wave at the closing door, like a big dork.

The door closed and Callan and I were left standing there, watching each other. One of us was trained to deal with criminals, angry people, and bureaucrats. The other had a barely-working verbal filter and several nervous tells. We both waited for me to say something.

I felt like I needed to confess something, although I didn't know what. Instead I went with an inane greeting. "So, what's new?"

"Just came by to say hi," he said as he sauntered over to the new release table again. I hadn't changed any of the books since the last time he pretended to look at it, yet he appeared to find it just as engrossing. He picked up the latest Michael Connelly tome to inspect. "I didn't get a chance to properly thank you for breakfast yesterday before I had to leave."

"My parents think we're sleeping together," I blurted out before I had a chance to censor myself. His head shot up and he stared at me, wide-eyed and mouth open. He dropped the book and it landed loudly on the floor.

He closed his mouth, then bent to pick up the book and put it back on the table. He cleared his throat, seeming to regain his composure quickly. Must have been all that meditation he did. "That's interesting," he said calmly.

"Well, you know, it was morning...and you had your shirt off..." I had the sense to stop before I ended up explaining the whole thing as if he hadn't been there. I wondered what would have happened if my parents hadn't shown up when they did. I kind of wanted a do-over.

"I remember."

"It's pretty funny, actually," I said, trying my hardest to find a bright side. "They totally got the wrong idea, of course. Except..." I thought of something that might cancel out any bright side.

"Except what?" he asked, sounding guarded.

"Well, it might make things difficult for you." I started walking toward him because he hadn't put the book he'd dropped back in the right spot, and it was driving me crazy. "I mean, I don't mind if they think something happened, because maybe now they'll stop setting me up on blind dates, at least for a little while. But my parents will talk. They talk a lot. It might be bad for your bachelor rep." I sidled up next to him and moved the book back to its proper place. He watched me do this, not saying a word.

We were standing very close to each other, and I swear I felt a little something-something. Not the kind of *thing* I'd felt when I ran into Mark, and not the same kind of *thing* that Danny had. This something-something was deeper than that. Like a fast-moving river, or lyrics to a Tom Waits song. Or maybe like a riptide. And I was in danger of getting pulled under.

When I looked at him, his expression had changed, and I could tell he'd felt it too. Well, this was interesting. "I wouldn't want anyone to get the wrong idea," I added quietly.

"That would be bad," he said. He kept looking at me.

It was perfectly quiet in the store; there was no noise from the furnace, or the computer or phone. Jimmy was quiet. I was quiet. The sheriff was quiet. I was starting to get that anxious feeling I got right before I started talking too much. As if on cue, my stomach growled. It was horribly embarrassing, but I was also grateful for my body's perfectly-timed comic relief. "Lunch time," I explained weakly.

He smiled. "I'm feeling a little hungry myself," he said. Oooh. Double entendre?

I was trying to screw up my courage to ask but as I opened my mouth to speak, the door opened too, and my part-time employee, Chuck, walked in. "Howdy!" he said, smiling at me. When he noticed I was with the sheriff, he lost the smile and started to look a little guilty. "Hi Sheriff, Sir," he said meekly, slinking in and taking his place behind the register. If I didn't know better, I'd have said that ol' Chuck "Banjo Man" Brown had something to hide. What college student didn't, I mused, thinking back to my own college days.

"Oh shit!" I said suddenly, and both Callan and Chuck turned to look at me, wide-eyed. "Sorry. I mean, dang! I'm late! I'm meeting Kelly for lunch. I've got to run!" I went behind the counter and picked up my bag.

"I'll walk you out," Callan said, eyeing Chuck suspiciously.

"Bye," said Chuck. "Hey, Bev, text me if you want me to do anything special this afternoon."

"I will," I called as I went out the door. I would be off for the rest of the day, so I made a mental note to text him a to-do list.

"Can I give you a lift?" Callan asked.

"That would be great, thanks."

He walked to the passenger side door of his SUV and opened it for me. I could get used to this, I thought. He walked around to the driver's side, got in, and started it up.

"Do we get to use the lights and siren?" I asked.

"It's only two blocks."

"Oh."

We were silent for the rest of the drive. I was nervous, but I managed to keep myself from making any stupid conversation. It was a first.

When we pulled up in front of Stacy's, Callan stopped his SUV and looked over at me. "Enjoy your lunch," he said warmly.

"I will, thanks. Maybe I'll see you around?"

"Maybe."

Such a dude, I thought. I shrugged my shoulders and smiled before opening the door and hopping out. Two could play that game.

"Don't order the catfish," he warned.

"No problem," I said lightly. "I never mess with bottom-feeders."

———

I had been running late but Kelly was running even later, so I still got to our regular booth first. I sat down and pulled out a book. I hadn't finished the romance I was reading, but I felt too self-conscious to read it in public. I was a Modern Woman and all that, but I still thought the busy restaurant wasn't the best place to display a book titled *Throb*. Instead I had brought the third book in the series by Robert Galbraith.

Molly eyed me with caution; I couldn't say as I blamed her. I smiled, and she came over with my water and a menu. I had even remembered to look over the specials board when I came in. Fried chicken. No thanks. But I reckoned Kelly would order it.

We exchanged pleasantries and I ordered a hot tea. So far, so good. I didn't feel a nervous breakdown coming on; maybe everything would be okay today. I was no closer to knowing what I should be doing about my novel or anything else, but right now it was lunchtime and I didn't want to think about it.

My new book was so good right off the bat that I didn't notice Kelly had walked up and sat down across from me, or that Molly had brought me my tea.

"Another propaganda piece from the patriarchy?" Kelly asked, nodding at the cover of my book.

"Actually, Robert Galbraith is the *nom de plume* for Miss JK Rowling, so your patriarchal conspiracy theories can suck it."

"Huh. Wonder why she wanted to publish under a man's name."

"Apparently, she wanted to get as far from her previous writing persona as possible."

"Oh yeah? Or maybe she just felt she needed to in order to win at a man's game."

There was no point trying to convince her that not everyone had an ulterior motive. Besides, why would a woman *want* to win at a man's game anyway? I'd rather make up my own game and win at that. "Well—"

Kelly held up one hand and interrupted me. "Male patriarchy one, JK Rowling zip."

I sighed.

Molly came back and sure as shootin', Kelly ordered the fried chicken. I got a chicken salad sandwich with a green salad. After Molly left to put in our orders, I asked Kelly how she'd been since we last caught up.

"Pretty good actually!" she said, and I could hear the enthusiasm for her job in her voice. "I picked up two new cases; they seem interesting. An ugly divorce and some kind of property dispute between your pal Al Turner and my new client—one of his neighbors."

"Well, good for you. I know how you love those ugly divorces. And anything involving Al is going to be very interesting." I thought back to my visit to his place on Saturday.

"It's already very interesting," she said cryptically, drumming the table with her fingers—a sure sign she was hungry. "But anyway, how's *your* week been? Are you still freaking out about being bored and boyfriend-less?" There was no lack of sarcasm in her voice.

"My week has been...interesting," I said flatly.

"Oh yeah? Spill it."

"Well, let's see. Where to start? I've decided I need a Life Plan because everyone keeps telling me I need one. My parents set me up on a blind date—with Sheriff Branch. Then Al Turner tried to hire me to perform my very first private investigation job. I got coerced into working on said mystery by Mark, under the guise of writing another Bigfoot article. So now I have to solve a missing barnyard animal mystery *and* write another Bigfoot article. Then I caught Al in what looked a hell of a lot like a *menage a trois* with his cousin Bill and Leona Tisdale. Oh, and now my parents think I'm sleeping with the sheriff."

I took a drink of water and checked out Kelly's expression over the top of my glass. I expected her to look utterly shocked, but she was just calmly smiling at me. "What, don't you believe me?" I asked.

"Of course I do. *Are* you sleeping with the sheriff?"

Before I could say, "Of course not," I had a brief vision of his bare chest in my kitchen. "No," I said with a hint of regret that I hadn't meant to put in there.

"I hear ya," said Kelly, picking up on my wistfulness. We shared a quiet moment and I knew what we were both thinking about. "He *is* pretty hot," she said slowly. We both nodded. "So, a typical week then," she added.

"Pretty much."

"See? This is real life in a small town. You can't make this shit up! But all that happened in only one week? That part is impressive."

"I know, right?" I said. I was a bit perturbed that she wasn't more surprised by all my news. But that was Kelly; she was unflappable. "You want to know the weirdest part? The Sheriff does *yoga!*"

"No shit! Well, actually, I'm not surprised by that either. He's in great shape—" She hesitated. "Yeah, he's always been in great shape."

I laughed. "You were going to say, 'for his age,' weren't you!"

She laughed too. "I was! But yeah, he's not too much older than we are, so..."

"So, you'd better watch what you say and stop looking so smug."

"I can't help it. You got so frustrated that things were boring. And now it sounds like they're definitely not boring." Then she started laughing so loud that she drew the attention of neighboring tables.

"What's so funny?" I asked.

"Your parents," she sputtered, "set you up on a freaking blind date..." She burst out laughing again.

"Okay, okay, I know. Ha ha."

"You have to admit they have good taste." She stopped laughing and used her napkin to wipe her eyes.

I wanted to deny it, but I couldn't. "Look, just don't say anything to anyone, okay? There's nothing to tell, anyway. He said he's not interested in seeing anyone right now, and I told him I wasn't, either."

Kelly shot me a look like she wanted to hurt me. "You've got to be kidding."

"Nope. I mean, I did invite him over for breakfast, but that doesn't count."

"In what universe doesn't that count?" she asked.

"I don't want to go out with anyone, okay? You people aren't hearing me."

"Fine, I hear you. I just don't believe you. So how did your non-date breakfast go?"

"I kind of spilled coffee on him and he had to take his shirt off, so I kind of saw him shirtless. And that was right about the time my parents showed up. They completely misconstrued the situation. It was so embarrassing."

"And so they think you and he..."

"Yeah."

She started laughing again. "Oh man, this is too good."

I furrowed my brow at her, but she didn't notice because Molly brought our food. We ate in silence for a few minutes.

"Wait, did you say Al, Bill, and Leona are having a *menage a trois*?"

"Well, I don't know for sure," I admitted. I told her the story of how I went over to Al's and I saw Leona and Bill leave in various states of questionable dishevelment, and how Al told me he'd been "taking a nap" during their "meeting."

"I know I said I wasn't surprised by anything you told me, but that is pretty weird."

"Tell me about it! I don't know what to think."

"What were you doing there?"

"Doing research for the damn article that Mark's making me write. Or working on a private investigator job. I'm not sure how to describe it, to be honest."

"You're not a private investigator."

"I tried to tell Al and Bill that, but they didn't seem to care."

"What are you investigating again?"

I was starting to feel full, so I pushed my plate away and watched Kelly inhale the last scraps of crunchy chicken breading off her plate. I told her about Al's missing sheep. Confidentially, of course.

"Do you have any leads?" she asked me, as if it were a real case.

"Just one."

She looked at me, waiting to elaborate. "Bigfoot," I said. Her mouth twisted into a weird shape as she tried not to laugh. "Oh," she said slowly. "Interesting."

Then I told her about the sheriff mentioning Danny's missing sheep.

"So, to summarize, you know Al 'borrowed' sheep from Danny before they went missing and you think Bigfoot took them," she said.

"Right," I sighed.

"Uh huh. Well, it's not out of the question." Unflappable.

"I think I might have gotten myself into something weird."

"What else is new? Just remember to be careful about what you wish for," she reminded me.

I glowered at her. "I don't even know what that means anymore. I'm not *wishing* to work on Bigfoot mysteries. I'm not *wishing* for my parents to be meddling busybodies. And I'm definitely not wishing for continued notoriety as the Bigfoot Lady. I do wish I had more of an idea of what I want to do with my life. But instead, I got all this crap." I turned one hand palm-up. "You told me I'm supposed to be thinking about what I want. I have no idea what I want. In the meantime, things just get weirder and weirder."

"That's because you're worrying about what you're supposed to want. You're sending out weird vibes to the universe, Bev. The universe is responding right back with its own weird shit."

"I had no idea you were a new age life coach as well as a lawyer," I snapped.

"I majored in law, minored in new age," she said, blowing off my crankiness.

I was silent again as I scowled at my chicken salad. Mercifully, Kelly changed the subject.

"So, what are you going to do about the sheep thing?" she asked.

"I don't know. I'm tempted to chuck it all and walk away. But that's not a good long-term solution. I do want to help Al and Bill try to find out what happened. I'd hate for them to get in trouble for something so...stupid."

"Well, that probably happens to them more than you realize," she reminded me. "You can't be there to save them every time."

"True. But maybe I can this time."

Suddenly she let out a little gasp and looked at me like a lightbulb had gone off in her head. "Oh my," she said slowly.

"What is it?"

"This property dispute that my client is having with Al Turner..." She stopped and reached for her bag, riffling through it and pulling out a manila folder. She thumbed through the papers inside, took one out and started reading it. "Just as I thought!"

"What? What *is* it?"

"My client told me that she found some decaying carcasses on her property, close to Al's side of her land. She said she thought Al had left them there on purpose as a threat, or maybe just to be mean, because they smell to high heaven."

"Oh," I said slowly. "Are they still there? Do you think they could be sheep?"

She pulled out her phone. "Let's find out," she said as she dialed.

An hour and one piece of blueberry pie later, we were at the Rogers' place, right up the road from Al's house. On the way, I'd called Mark to tell him that regrettably, I would be absent from the

Ledger staff meeting. He started to get angry, but I told him I was in hot pursuit of Bigfoot, and that did the trick.

Kelly informed me on the drive over that Betty Ann Rogers and her husband Eldon had been living on the property next to Al's for over thirty years. Betty Ann was the one with the money, the land, and the one who wore the pants in the family.

When we stopped at the house to talk to Betty Ann, she saw us come up the drive and walked out onto the front porch to meet us. She was literally wearing the pants—faded jeans tucked into rain boots, topped off with an old plaid shirt. Her white hair was piled up on her head in a messy bun. Eldon was sitting in a lawn chair on the porch without his pants.

"Eldon, for kee-rist's sake, would you go in and put your pants on!" she yelled at him. Eldon got up leisurely from his lawn chair, scratched his belly, and went in the house.

"Lord have mercy," she said to us after Kelly asked about the dead animal remains. "It's the most hugest, disgusting pile of stinky animal remains ever. It's like a bomb went off or something! One of those biological weapons like they got on the TV shows. Smells to high heaven. That damn Al Turner!"

Kelly tried to remind Betty Ann that it may not have anything to do with Al, but it was a losing battle. She had it in for Al, but bad. We told her we'd check it out and try to get to the bottom of it.

"I wouldn't say this to anyone else," Betty Ann said, looking my way. "But since you're an expert and all... I suppose there's a possibility it coulda been Bigfoot and not Al."

Oh, snap dangity. They were everywhere. "Right," I said, bobbing my head. "Sure." Kelly stifled a laugh.

We asked Betty Ann where exactly the biohazard pile was, and she pointed us toward Al's property, telling us to drive down the dirt road in that direction. She said we wouldn't miss the "giant mound of rotting flesh" as she hadn't had the chance to do anything about it yet.

"If I wait long enough, it'll get eaten up by varmints anyway," she told us. We all nodded in agreement.

We thanked her as we got back in Kelly's car, and drove down the road as instructed.

"I'm not sure I want to see it after how she described it," I muttered.

"Especially right after eating lunch," Kelly added.

"I told you we shouldn't have gotten pie."

"Lunch is not lunch without pie."

The road was bumpy, and it was slow going, but we finally stopped when we saw a messy pile of what looked to be organic material. It was a lot smaller than I'd imagined after Betty Ann's description and, truth be told, we almost missed it.

I couldn't help but notice that the fence separating the Rogers' property from Al's was only about forty feet away. It was the side of the fence that had a hole in it. There was a small copse of redbud trees and short shrubs between the fence and the pile of organic material, so when I had done my inspection of Al's fence on Saturday, I hadn't seen the carcass pile. I hadn't thought to look, in any case. Plus, this pile of gunk was rather tiny.

We got out of the car and walked over to the pile. It was indeed a mound of something that at one time had been alive. There were a few bones poking out here and there, and there were feathers. Lots of feathers.

"Eeew," I said.

"Damn, that smells!" Kelly exclaimed. "But it's not very big. I was expecting a huge pile of something gross; this is just a tiny pile of something gross. Can you tell what it is?"

"Looks like birds. Maybe chickens." We walked a little closer. I saw no sign of anything that could be considered once having been part of a sheep. But how the heck would I know, I reminded myself.

"Well, not that I'm a forensics evidence expert or anything," Kelly said, "but none of this looks like sheep bits to me."

We stood and watched the feathers rustling in the afternoon breeze.

Suddenly I felt fear deep down in my gut—maybe one of the chickens had been Beryl. It was possible; she did seem to get around. Could she have finally met her demise here? I wouldn't be surprised. But as I inspected the remains more closely, I noticed that all of the feathers in the pile were white or dark brown. Beryl was a rusty orange color. No Beryl. I breathed a sigh of relief. There was hope that she was still out there somewhere, making someone miserable.

I took my phone and my reporter's notebook out of my back pocket. "Did Betty Ann call the police about it?" I asked. As I was taking some photos, a text came in from Callan. Speaking of police. I'd look at it later.

"I don't think so," Kelly said. "At least not yet. I do know she wants to hit Al with a contract dispute and maybe a harassment complaint. There's a discrepancy over the border of the property—she claims her land extends past that fence there." She pointed to Al's fence.

I looked even more closely at the little pile. As I did, I spotted something that caught my eye, so I bent down to get a better look. It was a wisp of light brown hair. I reached for a stick and pulled the wisp of fur out and held it up.

"Curious," I mumbled. Kelly bent down to look too.

"Fur?"

"Yup."

She stood up again and moaned. "We need to get out of here. I think that pie is on its way back up."

Laughing, I stood up too. "I feel like if Al were going to send a message, he'd send a different one. Besides, I think these might be his chickens. Why would he kill his own chickens?"

"True. I mean the guy is weird, but that seems a little extreme, even for him."

"Yeah. Still weird though..." I got lost in thought.

"Don't tell me this has something to do with your private investigator job."

"I don't know," I confessed. "But I feel like it does, somehow. I don't think this is a message from Al for Betty Ann. He's not this sophisticated."

I made a few notes and took a few more pictures before we got back in Kelly's car and started back toward town.

"So, I'm still no further along in solving the Sheep Problem," I said as I stared out the window.

"If anything, you now have a Sheep and a Chicken Problem," Kelly laughed.

"Yeah..."

"So, you don't think Al did it on purpose?"

"I doubt it." He just didn't strike me as all that vindictive. "For now, tell your client to leave the dead animals out of her legal actions. Tell her there's been some reports of a coyote or a wolf in the area."

"Or Bigfoot," Kelly added.

I sighed. "As much as it pains me to say these words, I guess we can't rule that out either."

"Maybe he couldn't decide between chicken or mutton, so he went for both," she suggested.

"Ugh." I leaned the passenger seat way back and crossed my arms, pretending to sleep.

"I guess he's not vegan," she said.

"Just call your client," I snapped.

"Okay. I'll call her later this afternoon. I need to get back to the office first." When we got back into town, she dropped me off at Hoboken so I could get a much-needed coffee.

12

"I NEED A FLAT WHITE, STAT!" I said to Seth as I walked in the door of Hoboken. There were about ten people sitting at tables, and they all looked up at me from their laptops. I was surprised they'd heard me through their earbuds, but I had probably been pretty loud. Screw it; it was a coffee emergency.

Seth started making my drink, and as I waited, I sat down and tried to make a mental list of everything that was going on. Things may have been kind of weird before, but now they were getting *really* weird. Let's see. We had two missing sheep that were probably dead, possibly killed by the hand of a Sasquatch. We had a pile of chicken remains. Probably Al's chickens. We had what looked like a love triangle between Leona, Al, and Bill. My parents thought I was doing the deed with the local law man. Part of me wished I *was* doing the deed with the local law man. What was going on there? Of all the weirdness, this one was the most frustrating. I did not want a boyfriend. I did not want a boyfriend. I did not want—I wanted some aspirin because I was getting a spectacular headache.

I also had an article to write about Leona, one about Bigfoot, yet another about the sheriff, and then there was that damn novel thing. I was moving right past headache and straight for mental instability. Who the hell had time to even think about writing a novel?

As I continued to wait for my coffee, I remembered the text from Callan. I pulled out my phone and read it.

Callan: ***Do you have tome to talk later?***

I heard Seth call my name and by the sound of it, it wasn't the first time. I must have zoned out. I retrieved the drink from the counter, apologized to Seth, and sat back down to answer the text.

Me: ***Sure, what's up?***

I waited a minute or two but when I didn't get an answer, I put my phone back in my pocket and left the shop.

I sipped my coffee as I walked back to my car, which was parked by The Book Store. I was lost in thought but as I crossed the street in front of Craddick's Barber Shop, I heard someone call my name. A little further up the street were Al and Bill. They were standing in front of Al's truck, waving at me. I waved back and kept walking, but Al called out again and waved me over. Shoot. I wasn't ready to tell them I didn't have anything on the sheep yet, but I also couldn't escape, so I took a deep breath and started walking toward them.

I got about halfway there and suddenly I heard barking. Or it could have been an angry dinosaur. Or maybe a bulldozer. The noise was loud and ferocious. I almost lost the grip on my coffee cup, it scared me so badly. I looked around, expecting to see a crazed wolf barreling toward me. My body prepared to ditch the coffee and run for the hills. Then I noticed that the noise was coming from a cage in the back of Al's truck. My heart started back up.

"Come on over. He ain't gonna hurt you!" Al said proudly. "Come meet Smiley!"

Smiley?

As I got closer, the barking got even louder and the cage started rattling and shaking. I hoped they had latched it properly. "Hi guys." I stopped about ten feet away, rocking back and forth from my heels to my toes. Just to stay limber in case I had to make a break for it. "Whatcha got there, Al?"

"Meet Smiley Dawg! I found him as a pup a few years back, all tiny and scruffy and hungry." Al looked back at the cage adoringly, like he had his child locked up in there. "Didn't know he was gonna grow up to be so dang big though," he added thoughtfully. "Isn't he the cutest?"

I peered at the cage from my ten-foot safety zone. It was as close as I'd care to get in this lifetime. Inside was what looked to be a beast that I wouldn't have believed was a dog, if Al hadn't told me so. It was the size of a small horse and had teeth the size of my hands. His coat was a mottled mix of earthen colors ranging from cream to brown to charcoal grey. He was three tons of muscle and meanness, and he was still barking at me like he wanted to gnaw on me for his afternoon teatime snack.

"He wasn't at your house the other day, was he?" I asked, quite sure that I'd have remembered him if he was.

"Nope," answered Al. "I had to take him to the emergency vet last week on account of he ate the garden hose again and part of a lawn chair. And maybe some other stuff the vet couldn't identify. Anyway, ol' Smiley here had to stay at the vet for a while. We're lucky we didn't lose him!" He turned toward the cage and stuck his hand between the metal bars. My jaw dropped and I had a vision of having to rush Al to the hospital, with his severed hand in my paper coffee cup for safekeeping until someone could sew it back on. "Ain't that right, Smiley Dawg!" The monster stopped barking and started licking Al's hand. My heart started back up yet again. I imagined Al buying the dog from a mysterious traveling gypsy who had dinosaur eggs and two-headed snakes in the back of his caravan.

"So, didja figure out what happened to the, uh, subjects of the investigation?" asked Bill. I'd forgotten he was there until he spoke up. I turned to him, and again had to marvel at his t-shirt selection. This one was a royal blue, with white cursive lettering that said *Life's a Bitch, Then You Die.* Classic. The letters of the words curved around his beach ball belly.

And then an idea hit me. It wasn't like something big, like a train or bus, but more like a compact car. A Chevy Spark-sized idea hit me. "Not quite," I said to Bill. "But I think I'm making some progress."

"Did you do your particulate analyzation?" asked Bill. Smiley snuffled at Al's had again. I wanted to look away, but I just couldn't.

"Working on it," I said, never taking my eyes off the doggie. "I'll have something for you soon. But right now, I've got to run."

"Are you headed to your store?" asked Bill. "I'll walk with you! I need to talk to you about something."

"Okay then, let's go," I said. "See you tomorrow, Al." I raised my had to waive goodbye, and turned on my heel. Bill followed.

"Bye-bye now," called Al. "Smiley, say goodbye to the nice lady."

"Woof!"

I started walking in the direction of The Book Store with Bill in tow. I didn't think I was that fast of a walker, but he had a little trouble keeping up. He was a bit portly and carrying around a few more beers in his belly than I was, so I cut him some slack and slowed my pace. I wondered why he wanted to talk with me.

"So, you might be wondering why I wanted to talk to you," he started.

"I guess."

"Well, it's just that you're a real smart little lady and I had this business idea see, and I wanted to know what you thought of it."

"Okay, but in return, I have a question for you."

He paused for a second. "I guess that's fair," he conceded.

"Okay. What's your question?" I asked.

"You know how I got all these t-shirts, right? I got a ton of 'em. And people keep giving me more. And I don't know how it happens, but then I find good deals on even more t-shirts. So, I was thinking, why don't I sell some of my shirts? Because people are asking me to find them certain ones or they like the ones I got on. So...what if I started sellin' 'em?"

We had gotten to the bookstore, and we stopped in front of my car which was parked out front. I considered his idea. "Like, online? Or in an actual store?"

"I don't know anything about computer stuff," he scoffed. "I thought I might open up a little shop, like you did!"

I wanted to laugh heartily in his face. Bill? Run a store? Selling vintage t-shirts? Ordinarily, I'd say he was crazy to try it. But the more I thought about it, the more I thought the guy might be able to pull it off. He seemed to have a pretty fair share of dumb luck, except for when it came to stealing sheep. "Well, I guess it depends on what your overhead is," I said.

"My overwhat?"

"Like, how much your rent and utilities and other expenses would cost compared to how much profit you could realistically make on your shirts. And maybe you'd have to spend money on advertising and stuff like that. If you want to get rich off your shirts, I wouldn't bet on it. But if you're looking for something fun to do and maybe make a little extra folding money in the process, I say go for it."

His face brightened. "Really?" he asked.

"Why not? What's the worst thing that could happen?" I pictured his store going up in flames or being swallowed by a sinkhole.

"Great! I think I got a line on a location already. Maybe I could do this, for reals!"

I was all for encouraging the entrepreneurial spirit. "Just let me know how I can help," I offered. I hoped I wouldn't live to regret that offer. "Now, I have a question for you."

"Shoot," he said, his eyes big as latte cup saucers.

"You know the other day, Saturday, when I came out to Al's house to look around? You and Leona were there. And you, uh, kind of left in a hurry. And you looked a little, how can I put this? Disheveled." I watched his face closely. No reaction yet. I was going to go for it. "So, what's going on with you three? What was that about?"

Bill proceeded to turn pale and he looked down to the ground. "Well..."

I waited.

"I'm not sure I should say anything."

"Oh, come on, Bill. Who am I going to tell? We're friends, right?"

"All right," he said slowly. Oh yeah, this was going to be good, I could tell.

He took a deep breath before spilling the beans. "It's like this. I kinda got a thing for Leona."

"Okay..." I said slowly, waiting for the rest.

"And she kinda likes me too, only she doesn't want anyone to know about her and me. So that day, we arranged to meet at Al's for lunch. And Al fell asleep after we ate. So..."

Now this was making more sense to me. "So, you and Leona..."

"We had a little cuddle time, is all," he said sheepishly.

Well, wasn't that just the cutest? I could picture them as a couple about as well as I could picture putting spaghetti sauce in my flat white. She was so prim and proper and grumpy, and Bill was just so...Bill.

"Yeah," he sighed. "I got it bad for her. Only I can't tell how much she likes me. Sure, she'll get busy with me on the QT, but I want to share my feelings and tell everyone she's my girl." His chest puffed out a little as he spoke, and he seemed to get a little taller.

I held my breath in for a few beats, for fear of bursting into loud, inappropriate guffaws. "Yeah, that's tough. Women, huh? All you men want to do is share your feelings, and we're so difficult."

"I tell ya," said Bill, shaking his head. "Y'all are confusing A-F."

"I know, Bill, I know. But we're worth it. You stay strong, now."

"Thanks," he said, reaching out and putting his hand on my shoulder.

We stood there and both looked at his hand. He carefully withdrew it.

"Don't tell anyone," he cautioned me.

"I won't, I promise."

"Okay. Well, I better git. I got a store to open!" He looked a little happier as he waved goodbye and shuffled off down the street.

So, I'd been wrong about the love triangle, but this was just as good.

When I finally made it home, it was dark and I was hungry and tired. I made a beeline for the chicken coop, though, to say hi to the girls. Still no sign of Beryl. I gave them a little dinner. They were happy to see me, maybe a little more than usual. They were always friendlier when Beryl was missing. She could be such a bitch. I sure did miss her.

"You'll find a way to persevere without your alpha chicken," I told the remaining hens. I looked up at the starry sky, wondering where she was. "Godspeed, you crazy little bird," I sighed.

I went back in and pulled some homemade veggie soup out of the freezer, putting it in a pot to heat up on the stovetop. As it thawed, I sat at the kitchen table and made some notes. I took out my phone to check my messages—no new text from Callan. Well, first things first. The Sheep Problem.

What did I know so far? I made a list.

WHAT I KNOW SO FAR

1. Al is missing 2 sheep

2. Danny is missing 2 sheep. Reported to sheriff

3. Found at scene of disappearance: brown and cream hair, chicken feather, poop (origin: unknown)

4. Found on Rogers property: dead animals appearing to be chickens, one wisp brown hair
5. Al has large "dog"
6. Dog could easily eat chicken, sheep, small car
7. Bigfoot could easily eat chicken, sheep, large dog

POSSIBLE CONCLUSIONS
— Dog ate sheep, chickens
— Bigfoot ate sheep, Beryl
— Dog ate Bigfoot
— Everything is Beryl's fault
— Al stole the sheep from Danny
— Sheriff could arrest Al
—I like the Sheriff

I had started to go way off topic, but I didn't have much of a topic to start with. I was feeling lost, over my head, and out of ideas.

Did Bigfoot exist? Just the idea that the answer could be yes sent a new wave of dread through me. The authenticity of my encounter last year had been questionable at best and had happened long enough ago that I'd kind of forgotten about how much it had scared me. But now, I was scared all over again. My nervous system was spending a lot of time in fight or flight mode.

I pulled out my laptop and did a few searches to see if there was any new local Bigfoot chatter out there in the crazy section of the internet. I found a few new posts of more grainy photos, one new report of a giant footprint, and more talk of mysterious Hostess Cupcake thefts. I tried to search for information on what Sasquatches ate besides cupcakes, and it was a might bit scary. If I'd read that stuff before I went on my stakeout last year, I never would have gone. There was a lot of talk about how they liked bacon. That part made sense. Who didn't like bacon? So far, I was on board with Bigfoot's favorite foods. But then I read about how they liked to break the legs of their prey to immobilize them, so they couldn't get away and would be handy snacks for later. It sounded downright gruesome and terrifying. Kind of like a Sasquatch Mafia.

Well, it didn't prove Bigfoot had taken Al's sheep but none of it proved otherwise, either. I sure hoped that those poor sheep weren't stuck out there somewhere with broken legs, waiting to be eaten by a Sasquatch.

I considered simply going with the "Bigfoot did it" angle. It did seem as plausible as any other explanation. And it was the easiest conclusion to reach. I knew everyone would love it, and a story like that would make another great newspaper article. It would prove Al and Bill were right. And I had to admit, it would get me out of this mess a whole lot faster.

I was about to give up and pronounce Bigfoot the winner when I heard a knock on my front door. Oh my god. It was either Bigfoot or my parents. I wasn't sure which option would be scarier.

I turned the porch light on and looked out the peephole. A cowboy hat. I stepped back and tried to pretend I wasn't elated that there was a sheriff at my door. I had to play this cool, yo. I smoothed my hair and took inventory of how I looked. Oh well. It was too late to pretend I wasn't home. I opened the door.

"Hi, Callan!" I chirped. If I had been trying to play it cool, I'd just blown it. Quick! Proceed with diversionary tactics! "Am I in trouble or something?"

"You've got to stop asking me that," he said, taking off his hat.

"Sorry. It's just that...well, I'm surprised to see you."

"I hope it's not too late?" he asked, taking off his hat and stepping inside after I waved him in. He looked a little sheepish, like he really was worried he'd come over too late. It was 7:15.

"Not at all. I was about to have some dinner. Want some? It's just homemade vegetable soup."

"*Just* homemade?" he asked. "That's the best kind."

"I'll take that as a 'yes' then."

He nodded.

We went to the kitchen, and I stirred the soup while he started poking around, presumably looking for bowls and spoons.

"You're not planting evidence, are you?" I asked.

"You've got some guilt issues," he said calmly, placing two bowls on the counter next to me.

"You don't know the half of it. Have you *met* my mother?"

He smiled but didn't say anything.

After some small talk, the soup was ready, and I ladled it into the bowls.

"You're not going to dump any of that on me, are you?" he asked, eyeing the steam wafting out of the bowls as I brought them to the table.

"You've got some trust issues," I retorted.

"It looks hotter than that coffee was."

"I'll be extra careful." I managed not to spill anything, and we sat down at the table to eat our soup with some toasted bread and butter. He hadn't mentioned anything about why he had come over, and by this time, I was very curious.

I tried not to do my usual thing of filling all the silence with a lot of stupid words. It was going all right so far. The more time we spent together, the easier it got to simply enjoy his company. But I was still a little nervous as to why he had come by. I ate my soup and waited until he was ready to say something.

"Good soup," he said finally.

"Thanks, it's the 'throw everything in the fridge into a pot and cook it' recipe. Works every time—almost."

"What happens when it doesn't work?"

"I eat it anyway."

He was silent again, and we were nearing the end of the meal. I was almost at my limit and was about to say something dumb just to get the discussion going, when he finally spoke.

"I'm guessing you're wondering why I stopped by," he said, stirring the last of his soup.

"No... yeah, okay, yes." I got up, got two Emergency Beers, and put them on the table in front of us. Just in case.

"You know how I told you I wasn't interested in seeing anyone," he reminded me.

"Yeah, sure." I took a swig of my beer.

"Well, I changed my mind." He took an even bigger swig of his beer.

I felt like I'd stepped off a curb I hadn't seen was there, and now I was falling in slow motion. I put my hand on the table to break my fall.

"I'd like to take you out to dinner on Friday," he continued.

His voice was steady and calm, and he sounded like a man who knew what he wanted. I'd be lying if I didn't say I found that damn pleasing. What should I say? In a split second, I thought of all the things in my life that were a complete mess, which encompassed most things. A Bigfoot article. A Sheep Problem. A rented house and contraband fowl. A directionless life. An unwritten romance novel. An uncertain future. My lack of a plan for my life and my insistence that I didn't want to complicate any of it by adding in a boyfriend. Why on earth would I want to bring someone else into my messy life? It wouldn't be fair.

The sheriff gently cleared his throat, and I realized he'd been waiting for an answer for a good while.

"I don't think that would be a good idea," I said slowly, staring down at my bowl.

I looked up again, thinking that I should explain why I was saying no, but no words were coming out of my mouth. I tried harder. I owed him that much. But nothing was happening.

He looked up at me and when our eyes met, I saw disappointment. I hadn't realized he felt this way. Perhaps all of those things I'd been feeling for him, he'd felt them too. And here I was, shooting him down.

"I don't know what I'm doing," I said, gripping my beer like my life depended on it. "With the bookstore, with my writing, with my whole life. I can't add you into that mix; it wouldn't be fair to you. To either of us." I felt so adult. It sucked.

Callan nodded his head a few times. He looked almost as

unreadable as usual, except his shoulders looked a little droopier. I wanted to tell him that I was doing him a big favor by turning him down, that if we started spending time together it would be very bad for him, and I didn't know what I wanted and that he should avoid me like the plague. And I wanted to explain how I was obviously bad at relationships and scared to even try. But now I opted for silence. And so did he.

Finally, he spoke. He made an innocuous comment about the weather, and the awkward moment passed, sort of. He took one last swig from his bottle and looked at it thoughtfully before getting up to leave. I walked him to the door where he put his hat back on.

"Thanks for dinner," he said.

"You're welcome, anytime." He arched an eyebrow at me. "Oh. I mean, almost anytime. No, I mean...you're welcome."

He smiled weakly and walked out the door.

I closed it behind him and stood there, unsure of what to do next. I wished he'd have said something. I wished he would have agreed with me. Or maybe tried harder to convince me to go out with him. Oh hell, I didn't even know what I'd wanted him to say, but anything would have been better than his calm, kind silence. I knew I had made the right rational decision, though. I was saving him and me, but especially him, from a whole mess of grief. Yeah, I was doing us both a favor.

It was the crappiest-feeling favor ever.

13

Tuesday morning, I awoke from a bad night's sleep, full of dreams about Bigfoot eating sheep kabobs. It felt like Sasquatch would haunt my subconscious forever. Well, that was fine, I reasoned, as long as he stayed there and kept out of my backyard.

One of my dreams had been slightly different, though. In this one, I was working at a diner and Bigfoot came in to order his sheep kabobs, but before I could put the order in, Sheriff Branch arrested Bigfoot. My hero! I started feeling bad about the previous evening all over again.

I was so tired that I opted for driving to work again, and I slogged around the store all morning. I was distracted by everything that was wrong with my life. I knew I was just feeling sorry for myself, something I rarely did, but it seemed to be happening more often.

Most of the time, I knew that the only one responsible for how things were going in my life was me. But lately that had all gone out the window and everything—absolutely everything—felt out of my control. Even Jimmy felt it; he stayed in the little barn all day.

Around eleven, I got a call from Leona asking if I could meet her at 12:30 at Stacy's, instead of later in the afternoon as we'd originally planned. Luckily, Chuck was coming in for a few hours and I would be able to leave the store, so I agreed.

As soon as Chuck came in, I took off for Stacy's. I wasn't getting anything done in the store, anyway. I'd be early, but I had a book with me, and I also planned to get a little snack. Ideally one that came with fries.

Stacy's was crowded, but I had no trouble finding a booth in the back. I took the side that faced the door, so I could see Leona when she came in. I settled in, ordered a grilled cheese sandwich, fries and a salad, and pulled out my book.

Before long, however, I started to get the feeling that I was being watched. I looked up from my book, and the sheriff was sitting across from me in the booth.

"How did you do that?" I asked.

"Wasn't hard. You're really into that book," he said, leaning over the table a little. "Plus, I've been trained to be stealthy."

"I don't know if I should be scared or impressed," I said, closing my book.

"Both."

Molly came to the table and brought me my food, but his eyes never left me.

"Hi, Sheriff," she said. "Can I get you anything?"

"Hi, Molly," he said to her, still watching me with those deep brown eyes. "I'm good for now. Thanks though."

"Okie dokie," I watched her look longingly at him, like he was a warm chocolate chip cookie fresh out of the oven. I thought she might start drooling, but she finally turned and left our table.

I was feeling uncomfortable and wondering what he wanted. Why else would he come talk to me after I'd just given him the brush-off? "I'm sorry about last night," I said, looking at my fries.

"Don't worry about it," he said casually. "We can still be friends, right?"

I brightened at this idea. "Yes, for sure."

He nodded once.

I could smell my grilled cheese sandwich, and I looked down at it and then back to him.

"Looking good," he said.

"What, the sandwich?" I looked down at it.

"That too." Oh my. After everything, was he actually still flirting with me? I looked him in the eye; he did appear to look hungry. In fact, his eyes had a kind of smoldering quality that hadn't been there before. It was part romance novel smolder, part *I want that sandwich.* Either way, it was pretty hot. I felt myself starting to blush. I needed to say something that would change the subject.

"Want some?" I asked. Oh fiddlesticks! I was terrible at this. "Of the sandwich! You're hot. I mean it's hot! Wait." I took a deep breath. "You want some?" I was digging myself deeper into my hole. My face got hotter. "No, wait. I mean, would you like half of my sandwich?" That sounded okay. I was exhausted now.

When I finally had the courage to look at him, he was trying to hold back a smile. His eyes were bright, and he still looked hungry. "Okay," he said.

I pushed the plate to the middle of the table, picking up half the sandwich and taking a bite. I prayed cheese wouldn't ooze down my chin, memories of the Great Avocado Splooch Incident from last year fresh in my mind.

"We've been eating together a lot lately," he said, taking his half of the sandwich.

"Is that good or bad?"

"Depends on who's cooking."

I nodded and speared a fry on my fork. "In this case, it's a good thing. Help yourself to some fries," I offered. He nodded, and took one off the plate, holding it between two long fingers. He brought it halfway to his mouth, and then stopped and looked at me over the fry. Something about it felt kind of dirty. I liked it. He ate the fry and I reached for my ice water.

"Oh hey!" I said, remembering I had something for him.

"What?" he asked, taking a bite of his piece of sandwich. Half of the half disappeared.

I pulled out his shirt from my bag. "I've been carrying this around for a couple days now." I placed it on the table. I had repeatedly peeked in my bag at it since I put it in there Sunday evening. It was still folded neatly and smelled faintly of detergent.

"You didn't have to do that," he said, sounding genuinely surprised. I wondered how long it had been since someone else had done his laundry for him. I hoped it had been a while, and that no one had gotten a decent peek at his unmentionables recently. If it wasn't going to be me, I didn't want anyone else to see them either. "Thank you," he added softly.

"You're welcome. I'm sorry I spilled coffee on you. And that my parents think we're sleeping together."

"Oh, that's okay" he said. He was even more unflappable than Kelly. "Hey, I'm ready for a new book."

"You finished *The Cuckoo's Calling*? Did you like it?"

"Very much," he answered. "I want to read the next one in the series. Do you have it in the store?"

"I do! We should get together and talk about the first one." I said it without even thinking. I said it as if it was the most natural thing in the world, like breathing or eating donuts.

"About that," he said, sliding forward on the bench seat. He was about to say something else when we heard a slight cough that sounded very close by. I looked up and saw Leona standing over us. She had such a disapproving look on her face that I immediately felt guilty, but for what I wasn't sure.

"Sheriff Branch," said Leona flatly.

"Leona," he said, and popped the rest of his sandwich in his mouth.

She turned her attention to me. "I'm not *interrupting* anything, am I?" She couldn't have sounded more snarky if she'd tried. I wanted to tell her yes, she was interrupting, and could she please go away and leave us alone, but I knew if I didn't interview her today, she'd make my life hell and I probably wouldn't get another chance for the next six years. She looked at the table, Callan's neatly folded shirt sitting in front of him. I squirmed in my seat a little, like a third grader who just got caught passing notes.

"Sheriff Branch just came by to, uh..."

"Eat her sandwich," he added. He took a few more fries and popped them in his mouth before reaching for one of my extra napkins to wipe his hands. "I've got to run; you ladies will have to excuse me." He unfolded himself from the booth and towered over Leona, looking at her for a second before reaching down to the table to pick up his shirt. "Thanks for getting my shirt back to me, Bev."

"You're welcome."

Leona's jaw dropped all the way to the floor before she had the presence of mind to close it again. But her eyebrows were still up along her hairline.

"It was nice seeing you both," Callan said. Leona stared at him, and he tipped his hat at her. He then gave me a look that either said, *I want the other half of your sandwich real bad* or *I'll call you later*.

He started up the aisle, and both Leona and I watched him walk. I was admiring the sway of his hips and the pacing of his slow, deliberate steps. I realized I'd made a big mistake turning him down for dinner. Yup. Real damn big. And if I didn't know better, I'd swear that it had been his intention for me to come to this conclusion. He was that good.

Instead of leaving the restaurant, Callan waited by the front door until Molly came up to him and they started talking. She tossed her head back and let out a girlish laugh, and I felt a twinge of jealousy. When I looked at Leona, I noticed that she was still watching him too. Did every single female in Guthrie swoon over Sheriff Branch? I tried to regain my composure.

"Right. So, thanks for meeting me today," I said, gesturing for her to take the seat vacated by the sheriff. "I won't take up too much of your time."

"I hope not," she said. "I am a very busy person."

I had a flashback to Saturday, the vision of Leona leaving Al's house looking rumpled and flustered. Yeah, she was busy all right.

"Yes, of course. Do you want anything to drink?"

"No. Let's just get this over with." She scowled and wiggled her butt cheeks deeper into the vinyl seat. She stared expectantly at me.

I pulled out my reporter's notebook and pen and got ready to make some notes. "Okay then," I said defensively. "Let's go over some of the things you're involved with and talk about your vision for the city. You're a VIP around here; you must have some ideas on how to improve the community—"

"What's the big idea?" she interrupted.

"Excuse me?"

She jerked her thumb toward the front door of the restaurant. We both looked in that direction, but Callan was gone. "The sheriff. You'd better not be getting any ideas."

"He was hungry," I tried to explain.

"That's not what I meant. You better stay away from him, Beverley Green," she warned.

"Excuse me?"

"I'm talking about you and your romantic designs. You leave him alone. He's too good for you."

Romantic designs? Were we in art class? Did I just get schooled? Too *good* for me? My patience was thin and getting thinner. "I don't think my private life is any of your business," I said calmly.

"Oh, it's very much my business. I have a vested interest in how this town is run. And we can't afford to have our sheriff gallivanting around with the likes of you. He needs a local woman, someone who knows her place and doesn't cause trouble."

"Is that so."

"Yes. In fact," she said conspiratorially, leaning over the table, "I'm setting him up with my niece, Eunice. I think she's perfect for him!" She raised both hands in the air like she was on the most exciting roller coaster ride ever. She seemed to forget she was mad and had just insulted the living graham crackers out of me.

Over the last week, I had pictured the sheriff being set up on blind dates. Hundreds of them. But now I had a more specific picture in my imagination: Callan on a romantic date with a hot supermodel named Eunice, who had won a Nobel Prize for math.

I, in all my foolish wisdom, had turned him down flat. Technically, I shouldn't care who he went on romantic dinner dates with, but Leona had just told me I wasn't good enough for him. Them's fightin' words. Now I was angry with myself, even more angry with her, and had the urge to throw a piece of blueberry pie in her face.

"Let me get this straight. You think you know what's best not only for the entire town of Guthrie, but also for the sheriff? You don't think he can figure out his own love life?"

"Oh, honey," she snapped. "You know how men are. They don't think straight half the time, and the other half of the time they're not thinking with their brain." She gave me a knowing nod. "He might be mesmerized by your flashy, big city ways and those bouncy..." She looked me up and down before deciding on her next word. There were only a few things that you could say were "bouncy" when it came to a woman's body without pissing her off, and if Leona didn't choose her next word wisely, there might be a catfight in the restaurant.

"...curls of yours. But soon enough, he'd come to his senses and see that you're all wrong for him. You're outspoken, independent, and hard-headed. No man wants to put up with that crap," she declared.

She didn't like me, I got it. While her words were hurtful, they weren't exactly surprising. I was still an outsider to her. I was still not good enough to be a real citizen of Guthrie. But who was this wackadoo to lecture me on romance?

I didn't like to play dirty. It had never been my style. I always preferred to find ways to get along with everyone. The world worked better if we could be nice to each other; I truly believed that. But there was something about this woman. I had been trying for almost a year to play nice with her and had made very little progress. I was cranky now, and not in the mood to give her any slack. She wanted to go there? We would go there. On the express bus.

"I've got news for you, lady," I said, drawing up my courage. "You basically just described yourself. You're smart, independent, and, for better or worse, a leader in this podunk town. Your husband apparently loved you. And you've got Bill wrapped around your little finger. Clearly you possess some redeeming qualities, even though I can't see any right now. So you'd better think twice before talking to me like that again."

"Just what do you know about me and Bill?" Leona stood up from the table.

"I know you had some 'cuddle time' recently."

Her face suddenly drained of all color. "That's none of your business." Now she seemed more embarrassed than mad.

"Were you doing anything that you'd like *Ledger* readers to know about?"

"It was a private meeting." I thought she might start to cry.

"A meeting?" I asked innocently. "What, like for your knitting circle? Or 'Cuddlers Anonymous'?"

"Never you mind, Bev. We all of us got things we don't want to share, including you."

"Okay," I said. "I just thought it might be something worth mentioning in the article."

She leaned over the table again and glared at me. "You keep Bill out of this."

We sat in silence for a moment, but I couldn't let it go. "The man is head over heels. Honestly, I don't know what he sees in you, but there's just no accounting for taste. But that's *his* business, isn't it?" I glared at her. She sat back down heavily.

As Leona's heavy haunches hit the seat, Molly brought over a huge piece of blueberry pie and two forks. We looked at her, confused.

"We didn't order this," said Leona.

"Compliments of Sheriff Branch," Molly said. "He ordered it before he left and told me to tell you that if you didn't share this piece of pie, he would arrest you both for civil disobedience."

That was the most ridiculous thing I'd ever heard, yet I believed it. I glared at Leona and picked up a fork. "Fine," I sneered.

"Thank you," fumed Leona.

We started eating our pie. As we ate, Molly brought two cups of coffee. We sipped our coffee and as I ate a few more bites of pie, I started to feel my anger subside. It was delicious pie. It was so good I was starting to feel ever so slightly magnanimous.

"We really aren't so different, you and I," I said with a crap-ton of composure. "You're a strong, sharp woman, and you've made a huge positive impact on this town. And that's all I'm hoping to do, you know?"

"Hmm." she said quietly, taking another bite of pie.

I considered confessing to her that I'd turned the sheriff down, and she had nothing to worry about. I thought about telling her that she was right—he did deserve better. But on second thought, it might be best if we just avoided the subject, in hopes of prolonging our cease-fire.

As we ate the last bites of pie in silence, and it was as if a calm vibe settled over the table. I was tired of arguing with Leona. I was tired of worrying about what she thought of me and whether she was going to evict me over some damn chickens.

"Let's call a truce," I suggested. "Let me write a nice article about you. I won't tell anyone about you and Bill. He does like you a lot, and he confessed to me in a moment of weakness. I know it's private information."

She actually smiled. "He is a big ol' sweetie," she said. "but I'm not ready for it to be public knowledge."

"No problem," I said.

"And well, you're right—you and I are a lot alike. Maybe that's what irks me sometimes. You young folks are taking over everything; it's hard not to feel irrelevant the older you get." She stared at the pie crumbs.

I almost laughed at her thinking of *me* as a *young person,* but hey, I'd take it. "Yeah," was all I said.

"Well, let's get started on that article of yours then," she suggested. I nodded in agreement. We got refills on our coffee and got down to business.

It turned out that her story was pretty interesting. She was seventy-three years old and had been retired for the last eleven. Her parents had moved to Guthrie right after Oklahoma became a state; she really was an official "Guthrie Old Timer," my endearing nickname for her and her gang of seniors.

Her family had owned the newspaper at one point, but they sold it during the oil bust of the 1980s. Her husband had owned a drug store and did surprisingly well in the stock market, hence her early retirement. He had also bought a bunch of houses during the '80s bust, at bargain prices, which she still kept as rental properties. Like the one I lived in.

Before her husband died four years earlier, he'd set up a charitable foundation, which she now ran. She gave money to kids for school supplies and offered a few scholarships to local community and vocational colleges. It was impressive and I told her so. She practically glowed.

By the time she had to leave for her next appointment, I'd gotten everything I needed for a great article. We hadn't discussed the sheriff again, and I wasn't exactly sure where we stood on that other than I still felt it was none of her beeswax. Regardless, we had planted the seed of a friendship of sorts. It was still a teeny tiny sprout of a relationship, but I had hope that we could get it to grow.

I got back from lunch feeling about forty-seven different emotions. I was mad, frustrated, flustered, confused, and at the same time, hopeful. Leona was near impossible. Yet by the time we'd shared that piece of pie, something had changed. Somehow during that short time, we came to an understanding, as if we both realized at the same moment that it would be better if we could find a way to get along. Maybe we'd never be best friends, but surely there was some common ground there somewhere. It was as if Cal gave us the gift of a delicious, magic, conciliatory piece of pie. He was damn good.

And when I thought about him, I felt a lot of the same emotions—anger, frustration, confusion. I also felt sad, regretful and embarrassed. The day before, I'd been so sure that turning him down had been the right thing to do. So why did I feel so lousy about it now?

All I could do for the next hour was slouch behind the counter. A few customers came in and I did a fair amount of business. I was, of course, friendly and helpful to everyone but when no one was in the store, I moped. This sucked.

I didn't know what to do about Al and Bill, Leona, Bigfoot, Beryl or global warming. And I really didn't know what to do about Callan. I'd effectively told him to go jump in a lake. Why did I do that? He was nice and very handsome. He was smart and I was sure there was much more to him that met the eye; his laconic, laid-back persona hid a thoughtful, funny, kind man. His eyes didn't sparkle like two inviting blue pools of water, but they had depth and warmth. And did I mention he was handsome as all get-out? What in the name of everything that was good and chocolate-coated had I done?

I started pacing the store. I needed to walk this all out. I walked the outer perimeter of the store; then I walked up and down each aisle. Everything felt out of control and I didn't like it. Where was my stupid life plan, dammit? If I could just figure out what I was supposed to be doing, all this stress would magically disappear, and I'd be on track. I'd also grow two inches taller and be able to read minds.

What would New York Beverley do? When I lived in New York, I was under a lot of pressure as an editor. I had a huge workload and a lot of responsibility. All the time. Yet I didn't remember ever feeling this pressured or stressed.

I walked past the self-help section of the store. I used to read a lot of books from this section until I concluded that they weren't helping my Self. The very name of the subject "self-help" implied that there was something wrong with me and all I was doing was looking for problems so I could fix them. I had eventually stopped reading those books. Now I was reconsidering.

I continued to pace the store. I was falling even more behind on everything that needed to be done, but I couldn't concentrate on anything. I didn't even feel like reading a romance novel. I felt like a slow-motion train wreck in progress when I thought about everything that was going on, and all the things that weren't going on.

The store had been empty for about thirty minutes. I went behind the cash wrap and sat back down to mope some more. Just as I rested my arms on the counter and laid my head on my hands, I heard the door open. With a deep breath, I prepared myself to transform back into the happy bookstore owner. When I lifted my head, Callan was standing in front of the nativity scene. He smiled, but quickly bent down to look for Jimmy, who still hadn't come out of the little barn.

I watched him as he watched my turtle. His long, lean frame was bent at the waist. His coat was open, hanging down his sides. The lines of his long legs ended in work boots. I sighed under my breath. *Train wreck.*

"I brought your turtle a present," he said. His voice was even, and his gaze never left the manger. My eyes went to his hands, to see what he'd brought, but they were empty except for his left one, which was holding his hat.

"Really?" I got up and walked around the counter. I wanted to run over to him and leap into his arms, but I opted for staying put. I felt a sudden sense of whimsy and climbed onto a box next to the register before hopping up to sit on the countertop, my feet dangling above the ground.

Callan straightened up and looked at me. "Yup."

"That was nice of you," I said, now even more curious.

He walked toward me, then stopped and stood a few feet away. "Look," he said. "I know I said last week I wasn't looking to go out with anyone."

"Right. Me neither."

"Yeah. And then I asked you out to dinner anyway."

"Uh huh."

"And you said no."

I felt like I needed to start explaining myself again, so I opened my mouth to say something, but he held up his hand. "Let me finish," he said. I closed my mouth.

"Maybe you think I'm crazy. Hell, maybe I *am* kinda crazy. But I'd be crazy for sure if didn't at least try to see you again. I like spending time with you. And I can't say that about a lot of people." He shifted his weight from one leg to the other, his eyes never leaving mine. They were clear, warm, serious, honest. My cheeks flushed. I started to say something again, but again he stopped me.

"Here's what I think," he said, taking a step closer. "I think you're still trying to get used to living in a small town. You're still trying to fit in and figure out what you want next. You think your life is a mess, and that you're doing me a favor by saying no. But I don't need you to do me any favors."

He took another step closer, his legs almost brushing my toes. His movements were so deliberate and graceful I almost couldn't stand it. I might have gasped slightly.

"Just remember one thing," he said, stepping even closer. He put his hat on the counter next to me. He was way into my personal space bubble. Normally I couldn't stand it when people did this, but right now I didn't mind one single iota. I didn't even spend much time being mad at him for trying to give me advice, like everyone else had. I didn't say a word.

He moved in closer still, his eyes becoming bigger and browner, and I was hardly breathing. "It's simple," he said, "you just need to be sure of one thing." He leaned in like he was going to kiss me, but instead he paused there. Then he moved again, so his mouth was right next to my ear.

"Just be sure," he continued in a whisper, "that your feet keep pointing in the direction you want to be going." His voice was so soft and close to my ear that it gave me goosebumps. He smelled like forest and chocolate chip cookies. Like a man who knew what he wanted.

Then he stepped back a little, and we both looked down at my feet, which were pointing right at him. We looked at each other again, and he smiled a half smile that was one of the sexiest smiles I'd ever seen in my entire life.

He reached a long arm out toward me, and for a split second I thought he was going to draw me into an embrace. But instead he picked up his hat, turned, and left the shop. I looked at the counter, and he had left a fresh bunch of spinach where his hat had been. It was even better than giving me flowers: he'd seduced me *and* left a snack for my turtle. What a man.

For the first time in a long while, I felt like the complete opposite of a train wreck.

14

WHEN I OPENED the store on Wednesday morning, I had a tiny bit of hope that it would be a drama-free, easygoing, smooth-sailing Wednesday. That small hope disappeared completely by 10:30 when the UPS man came and brought me books that were meant for a different bookstore.

To be fair, it wasn't his fault; I'd been waiting on a shipment from a small publisher, and they'd sent me an order for a store in Milwaukee. I tried not to take it out on Mike; he'd been very good to me since my store opened. But I was probably snippier than I should have been. After he left, I realized what I'd done, and promised myself I'd stop at Missy's sometime this week and get him a present that had plenty of chocolate on it.

I wasn't in the best mood, to say the least. I was trying, but it just wasn't happening. Not even pacing the store helped. So I tried the next thing on my procrastination list: dusting. I picked one aisle and started dusting shelves, books, and endcap displays. I'd randomly chosen the self-help aisle again. As I dusted the books, I looked at the sub-categories. Mindfulness. Happiness. Stress Management. Personal Transformation. They all held promises of a better me. So did the idea of thinking really hard about what I wanted out of life and putting a plan together.

Callan's words from the evening before still seemed rather cryptic to me. Make sure my feet were pointing in the direction I wanted to be heading? That was almost as bad as everyone telling me to be careful what I wished for. All this advice. Gah!

What had he meant? I wasn't sure, but on some deeper level, it had felt right and it had made sense. But I couldn't put it into words yet. I'm a slow learner, what can I say?

As I stood there feeling sorry for myself and my lack of direction, a book that was stored on top of the shelves in the overstock area fell down. Onto my head. The hard spine of the book hit me square on the top of my skull. The book bounced off my head and landed on the ground, front-side up. I read the title. It was called *The Life Plan.* Oh. Turns out life plans hurt like a mofo. What the hell did this mean?

My head was hurting too much to think about it. I was no closer to figuring anything out, and my to-do list wasn't magically getting any shorter. It was all still too much. The only thing that could help at this point was an after-lunch flat white.

Neither Julie nor Chuck were coming in today, so technically I shouldn't have closed up the shop, but these were trying times. After eating my lunch behind the counter, I left for Hoboken. The sky was cloudy today and the breeze was almost cold. It looked like it was going to rain again, and soon. I picked up my pace.

I ordered my drink and asked Seth to put it in a to-go cup, so I could get back to the shop, planning on a quick turnaround. That plan vanished when Al walked into the coffee shop.

"Hiya, missy," said Al.

"Hiya, Al," I sighed.

Bill walked in behind his cousin, decked out in another fine t-shirt. I'd seen him in an 80s Madonna t-shirt before, and this one was also from the 80s except it was for the hair band Cinderella. I had to give him props once again. "Dang, Bill, that's quite a shirt. Do you even know who Cinderella is?"

He shot me a look like I was an idiot. I had no idea he'd know of a band like that. And I had no idea that an 80s metal band would make shirts that large.

"How's plans for the shirt shop going?" I asked him.

"Oh, real good. I got my lawyer starting all the paperwork to make it official and get all my tax stuff set up. It sure is complicated!"

"Yeah, for sure," I agreed. "You found a good space yet?"

"Yup! Did you know Leona owns the building you're in, plus about half the rest of the block? She's gonna give me a sweet deal on a little place a few doors down from you. Just think, we'll be neighbors!"

"Cool!" I said with way more enthusiasm than I actually felt. "Hey, do you have any Black Flag shirts?" I asked on a whim.

Bill looked up at the ceiling thoughtfully. "Well, yeah, I think I do! Want one?"

Before I could say yes, Al interrupted. "We didn't come here to talk t-shirts," he snapped.

"That's true," agreed Bill. "We came here for a cortado!"

"No, we didn't, Bill. We saw Beverley in here and came in so's she could tell us what happened to the, uh, 'items.'"

I had been hoping to put this off, like, forever, but now was the time to get it over with. I hadn't known what I would say to them, but as I thought about it now, I knew where this was headed.

"Okay, guys. Let's sit down for a minute," I said, looking at my watch. I pulled out a chair at a nearby table and took a seat. Seth brought me my drink, a look of sympathy in his eyes.

Al and Bill ordered their coffee before joining me. When they sat down, Al had a plate with a delicious-looking muffin on it. It looked like it had some kind of berries in it and had a crumbly topping. I found myself wanting one very badly, but I pressed on. "So, it's like this," I began. "I'm not exactly sure what happened to your sheep. But my gut feeling is that they are no longer of this world, and their demise may have been an unhappy one."

Bill gasped and brought the back of one hand up to cover his mouth. Did he think the sheep had been on vacation or something? I tried to refrain from rolling my eyes.

"What kind of proof you got?" asked Al. "What did all that evidence tell you?"

"I don't have any actual proof of anything, but I have some theories. The first one, you're not going to like very much."

Al frowned. "What is it?"

I took a sip of my flat white for fortitude, as Seth came over and brought the two cousins their drinks. "Well, Al, have you ever stopped to think that maybe your cute little doggie eats more than garden hoses and patio furniture? And before you answer, stop and think real hard. That dog is a *monster*."

To his credit, he did appear to stop and think real hard. "Well, he does seem to eat a lot of weird stuff..."

"The thing is, I don't think I've found any signs of sheep remains."

"What do you mean you *think* you didn't find any remains?" asked Bill. He took a slurp of his cortado.

"Al, did you know there's a pile of dead animals right over your fence on the Rogers' property?"

"What?" he asked incredulously.

"Yeah, Betty Ann found them the other day and she thinks you put them there," I explained.

"Why on earth would I do that?"

"How would I know? Regardless, none of the dead stuff looked big enough to be a sheep. I think they were actually your chickens. And I think your dog dragged them over there, after using them as chew toys."

"Oh..." The little hamster in Al's brain was working overtime. "Well, that certainly would explain why they all disappeared..."

"Little Smiley likes chickens," I added. Bill snorted.

We sat in silence for a few minutes, then I decided to spring my second theory on them. "As far as the sheep are concerned... maybe Bigfoot did it." By this time, Al had almost finished his muffin, but he dropped the last piece of it on the floor. A smile spread across his face.

"You don't say," he said slowly.

"As much as it pains me to say, I can't rule it out."

Al and Bill both nodded silently.

"I also can't rule out alien abduction, spontaneous combustion, or the possibility that you guys made this all up."

"True," mused Bill.

"The thing is, regardless of what happened to them, you guys need to think about how to make this right. You owe Danny two sheep."

"We never told you we borrowed the sheep from Danny," Al said, holding his hands up in a *wait one cotton-pickin' minute* gesture.

I sighed. "I'm a reporter, guys. I find stuff out. Danny knows his sheep are missing, and he told the sheriff. You guys could get into a lot of trouble."

Al and Bill looked at each other, sharing a concerned glance.

"Don't worry," I said. "I'm not going to tell either of them it was you two. I still want to help you make it right."

"We gotta go get two new sheep and then take 'em back to Danny's," Al suggested.

"No." I said, trying to think it through.

"But that's the easiest..."

"You could get caught!" I exclaimed. "There are so many problems with that idea, Al. If someone calls the sheriff, you could get arrested. What you did is wrong, but I'd still hate to see you end up in jail over two stupid sheep."

"Oh," mumbled Al. "I hadn't thought about that."

"You're darn lucky you didn't get caught when you took them," I reminded him.

Silence again. Bill scratched at his head. "Yeah, I don't know how we managed to pull it off, to tell you the truth."

"I think I have a solution to all this," I said. "Let me mull it over a bit more. But I think I can talk to Danny and get something worked out."

"That would be swell!" said Al.

"In the meantime, start looking around for a place to buy two sheep. And they need to be good ones. Rambouillet or Teeswater or something." Yes, I had done some research into what sheep were commonly owned in Oklahoma. I couldn't ask anyone what Danny owned without raising way too much suspicion, so I just had to hope we could get close.

"Okie dokie, missy. We're on it," Bill said eagerly.

I stood up and stretched, getting ready to hoof it back to the bookstore. "Okay, I'll be in touch," I said.

Al and Bill stood up too. "We appreciate it," Al said. He looked serious, and I believed him.

I smiled and raised my hand by way of a wave goodbye as I left the coffee shop. It started to rain on my way back.

I got back to the shop only slightly drenched. I sipped the last half of my flat white while I slowly unpacked boxes of books, adding some to the front display tables and sorting the rest into piles to be shelved later. My personal phone sat on the counter, next to the shop's landline phone. I kept staring at them, but neither rang. I wasn't sure why I was expecting them to. Maybe I hoped that the sheriff wouldn't give up so easily after I turned him down. Oh geez, that was so romance novel-y. If I wrote a romance novel, I'd write about a woman who wouldn't wait around to be pursued. She would know what she wanted, she wouldn't be afraid to admit her mistakes, and she'd be brave and smart enough to make them right.

Huh.

I stopped unpacking books, picked up my phone, and made a call.

"Bob's Tow Service," said the deep voice.

"Oh! Uh, I think—"

"Hi, Bev," said the sheriff.

"Callan?"

"Easier than checking the caller ID sometimes," he explained. "Weeds out the undesirables."

"I sure hope this is your personal phone, otherwise anyone needing something other than a tow in Logan County might have a serious problem."

"The citizens of Guthrie are safe. What's up?" he asked.

"Yeah, so..." I began. I started pacing the store, one hand stuck in my jeans pocket, the other holding the phone. I wasn't sure where to go from there.

"Is everything okay?" There was a tinge of concern in his voice. I didn't dislike it.

"Oh yeah, fine, fine. I was...just wondering if you'd like to have dinner with me on Friday."

There was a pause. "Are you asking me out, Beverley Green?"

"Yup."

"Can I get back to you? I have to check my calendar. I'm not sure if anyone has set me up on a blind date this weekend."

My stomach dropped to the floor. It hadn't occurred to me that he might make other plans. I had royally messed up. Figures. *Way to go, Bev.* "Okay," I said meekly.

"Just messin' with you," he said in that relaxed, stoic voice. "I'd love to have dinner with you."

I was too relieved to be mad. "Good," was all I said.

"I'll pick you up at six."

"Good."

We ended the call, and only then did I start breathing again.

My grandma used to have a foolproof way to decide what to do when making a difficult choice. She'd flip a coin. But instead of simply going with what side the coin landed on, she paid attention to how she felt about the result. Either she felt relieved, or disappointed. Depending on how she felt, she'd make her choice.

When Callan told me he'd have to check his calendar, I had felt absolute dread. I guess that said it all. Once I caught my breath, it sank in. I was going on a real date, not one that was engineered by my parents! I was happy and already nervous. I was also feeling inspired, so I pulled out my laptop and began to work in earnest on the article about Leona.

When this journalistic masterpiece got printed, people were going to think Leona Tisdale was a real live angel, sent straight down from heaven to bless the town of Guthrie. Prior to our meeting, I thought I was going to have to fake my way through the whole thing, but as I started to write, my admiration of Leona began to feel sincere. Maybe she wasn't so bad after all. I mean, sure she had tried to get me evicted before my store even opened. And yes, she would kick me out of my house if she knew I had chickens in my backyard, and all right, she also didn't want me to be within twenty miles of Sheriff Branch. But still. Maybe she was a real sweetie. Bill was a little out there, but he was a nice guy and he saw something worth loving in her, so...I wasn't completely sold, but it was a definite improvement.

Worst case scenario, if ever things got murky between us again sometime down the road, I could use her unconventional love affair as blackmail—I mean bargaining chips.

I worked by myself for the rest of the day in the store; it was pretty dead. A few people came in asking if I had the new Oprah Book Club selection, but I had to tell them it wasn't due out until the following Tuesday. They were sad and so was I. I would have liked to ring up a few more sales. For the rest of the afternoon, Jimmy and I were alone in the store.

I managed to finish the article and I emailed it to Mark. I followed it up with a text, to let him know.

Me: ***Leona article done. Sent in.***
Mark: ***k***

I had learned to be as brief as possible with Mark. He didn't like extra words in text conversations or real-life ones either. And I had become an expert at understanding his brand of texting language. For example, *k* meant, *Great, thanks! I really appreciate you as an employee and friend.*

Me: ***No progress on BF piece.***
Mark: ***WTF***

This meant, *it's okay, Bev, I know you're having a hard time with that one and I wish I could help you out, but my hands are tied, so take your time and let me know how I can support you.*

Three more messages came in quick succession.

Mark: ***finish tomorrow.***
Mark: ***no, I'm not kidding***
Mark: ***I don't care just do it***

The first text translated as, *Anytime next week is fine.* The second one was, *Actually you better get it done by Monday or I might get a little mad.* And the third one meant, *I know you are going to come up with twelve great excuses as to why you need more time, but I don't give a shit,* and *My kids are with me this week and are driving me crazy.*

I felt momentarily bad for Mark. Since his divorce a while back, he had his kids every other week. They were good kids, but they were in that weird, liminal teenage space where they were testing boundaries and not being real happy about their parents' divorce. It got to him sometimes.

Me: ***k***

This should have been the next thing on my list. Another freakin' Bigfoot article. Fortunately, I was still an Olympic-level procrastinator, so I promptly forgot about it.

15

In New York they have snowstorms, or nor'easters. In California, they have earthquakes. In Oklahoma, there are spring storms...and tornadoes. So it wasn't too much of a surprise when I woke up Thursday morning to my phone alerting me that Guthrie was under a Tornado Watch.

I had been dreaming about Bigfoot again, so waking up to rain and wind and the threat of a twister was a welcome change. I was starting to wonder if all of these weird dreams I'd been having about Bigfoot were stirring up the collective consciousness of the entire human race and were the reason all this Sasquatch kerfuffle was happening again in real life. It all started with that stupid Novel Police dream. *What you resist, persists*—isn't that what they say? As long as he was only lurking around my subconscious and not my backyard, I'd be okay.

Chuck was in charge of opening the store, which was a good thing because I'd forgotten to set my alarm and had slept later than usual. I texted Chuck to see if he would be okay making it to the shop. Tornado Watches were just suggestions to be extra careful, whereas Tornado Warnings were when you needed to grab your motorcycle helmet and head for the bathtub with a heavy blanket and a bottle of Scotch. I always used to get "Watch" and "Warning" mixed up, but now I was pretty sure I could remember the difference. Probably.

After I sent the text, I looked over the calendar on my phone. And there it was, highlighted with a bright red background: dinner with the sheriff the following evening. A real live date. What should I wear? Would my hair behave? Where would we go? What if he made a move on me? Should I make a move? What will we talk about? I felt like I was in high school again. Except that in high school, none of this kind of thing actually happened. I'd had a boring high school life. Very few dates and not much of a social life. I'd never been very good at this stuff. But the important part was, I had a date! With the sheriff! For all my worrying, I also felt relief, like a burden had been lifted off my shoulders, and I felt lighter. What was that about?

Then I had a scary thought. What if my parents found out? Then I'd have to admit my mother was right that the sheriff and I might be a good match. Damn parental meddling! My mom would be impossible to deal with; her gloating would be off the charts. Maybe there were worse things that could happen...but I couldn't think of any.

In order to not have to deal with the whole Sasquatch thing, I found myself slipping into dangerous procrastination territory once more. I still had nothing. Less than nothing. In accordance with my attitude of avoidance, I decided to go on a quick run. It was warm enough that if I got drenched by a sudden thunderstorm, at least I wouldn't freeze. I did a few miles through the neighborhood and it didn't rain a drop.

But when I got back it began to drizzle, and the drizzle quickly turned into a downpour. A storm front was passing through. While I was in the kitchen making breakfast, the room kept flashing brightly from the lightning and the thunder rumbled across the sky, rattling dishes in the cabinet and a few glasses that I'd set to dry too close together in the sink. I sat down to eat and Chuck texted back, letting me know he had made it to the shop and everything was fine. I let him know I was going to work from home for a bit longer.

I thought about calling Danny to see if he'd heard anything about any more Bigfoot sightings, but I knew the answer would be no, since the only reason I was writing this dumb thing was because Al and Bill had lied to Mark about seeing one. Plus, he'd probably give me a hard time about even asking. I was going to have to call Danny soon, though, as part of my plan to mediate the sheep debacle. I'd worry about that later, too.

After breakfast, I figured I'd be ready to think about all the things I was supposed to be thinking about, but I wasn't. I decided to procrastinate even more. In between patches of rain, I kept busy by working in the backyard. As long as I didn't hear tornado sirens, or get blown over by a strong wind, or pelted with hail, I could at least make sure the chickens were all right and the flowerbeds were weed-free.

I stood on the covered porch while putting on some gardening gloves and looked over at the picnic table. The cupcakes I'd forgotten about last week were still there. I really needed to take those inside later...and eat them.

After about thirty minutes, the rain rolled in and the sky looked like the downpour wasn't going to let up anytime soon. Still no tornado sirens, but it was windy and I was drenched, so I called it. The hens had fresh food and water, a new head of lettuce, and they were tucked into their coop with no intention of leaving. I headed back inside and took a shower, getting ready to get ready to write that piece of Squatch article.

But before I could start making stuff up for the article, I got a call from Chuck asking where I was, because I apparently I was scheduled to meet with the elementary school librarian at eleven, and even thought it was only 10:45, she was there waiting for me. Oops, I'd forgotten about that. So much for looking over my calendar this morning.

I made sure I looked presentable, then jumped in the car to drive over to the shop. As I drove, I heard my phone chime that I got a text, but it'd have to wait till I got out of the car. I hoped it was from Callan. Oh, but if it was from him, maybe he was texting to tell me he was working tomorrow night and couldn't go to dinner. Or worse, maybe he was texting to tell me he had changed his mind. Or just as bad, maybe it wasn't Callan at all, and I was already making up things that could go wrong. This was going to be a long couple of days.

I wasn't able to check the text until midday because my meeting went long and then I forgot. It turned out to be from Al, letting me know that he and Bill had managed to find two very nice Wensleydale sheep from a rancher south of Oklahoma City. I had thought Wensleydale was simply a type of cheese, but hey, whatever. I texted him back, telling them to stand by with the sheep and I'd let them know what to do with them as soon as I figured out what to do next. Which meant I was going to have to figure out what to do next. I felt my to-do list getting longer again.

The rest of the afternoon was busy at The Book Store; we had a lot of foot traffic and sales were brisk. I couldn't account for the reason—maybe rainy weather got people more in the mood to read. It was so busy I had very little time to daydream about Callan. I had even less time to worry about going on a real live date with him, and absolutely no time left over to worry about whether or not it had been a bad idea to say yes.

When I got home that night, I made myself a quick dinner of a veggie and cheese quesadilla and washed it down with an Emergency Beer. Then I called Danny. I would rather have texted, but this would probably go over better as a call. When he picked up, I tried to sound causal.

"Hi, Danny. It's Beverley," I began.

"Hiya, Bev! How are things?"

"Oh, pretty good, pretty good, you know, the usual. Everything is normal. Everything's fine..." I was off to a great start.

"Great," he said patiently. "What can I do you for?"

"Listen, I was wondering if you had time to swing by my place tomorrow afternoon? I was hoping to talk to you about something." I figured the less I said now, the better.

"Well, I'm out of town right now. Could we meet up on Saturday? What's up? Is something wrong?" He sounded worried.

"Oh no, everything is fine, but I need to talk to you about something, I'll tell you when I see you. It'll just be easier that way. Saturday should work."

"Are you sure?"

"Yeah, sure! What time on Saturday?"

We made plans to meet up around noon, and I offered to make us a little lunch. I was hoping to ease the whole *Al and Bill stole two of your sheep* news with a sandwich and chips. So, I had one more day to put it off. I called Al next, to tell him to bring the sheep over on Saturday morning. I figured I'd have them ready to go when Danny came over, and I could give them to him as a peace offering, hopefully avoiding jail time for Al, Bill...and me. But Al wasn't answering his phone, so I left him a message telling him to bring the sheep at ten o'clock Saturday morning.

16

Friday morning I woke up with a start. *Date night!* This was either going to be epic...or epically disastrous. It was like the electricity in the air before one of our springtime storms. You could get some nice rain and a pretty lightning show...or total disaster. Whether it was an impending date or an incoming storm, you had to keep an eye on the radar and be ready to take cover.

As I sat up in bed, I could feel all the butterflies flitting around in my stomach. I'd thought I was too old for this crap, but apparently not. Instead of going for a morning run, I walked through my neighborhood. The air was cool but dry and pleasant. My mind kept wandering back to the words *date night.* Was that what this was? At some point, didn't you reach an age where you called it something else? *Special friend dinner? Adulting time?* Ugh. Whatever you called it, it still felt the same: nerve-wracking.

I felt a little better after my walk, and as I went through my morning routine of shower, breakfast, and chicken tending, I almost felt calm. It would be a good day, I tried to tell myself, and an even better evening. Positive thinking and all that.

I drove to work and accidentally ended up at Missy's again. I was going to have to start using GPS to get me to work so this didn't keep happening. But while I was there, I might as well sample some of the goods. Just to mix things up a bit, I chose a cheese danish instead of a chocolate donut to go with my coffee. And I picked up a few things for Mike the UPS guy, as a peace offering for my bad mood the other day. I got it all to go and continued on to the bookstore.

When I pulled up and parked in front of the shop, I had to smile. My handyman Jake had been out and had taken care of the job I'd requested. I got out of my car and surveyed his work. He had added some lettering to my front windows. Under the plain block letters that spelled out *The Book Store* were the words *Read the Fine Print* in beautiful scripted lettering. My bookstore now had a tag line, and it was perfect. The place suddenly looked and felt that much more special. Yes, it would be a good day.

To say that I had a hard time concentrating on work would be an understatement. I might as well have pulled out my novel-writing notepad and started drawing little hearts and smiley faces all over it. I did try to shelve some books, but lord only knows if I managed to get them in the right alphabetical order, let alone the right area of the store. I was nervous and scared, but also excited. I was scared of putting myself out there, since it felt a lot like making myself vulnerable and I wasn't used to that. I was also scared that my indecisiveness would hurt someone else. Someone who, from everything I could tell, was a very nice, honest, sincere, and respectable person. Someone who had the power to arrest me if I pissed him off. On top of all that, I was excited because no matter how I looked at it, I came up with the conclusion that I really liked the sheriff.

At one point in the afternoon, when it became apparent that there was a lull in store traffic, I did pull out my novel-writing notepad, and blew the dust off of it. I got out my favorite pen and prepared to work on some museum-worthy doodles. But instead, actual words started to appear on the paper. And after about thirty minutes, I realized I had something that looked suspiciously like a very rough outline for a romance novel. How on earth had that happened?

I took a break to check on Jimmy Perez. He was sitting next to his water dish, with a piece of lettuce sticking out of his mouth. It made him look very thoughtful and intellectual, and I told him so. He liked compliments.

"Do you think this dinner thing is a good idea?" I asked Jimmy. Jimmy thought about it. Then he moved his head to look up at me, and the rest of the lettuce slowly disappeared into his mouth. "I'll take that as a yes." He was a smart little guy and had never steered me wrong before.

Jimmy and I held down the fort for the rest of the day. Right before five, I got out my phone and texted Mark, telling him flat out that I wouldn't be able to write the Bigfoot article. I told him that the sightings were fake, and there was no news story. As I locked up the store, I felt my phone buzz three times in my back pocket—I knew without looking they were all from Mark. I ignored them and headed out.

I arrived home thinking I had plenty of time before Callan would pick me up for dinner. I dropped my stuff in the kitchen, walked out the back door to say hi to the chickens, and almost tripped over a sheep. At the last second, I caught myself from falling right on my ass; the sheep looked at me calmly like I had just asked him what time it was and he wanted to tell me that really, I had my own phone and could bloody well check the time myself. As I was staring at the sheep, I heard a snarfly sound behind me. I turned around, and there was a second sheep.

"*Baaaaaah,*" it said by way of a cheerful greeting. I was so stunned that it took a few seconds to sink in. Of course, Al and Bill were to blame.

I sat down at my picnic table and watched the sheep. They were milling around, nibbling on grass, minding their own business. Their fleeces were a nice cream color, and their faces were a dark bluish-grey. I knew next to nothing about sheep, but I guessed these two to be pretty young. I shook my head as I pulled out my phone to call Al. No answer, of course. I tried Bill.

"Oh hiya, Bev, what's cookin'?"

"Bill, what the heck! There are two sheep in my backyard!"

"Yeah, one ram and one ewe! Aren't they the cutest?"

"No! Well, I mean yeah, but shoot, Bill, you were supposed to bring them over *tomorrow!*"

"Yeah. About that..."

Oh, sweet relish on a cracker.

"What, Bill? What!"

"Our delivery fella couldn't do it tomorrow. We had to do it today. Al said he was gonna call you. He didn't call you?"

"Yeah, no," I sighed. There was nothing I could do about it now anyway. I didn't have time. Oh, holy heck, the time! "Listen, I am not happy about this."

"Why, don't you like them sheep? They're cute!"

"I can't keep sheep in my backyard, Bill; it's not allowed!"

"It's just one night," he scoffed. "They don't eat much. It'll be fine! Listen, gotta run. I think Leona's here." And he hung up.

I sat for another minute in stunned silence, watching the sheep. They were still calm and collected and didn't look like they could get up to anything too sinister. Maybe this would work. It wasn't like I had much choice at the moment, so it had better work. Maybe they would be quiet, and maybe the Sheriff of Logan County wouldn't even notice they were back here. It was a neighborhood and city violation that was probably worse than harboring a few chickens, though. If he did happen to find out, maybe he wouldn't be mad, or ask me why I had them...

The longer I sat there, the more ridiculous it all seemed. What a mess I'd gotten myself into. I was just trying to help, for cripes' sake! I laughed. Guthrie was definitely *not* boring. Things were so interesting now that I began wishing for the time when I'd thought it was boring.

"I have to go now, but you guys better be on your best behavior," I said to the sheep. They didn't even turn their heads toward me. They sure were cute little guys. If they were Wensleydales like Al had said he was getting, they looked nothing like the cheese.

I watched them a little longer. "I'm going to call you Burt," I said to the one I guessed was a ram. "And you're Loni," I said to the ewe. "Don't embarrass me tonight, Burt and Loni." I took a deep breath and started humming that Jerry Reed song from *Smokey and the Bandit* as I went back inside.

I had less than an hour to do all those girly, pre-date things I was supposed to do, like get a manicure and pedicure, wash my hair, make sure I had my nice underwear on, obsess over what to wear, get a facial, do my makeup, blow out my hair, change clothes three times, call my closest girlfriend to ask her what I should wear, and decide to go clothes shopping but instead change clothes two more times. All in time to be comfortably seated on the couch the moment my date arrived.

Instead, I had just enough time left to stress-clean the kitchen, give my hair a stern talking-to about being on its best behavior for the night, apply a little makeup, and find a clean pair of dark jeans which got paired with a clean t-shirt, new cardigan, and my best pointy flats. As I slid my left foot into my shoe, I heard a knock at my front door. This was it.

We had eaten dinner together before. We'd gone on walks, texted, and flirted. Heck, we'd even shared a grilled cheese sandwich, and in some cultures that was practically a promise of marriage. So why was I so nervous now as I walked to the door? Why did this feel like such a big deal, and why was my heart racing? Maybe it was because this dinner *was* a big deal. Or maybe it was the contraband sheep in the backyard.

I opened the door, and hardly recognized Callan. The cowboy hat was gone, and the boots and long coat had been replaced with leather chukkas and a light grey wool sweater. He looked devastatingly handsome.

"What?" he asked.

"What?" I asked.

"You're staring at me." He looked down at himself self-consciously.

"Oh! Sorry. Come in," I said, trying not to ogle any more than I already had. As he stepped into the house, I realized I shouldn't have asked him in. I had no idea if the sheep would stay quiet or not, and now I was playing with woolly fire. "Let me get my bag, and then I'm ready to go," I added.

"Actually, would you mind if I grabbed a glass of water?" he asked as he started walking toward the kitchen. "My throat's scratchy."

Oh dear. Normally I wouldn't mind, but tonight I minded. He might see my visitors out back through the kitchen window. "Sure, sure! Let me get it for you. Have a seat!" I cut him off from entering any further into the house and redirected him to the couch before I went to the kitchen. I got a small glass from the cabinet, filled it with water, and brought it to him.

"Here you go," I said. I almost suggested he drink it on the way to the door but thought that might be too weird. I stood watching him sip the water, making no move to get up off the couch. "So, where are we going for dinner?" I asked. "I'm starving!"

Callan opened his mouth to answer, but before any words came out, a distinctively sheepish bleat came from the back of the house. I coughed loudly. *God dammit, Burt!* I thought angrily. What should I do? Should I try to pass it off as a sound resulting from some weird bodily function? Should I admit right then and there that I had illegal sheep? Should I ignore it altogether? That last one sounded the easiest.

"Italian," he said slowly, giving me a questioning look.

"Great! Well, let's get going then!" I reached for my bag and coat and stood by the door expectantly. Callan stood up and looked even taller than usual. I wondered if it was my guilty-feeling imagination. I smiled. "You look very handsome," I said softly. I hadn't even meant it as a distraction from the sheep. He did look great.

He smiled and moved to the door. I locked up as he waited. "You look pretty damn good too," he said.

"Please, Sheriff," I said as I walked toward his truck, "at least let me get some food down before you feed me a line like that."

"Dammit," I heard him mumble as he started to follow me. I smiled.

"So, this is a different vehicle," I noted, as we drove down the street.

"It's my personal truck. I thought it might be nice if we were incognito tonight."

"Good idea," I agreed. But then I wondered if he wanted to be incognito because he didn't want anyone to know we were going to dinner together.

"Not because I don't want anyone to see us together," he continued, as if reading my thoughts. "I just don't want to be bothered by anyone, is all."

I nodded my approval. "So, where are we going for Italian?"

"Oh, I thought we'd get out of town. Again, for privacy. There's a nice little place down toward Edmond. Not too far, not too busy."

Sounded perfect.

We made the drive in good time and ended up in a corner booth at a dark, quiet restaurant. A fire was going in the fireplace at the bar and in the wood-fired oven. As we got settled, our server brought us menus.

We looked over the offerings together; everything sounded delicious. It was difficult to decide, but Callan assured me that the chicken piccata was the best he'd ever had, so we both ordered it. After a few minutes, our server brought over a plate of bruschetta as an appetizer.

"We didn't order an appetizer," Callan said, sounding confused.

"No, sir. It's compliments of that gentleman over there." She pointed to a table across the room, and there was Danny Cadence, sitting in the opposite corner, next to a dark-haired woman who appeared to be very pretty. He was clearly also on a date.

"Um, tell him thanks?" I said, not knowing what else to say. The waitress smiled and walked away.

"Well, this is weird."

"Why?" Callan asked, testing out a piece of bruschetta. "It's delicious."

"No, I don't mean the bruschetta is weird. I mean it's weird that Danny is here." I didn't know if I should look over there again or not.

He shrugged. "He's got a car."

"It's interesting that you both have the same date restaurant in your repertoire." I smiled.

He shrugged again. "What can I say? We have good taste."

I looked at Callan, who was watching me closely. He had that strong stubbled jaw and those eyes which revealed just a hint of mischief. His long fingers delicately held a piece of bruschetta. He was dreamy, and it was cute that he'd been a little jealous.

He scooped up another piece of bruschetta. "You should try this; it reall is delicious. Tell Danny thanks next time you see him."

"I'll send him a thank you card," I said, taking a piece. I looked at Callan; he was smiling. As I ate the bruschetta, I had flashbacks to our blind date dinner with my parents, and I hoped I would be able to eat my meal without spitting any of it out all over the table. I had a 50/50 chance, based on past performance.

Our server brought our meals. We ate slowly, keeping the conversation light. When I first met him, he came across as aloof or even grumpy. But the more I got to know him, the more he began to open up. He told me a little more about his personal life, like how he had a daughter who was in college in Denver and an ex-wife of ten years who was living in Fredericksburg, Texas, whom he occasionally ran into when he went down that way to visit family. I wanted to ask him if he'd dated much in the ten years since his divorce, but then I might have to answer questions like that and be forced to admit that my personal history indicated I'd been a failure at relationships for most of my life.

"Have you ever been married?" he asked me at one point. His voice was level like it always was, but when I looked at him, I saw a fleck of real curiosity in his eyes.

"Well," I started, reaching for my water. Instead of wrapping my fingers around the glass, I knocked the glass over, spilling the contents all over the table. And I mean, *all* over it. I also spilled it on my lap. And Callan's arm.

"I'm so sorry," I said, trying to wipe water off his sleeve.

"Are you wanting me to take off my shirt again?" he asked, gently removing my hand from his arm, indicating that he was fine.

"Trust me, I have better moves than this if I were really wanting to undress you," I said absently.

"I believe you," he said.

Our waitress came over with some extra napkins and helped us clean up the mess I'd made. Instead of spilling the beans, I'd spilled the water.

"I'm sorry," I said again.

"It's all right, really."

"I'll be right back," I said, reaching for my bag and getting up from the table to walk to the ladies room. I tried to dry off my cold, wet pants, but it didn't work very well. Smooth, Bev, smooth.

When I came out, Danny was standing along the wall across from the door, waiting for me.

"Hi, there," he said, smiling broadly.

"Hi, Danny," I said, slinging my bag over my shoulder.

"I was surprised to see you here. With the sheriff, no less."

I shrugged. "I was surprised to see you here too, with...whoever that is."

"Her name's Stephanie. She's a new accountant at the firm I use for the ranch. I'm not sure, but I think she might be interested in more than numbers."

"Cool." I wasn't sure if I thought it was cool, but I knew for sure it wasn't my business.

He looked back toward the main room of the restaurant. No one could see us from where we were standing. "Is he your...boyfriend?"

"I'm not sure," I said. "I didn't really want to start seeing anyone, but..."

"...But sometimes things just happen," he finished my sentence.

"Yeah, sometimes things just happen."

We looked at each other, not knowing what to say next. We were silent, but things were still said. We acknowledged that we were more surprised to see each other here than we'd let on. We admitted that we were a tiny bit jealous of each other's dates. We also knew that technically there was no reason to be. The silence was also an admission that we had liked each other, but we missed our opportunity to do anything about it. If there had ever been any question about us before, it had been answered tonight.

"Well I guess I'd better get back." I tilted my head toward the dining room.

"Yeah, me too. But hey, what did you want to see me about tomorrow? Can we talk about it here?"

"You know, it would be better if we waited. Just come by my place tomorrow for lunch like we planned, and we'll talk then."

"Okay, I'll be there. It's good to see you, Bev."

"Good to see you too, Danny."

He nodded his head, turned, and walked away.

I waited a few seconds, and then followed him back to the main room, returning to my table where the sheriff was waiting.

"Did you get everything worked out?" he asked me.

"Well, my pants aren't quite dry..."

"I meant with Danny."

"I can't put anything past you, can I?" I said, trying to sound exasperated but secretly appreciating his concern. He didn't answer, just glanced my way with a half-smile. "That's okay," I continued, "because I don't want to put anything past you. Everything is worked out because there was nothing to work out in the first place." I reached my hand across the table and placed it on his.

He interlaced his long, calloused fingers with my shorter ones. We both looked at our clasped hands resting on the table. I liked the way it looked and felt. His skin was surprisingly soft and must have had magical heating powers because my temperature was rising.

"Then I guess everything is okay." He lifted his brown eyes, his eyebrows following.

"Yes." I met his gaze and, in that moment, we both realized something had changed. See *palpable mood changes* in the Manspeak Dictionary index.

We shared a small piece of tiramisu for dessert, and he ordered a Scotch.

"This is nicer than our first date," he said.

"Mostly because my parents aren't here," I agreed.

"Not only because of that." He smiled at me before taking another small sip from his glass. He was nursing his Scotch, making it last.

"If I didn't know better, I'd say you were drawing this evening out," I said lightly. Hardly anyone was left in the whole place.

He looked pensively at the remaining Scotch, then looked at me over the top of the glass. "Maybe." He took another small, slow sip. I laughed.

We sat in silence for a few beats before he spoke again. "Leona said she thought the article you wrote about her was okay," he said. I guess that Mark had sent it to her to look over before he published it.

"When did you see Leona?" I asked. "Did she file another complaint about me?"

"Nope," he said. "Grocery store."

"Oh."

"She said she thought you did a good job," he continued.

"That's because I left out the weird stuff."

"Oh yeah? Like what?" He put his elbows on the table and leaned in closer.

His face looked so open and friendly and downright cute that I almost told him about the covert love affair thing. But Bill had asked me not to spill the beans, and he was my pal, so I honored his request. Even though I really, really wanted to tell Callan. "Oh, just like how she is addicted to Ramen Noodles," I said, waving off his question with my hand. "Anyway, I'm glad she thought it was *okay*."

"That's high praise coming from her."

"It was the magic pie you sent over to us at Stacy's. It had conciliatory crust."

He let out a laugh. "Well, I guess since she approved of the job you did, I'll go ahead and let you interview me, too."

"You will?"

"I'm not real excited about it, but sure."

"That would be great, because Mark is pestering me about your story being late, and I'm kind of ditching another assignment, so if I could placate him soon, I might not lose my job."

"What's the other story about?" he asked.

I shouldn't have said anything. I *could* lie, I supposed, but that would be dumb. Dumber than the article would be. "It's about Bigfoot," I mumbled.

"I'm sorry, I didn't catch that," Callan said. He was smiling and I knew he'd heard me; he just wanted to hear me say it again.

"Bigfoot. An article on Sasquatch, okay?"

He pressed his lips together to try not to laugh.

"Al and Bill said they saw one," I tried to explain, "which is a load of horse poop because they didn't see one, they just—" And that's when I realized I might have said a little too much. That's all I needed—to incriminate myself on a first date. As if the sheep announcing their presence in the yard earlier hadn't been bad enough.

"They just what?"

"Oh, uh, they're just a few slices short of a full loaf, if you catch my drift," I said, looking at him over nonexistent smarty-pants glasses perched on the bridge of my nose. "Anyway, there's nothing to tell, so no story to write. And I won't bother interviewing you for that article," I said, reminding him of my previous attempt to do so last year.

"About that. I'm sorry. I don't have much to say sometimes, but that doesn't mean I'm not thinking about things." His tone suggested innuendo, and when I looked at him, so did his face. Was it getting hot in here? "Ready to leave?" he asked.

"That would be great."

I insisted that we split the bill, so we each put some cash on the table and then pulled on our coats. As we walked to the door, Danny nodded at us from his corner table and the sheriff nodded back.

We drove most of the way back to town in silence, but there was a tension between us. It was the good kind of tension though; not the kind like when you're watching a horror movie and you're waiting for the main female character to get her left arm hacked off with a butter knife. It was the kind of tension that happens when a handsome, smart, thoughtful man is taking you back to your house after a nice dinner, and you're sort of wondering what will happen next.

When we pulled into my driveway. I started talking without thinking about what I was saying.

"Would you like to come in for a nightcap?"

"Yes," he said.

We walked to my door and I unlocked it as quickly as I could, because it had gotten quite cold and I'd already started shivering.

"By 'nightcap' I actually mean tea," I confessed. "I don't have any hard liquor in the house. I might have some Emergency Beer though."

"*Emergency* beer?"

"Yes. You know, beer for emergencies."

"This is not an emergency; tea would be great." He took off his coat and put it on a chair by the door. I prayed to everything holy that the sheep were asleep in the backyard and would stay quiet. I wondered if sheep slept lying down and made a mental note to check on them later to verify.

I told him to make himself comfortable in the living room as I went to put on some water for tea. But after about thirty seconds, he had followed me into the kitchen. If I didn't know better, I'd have guessed he was nervous. I wondered if he could tell that I was nervous too. How ridiculous, to be this nervous. I mean, how many times had we both done this? With other people, that is. Ugh. I didn't want to think about that, either.

"What kind of tea would you like?" I placed a few boxes on the kitchen table for him to choose from. He walked over and stood next to me. I felt like I might catch fire.

"This one." He handed me a box. Then he took the box back and put it on the table. He put his hand on my shoulder.

"One Lemon Zinger coming up," I said quietly

"Look, Bev, I don't know what this is. I almost didn't want to do this, whatever it is." He waved his hand around the room. "But I can't stop thinking about you."

I took a deep breath. "Me neither." He moved a little closer, towering over me. His breath sounded a little quicker than normal. I knew mine definitely was. "I'm sorry," I said.

"For what?"

I wasn't sure what I was sorry for. For him liking me? For me liking him? For me not having the emotional or hormonal fortitude to stick to my original decision not to go out with him? For admitting that maybe I'd like to have someone to spend time with? For realizing that I liked this person and, to be totally honest, that I wanted to jump his bones right there in the kitchen?

"Okay, I'm not sorry," I said.

He looked down at me, lips slightly parted, eyes narrowed. He took a deep breath and held it for a few beats before letting it back out again. His hand was still resting on my shoulder, and I could feel each finger. His thumb on my collar bone, the other four fingers pressing lightly into the top of my shoulder.

I had read enough romance novels to know what should come next. And just as in a romance novel scene that happens early in the book, when things are first heating up, so to speak, the kettle chose that exact moment to start boiling and whistling. We laughed and his hand dropped away. The tension was temporarily broken. I was pretty sure it would return at some point soon.

We made our tea and sat down on the couch in the living room. I held my mug between my hands to warm them.

"That's quite a collection of books," he said, nodding at my floor-to-ceiling bookshelves.

"Well, they're kind of my life."

"A lot of romance novels, it looks like." He put down his mug of tea and squinted a little at the shelves. Then he put a hand on my thigh as he stood up to go get a closer look. Smooth move. I was impressed. And really okay with it.

"It's, uh, research." I confessed. "For my writing project."

"How's that going?"

"Not great."

"It's a romance novel, right?"

"I guess it's supposed to be. But I can't get it going."

"I doubt that," he said without an ounce of sarcasm. There might not have been sarcasm, but I wasn't so sure that there hadn't been some innuendo in there somewhere. "Just give it some time. What's the rush?"

Just what Kelly had said. Everybody loved to give me writing advice, I thought to myself. I sighed.

He turned around and fixed his gaze on me. "Are you impatient?" he asked, leaning against the bookshelf. He looked so good, standing there. I wasn't sure exactly what we were talking about anymore.

"It's frustrating," I said, holding his gaze. I could play the double entendre game, too. He raised an eyebrow, and then looked back at the books. "New Yorkers aren't known for their patience," I continued.

"But you're from Oklahoma. The pace of life is pretty slow out here."

"Yeah, but you can't spend over twenty years in Manhattan and not get accustomed to a fast-paced life. It's just...different now.

When I first got here, there was so much to do—getting the store set up, getting settled in at the paper, spending some time with my parents. Now, I feel like I should be doing something more."

He slowly walked back to the couch and sat down so close to me that our legs were touching. "Like what?"

"Like writing a novel, I guess. Beyond that, I don't know."

He turned to face me, and his leg pressed into mine. My leg was sending my brain urgent messages. *More! More!* I started to feel slightly panicky as that good kind of tension rose.

His honey-brown eyes were warm, and upon closer inspection, they appeared to have an ulterior motive. "You don't always need to have everything planned out to the last detail," he said. "Once you know what you want, all you have to do is sit back and let it unfold naturally." He sounded so wise.

"Besides, you can't rush a good thing," he said in his slow, espresso-rich voice. "Anticipation is the best part, you know. It's all about the getting there." He smiled an easy smile and looked at my lips. I wanted to melt.

I was less patient than he was. "Clearly, you've been misinformed, Sheriff. I can probably set you straight."

"Stop calling me Sheriff. You're a very sexy woman, Beverley Green." His voice was soft as cotton now. I smiled, and then we heard it—a soft, lonely-sounding *baaaaaah* from the backyard. Oh my goodness. I had forgotten all about the damn sheep back there!

It had to have been Burt again; there was no way my sister Loni would let me down like that. On the plus side, it hadn't been very loud. But on the minus side, it sounded like I had illegal sheep in my backyard. I wondered if I should rip my shirt off and throw myself at Callan so he'd forget he heard it. Maybe we could steamroll right over it by making out like teenagers.

But before I could make my move, he pushed off the couch and stood back up, looking toward the kitchen. He started to point his thumb back toward the yard, but I just shook my head and stood up too. I wasn't sure I could breathe anymore. But it was only two stupid sheep, right? I mean, it wasn't like I was trying to hide nuclear missiles in my storage shed. *Let's keep everything in perspective here, Bev.*

However, I also knew that it was a good thing to feel bad about the sheep. There shouldn't be any secrets between friends. Or lovers. Or sheriffs and citizens. Or whatever we were. I promised myself that when it was all over and the sheep were returned to Danny, I would tell Callan everything, and it would all be okay. *It was just two sheep.* I was probably making a mountain out of a molehill. Or maybe a shitheap out of a sheephill.

"I should probably get going," he said. Was this code for *I've changed my mind about you?* But he'd just finished extolling the virtues of being patient...hopefully that was it.

"Are you sure?" I asked. "I mean, my parents already think you're my new overnight guest."

He took my hand and walked me to the door. I watched him put his coat back on.

"Thanks for taking me to dinner," I said softly.

"Thanks for asking me out to dinner." He looked down at the floor, and we both stood there, as if neither of us was sure what came next, but we could both take a guess.

"Can we do it again?" I asked.

"I certainly hope so." He took a single step forward, covering all the ground that was between us. He put his hand on my shoulder again, then moved it up to the back of my neck, pulling me closer. And before I knew what was happening, he kissed me. On the cheek. The stubble on his face scratched my skin ever so slightly, and I had to admit the sensation that was not unpleasant. In fact, I wanted to explore this sensation more.

Apparently, Callan decided that his aim could have been better, because he tried again, this time with wonderfully satisfying accuracy. It was one slow, soft kiss. On the lips. Full of so many things, like affection, thoughtfulness, confidence, and just a hint of flat-out desire. Without using any words, he had told me a novel's worth of information. His lips were soft, but I could tell they would definitely get down to serious business when the occasion called for it. He pulled away and looked at me, his face flushed and his lips still slightly parted.

"Don't put that in the article," he whispered.

"What article?"

"That's my girl." He ran his fingers through my hair. "See you later," he said. And then he was gone.

After I locked the door behind him, I stumbled through the house to my bed, where I fell onto the soft comforter and into a deep, Bigfoot- and sheep-free sleep.

17

It turned out I had grossly underestimated my new hometown. Originally, I'd thought it was quaint, charming, slow-paced, authentic, and homey. But it turned out I was wrong. It was all that and so much more. It was also weird, quirky, puzzling, and a little bit salacious. When I moved to New York, I expected it to be bustling, crowded, kind of seedy in places, and expensive. And that city lived up to my expectations. Guthrie was exceeding my expectations.

I reflected on this as I lay in bed Saturday morning. I thought about the night before and I couldn't help but smile. Everything was going to work out just fine.

Leona had liked my article. I had two sheep to give to Danny, and I was sure he would be gracious and kind about the whole mix-up. He'd take the sheep and all would be well. And I'd start my article about the sheriff, too. And Mark would tell me I didn't have to write about Bigfoot again, and Al and Bill would thank me for my all help by bringing me donuts. I had a rough outline for a book, and soon I would be on the New York Times Bestseller list. Yes, all was well with the world this morning.

I had made a deal with Julie that if she took care of the store with Chuck this morning, I would come in after lunch and give them the rest of the day off. This way, I had a few hours to go grocery shopping, relax a little, and make some lunch for Danny and me. Before I got out of bed, I tried to think of what I would say to Danny. *I know Al and Bill are idiots, but hey, they're cute...*Well, I would try to think about it later. I started to get a little nervous.

I got out of bed and didn't get more than three steps before banging my toe into the wall right outside my closet. It hurt like a sonovagun, and I cursed like a sailor at the wall. I felt this did not bode well for the rest of the day. Then I heard a very distinct sheep bleat from the backyard, followed quickly by two more. *Burt, shut the heck up,* I thought. My mood was leaving optimistic in the rearview mirror, heading toward doomsday preparedness. So, it didn't come as much of a surprise when I walked to the kitchen, looked out the window, and saw four sheep. Two of them had chickens sitting on their backs.

Yup, status quo.

Two of the sheep were Burt and Loni, but now they had two more friends. And one of the chickens was Beryl.

"Huh," I mumbled as I slipped on my Vans. I was more surprised by Beryl's return than the addition of two more sheep.

"Hi, Beryl," I said as I got closer to her. She eyed me cautiously but didn't try to fly away. She didn't even look like she wanted to kill me. "How on earth did you get here?" Her beak stayed shut tight. She would never tell.

I looked at the other chicken and realized it was a rooster. He eyed me cautiously also, then flew off the back of the sheep he'd been sitting on. He strutted across the lawn and flapped up to sit with Beryl on her sheep. Man oh Manischewitz. Beryl had found herself a boyfriend. My chicken was getting some.

"Where did you pick up this fella?" I asked her. I'm pretty sure she smiled at me; it was one more secret that she was never, ever going to tell me.

The two new sheep had tags on their ears. They were a different breed than Burt and Loni, but they looked to be in good shape. I searched my mind for the weirdest, yet simplest explanation. They must have been Danny's sheep.

All right. Okay. I needed to process this. I sat down heavily at the picnic table to think. What was going on? The very first thing came to mind was two people. Two people who were cousins, and who were known to do some pretty ridiculous things. Two people who seemed to have played a prank on me. I was going to wring Al and Bill's necks the next time I saw them.

If this was their idea of a joke, it was *so* not funny. They'd taken me on a wild goose chase—or in this case, a wild sheep chase. They'd pretended to hire me to look for their damn sheep. They'd gotten me in trouble with my boss and forced me to write another Bigfoot article. They'd made me see things involving Leona that I couldn't un-see. I had baggies of weird fur sitting on my desk. I'd taken pictures of animal poop. I was pissed.

I was about to jump in my car and head to Al's so I could beat him to a pulp with the spare umbrella in my trunk, when a short burst of reason took over, causing me to pause and take a few deep breaths. Maybe, just maybe, there was another explanation? I could think of one other possibility...but I liked that one even less than the first one.

If Al and Bill hadn't pulled a fast one on me, maybe—and I couldn't believe I was even thinking these words—just maybe, Bigfoot had. Maybe Justin Miller's extraterrestrial Bigfoot theory was right. Maybe these sheep had been abducted by space creatures and then deposited in my backyard. I looked at them closely; they didn't appear to be glowing.

I thought I might start to hyperventilate, or that my brain might melt, or both. And this was all happening before breakfast. I couldn't deal with it. And that's when I looked down at the picnic table and noticed the Hostess Cupcakes were gone. I'd forgotten about them for a while, but I know I hadn't moved them or eaten them. Now they were gone, and all that was on the table was a brown smear of what I desperately hoped was chocolate icing. I sighed and wondered who exactly had enjoyed eating my cupcakes.

This was all too much. My brain was not equipped for this level of weirdness. Giant lawn chair eating dogs, sure. Senior citizen clandestine love affairs, okay. But the rest of this was getting to be way too much. *It's okay, Bev. Just breathe*, I told myself. I needed to think rationally. *What needs to be done right this minute?* I needed food and coffee.

Before doing anything else, though, I put Beryl and her boyfriend into the chicken pen and made sure the gate to the backyard was secure. As I closed the pen back up, I smelled pot smoke wafting over the fence from next door.

"Zach?" I called out toward the fence.

"Hey, what's up, dude," said Zach from his backyard. Zach and his wife Zoe were a young, cute, pot-partaking couple who rented the house next to mine. They also had non-approved chickens and were really nice people. One time a few months earlier, they'd brought me some homemade cookies, and I didn't notice until I'd eaten two of them that they were *special* cookies. It had been a fun night.

"Hey, Zach, are you by any chance missing a rooster?" I asked him.

"Um, let me check," came the reply. I heard some steps, the sound of a gate unlatching, and Zach's voice as he spoke to his birds. Then he called back to me. "No man, everyone's here. How come? Usually you're losing chickens, not finding extra ones."

"Haha, true," I said, trying to sound amused but not doing a very convincing job of it. "Nothing's up over here. I was just curious. Thanks though." I didn't feel like explaining everything at the moment.

"Okay," he answered. "Hey, do you have, like, sheep over there? I swear we heard sheep last night."

"Sheep? Here? No way! That would be weird. You must have been imagining things." I *really* didn't feel like explaining all that stuff.

There was a pause. "Dude. You're probably right. We did take some mushrooms." For a second, I thought back wistfully to my college days. People were still doing mushrooms. Good to know.

"Well, guess I'll talk to you later," I said.

"Later, dude."

Dude. I needed food and coffee.

I made sure the four sheep weren't going anywhere. Well, as sure as I could considering there weren't any guarantees when it came to losing *or* gaining sheep these days, and went in for an EBB, or Emergency Big Breakfast. Eggs, bacon, English muffin and coffee. It had to be done. I was gonna need the extra carbs today.

By the time Danny was scheduled to arrive, I had prepared lunch, finished three loads of laundry while baking cookies, scrubbed my shower, cleaned the crumbs out of my toaster oven, and vacuumed the entire house. I'd considered cleaning out the garage, but I kept stopping to stare incredulously out the back window. I had a whole damn farm out there. Thank goodness this would all be over soon.

Right around noon, there was a knock on my door—Danny was right on time. But when I opened the door to let him in, I stood face to face with Al and Bill.

"Hiya!" said Al, raising one hand in a greeting. He stood like that for several seconds before I realized he was waiting for me to give him a high five. But I was too late. By the time I raised my hand to give him one back, he'd lowered his. He shrugged and pushed on past me to enter my house, Bill in tow.

"What the heck are you doing here?" I hissed. "This isn't a good time!"

"Oh, really?" Al looked back toward his tiny Ford Ranger, but it was the only car in the driveway. It still had some big scratches on the passenger side, which he'd claimed had been made by a lady Bigfoot last year.

"We was missing the sheep and wanted to come by to see them," Bill said. "They're so dang cute." I couldn't help but notice his t-shirt. It was brown, and had a drawing of a hedgehog on it, with the words *CAN'T TOUCH THIS* underneath. I was still upset about their unannounced visit, but I silently gave him props, once again, for his shirt. He was going to have a successful store.

"Which sheep were you missing?" I asked.

Al looked confused. "The ones we had delivered to you. What other sheep are there?" He looked over my shoulder as if expecting the sheep to be sitting on my couch. "Are they still here?"

"I've got some news for you guys," I said, motioning for them to follow me through the house to the backyard. I probably shouldn't have invited them in, since Danny would be there any minute. But I wanted Al and Bill to get caught out and confess to being involved in all this. As I led them outside, I waved my hand to encompass the whole yard. "Tell me what you see," I said casually.

Bill and Al stood by the picnic table, surveying the scene. "Well," said Bill, "that's an awful lot of sheep you got there."

"Uh huh, I said calmly. "And do you recognize them?" I watched Al as he processed the question.

"Wait," he said slowly. "Is that...?"

"You tell me, Al. Are they?"

"Sure looks like it..."

"And do you mind telling me how they got here?"

"How what got here?" said a voice behind us. There was Danny, standing by the backyard gate.

Al, Bill, and I stared at Danny as he walked into the yard. My eyes grew wide in surprise, and I'm guessing Al and Bill had similar looks, because then Danny asked, "What's wrong with you people?"

"We're, uh, surprised to see you," I said flatly.

"Weren't you expecting me?"

"Oh. Right." It was slowly coming back to me. "You're late!"

"I'd say that's the least of our worries right now," said Al.

"What's the least of your worries?" said another voice. It came from the back door of the house. All four of us looked in that direction, and there was Sheriff Branch, standing tall, hands on his hips. I didn't have to look at him very long to be able to tell that he was enjoying this, and that he was expecting it to get pretty darned interesting before it was all over. I had no idea what he was doing at my house, but the way this was going, I wasn't at all surprised.

"Danny was late!" yelled Bill. Way to stay calm, Bill.

We all stood stock still except for our eyes, which were darting from person to person. Everyone was waiting for someone else to say something. Well, it sure as hell wasn't going to be me who was going to go first!

"Sheep!" I blurted out.

"Bev, what's going on?" asked Danny and Callan in unison. I was starting to feel faint and about to begin babbling uncontrollably, but another voice piped up from the gate.

"Yes, Beverley, what *is* going on here?" asked Leona.

I had been perplexed by why the sheriff had shown up, but now I was nearly hysterical about an unplanned visit from my landlady. What were the effing odds? I needed to sit down, but I wasn't near the picnic bench. Instead, I shifted my weight to one leg and surreptitiously tried to prepare to make a run for it. All my exits were blocked, but I could still try to hop the fence.

"Sheriff, what's going on here?" Leona snapped, walking further into the yard. Just then, Burt let out a sweet, smooth, sheep bleat. We all turned to look at him.

"That's Burt," I said weakly.

"I don't care if it's the Queen of England. You've got some explaining to do," said Leona. She sounded a little like Desi Arnaz, and I was feeling a lot like Lucille Ball.

"Now, sweetie," said Bill, stepping toward her and reaching out to touch her arm. "Take it easy, hunny bunny..."

Well, that was that. If Leona had wanted to keep her romance with Bill under wraps, any chance of that was now shot to heck. And the most remarkable part was, it hadn't been my fault.

It felt like something bad might happen now. I thought she might start spewing steam from her ears, and then swell up and explode all over the yard. She did turn dark red and shot a look at Bill that would have withered the manhood right off of any red-blooded male. I felt bad for Bill, but I hoped this would make everyone forget that there were four sheep and twelve chickens watching us.

"Bill, what the hell?" said Al. I guess he hadn't gotten the full memo from Bill and Leona. He was turning red too and heading straight for his cousin.

I shot a pleading glance at Callan, hoping he'd step in and keep the peace, seeing as he was the one who had a gun and all. And to my great relief, he did take charge.

"All right, let's take a couple of deep breaths here, shall we?" he said, stepping between Al and Bill. "Clearly we've got some things to talk about." He directed everyone to the picnic table, where we chose sides and sat down. I sat between Al and Danny, while Leona and Bill sat across from us. The sheriff remained standing, towering over us all.

"Bev, why don't you start?" he suggested, once we were all settled. Everyone looked at me expectantly. I seriously considered breaking up with him.

"Well, it's like this, see," I started, not having the foggiest idea where I was headed. I looked toward the back door—all we needed was for Mark and Kelly to join us, and maybe Seth from the coffee shop, and Julie and Banjo Man...and Bigfoot. I was still scared to death of Sasquatch, but if he were going to show up at my house, now would be a good time.

This was it. The culmination of the past several weeks boiled down to this moment in my backyard with five people staring at me, waiting for me to explain everything. My stress level had been 2 out of 10 this morning. Now it was 8.7 and rising. I could feel fear deep in my gut. I didn't want to let anyone down. These people were my friends, my neighbors, and people who could evict or arrest me.

How had I gotten here? All I had tried to do from the get-go was to make sense of where my life was headed. But then everyone else's lives had gotten mixed up into mine. It was like a giant tangle of yarn except instead of having two ends, it had six. Any place I would try to pull to loosen the knot would tighten it somewhere else. I was on the verge of losing a new boyfriend, my job at the paper, some quirky friends, my home, and twelve chickens. No big deal. Lesson learned: trying put together a stupid "life plan" only got you so far. Because who could plan for *this* shit?

If there was a time to give that all up, it would be right now. If ever there had been a time to give up trying to control everything, today was that day. If I had been looking for an opportunity to wave the white flag, cry "uncle," let go and let God, and throw in the towel, it would be right this minute. I had absolutely nothing to lose. And by nothing, I meant everything, but what was the difference, in the end?

The sheriff gently cleared his throat and I remembered where I was.

"Can I call my lawyer?" I asked tentatively. Callan stared at me blankly.

"Fine. Let me see if I can run through this without a white-board," I began. I stopped for a beat, hoping someone would laugh, to lighten the mood. No one did. I continued, telling the truth as I knew it to be.

"Al and Bill borrowed a sheep, which happened to belong to Danny. They swore they'd return it, only it went missing. So they borrowed another one. It went missing, too." I looked at Al. He nodded vigorously. Bill tried to fiddle with Leona's dress sleeve, but she slapped his hand away like it was a mosquito.

"They asked me to look into what happened to the sheep," I went on. "But I didn't want to. I suggested they call the sheriff to report the sheep as missing. But once I heard how they'd acquired the sheep, I could see why they didn't want to do that. I still didn't want to help, but then *someone*—" and here I glared at Bill, "—called in a Bigfoot sighting to the paper and Mark assigned the story to me. Al and Bill insisted Bigfoot had taken the sheep. So now I was forced to look into it."

I looked around to see if I was getting any traction. Nothing but intent staring. I *really* wished Bigfoot would visit right now.

"But the sheep are right there," said Danny, pointing to his animals.

"Yup," I agreed. "They showed up here this morning. And honest to goodness, I have no idea how they got here. I think Al and Bill played a stupid trick on me, just so I'd have to write another stupid Bigfoot story," I said angrily.

"Now, why on earth would we do that?" asked Al.

"Oh, I don't know Al," I snapped. "Maybe you were bored because you were left out of Leona and Bill's love life?"

"Hey, stop it!" yelled Bill. "No one's supposed to know about me and my sweetie lips." Leona reached over and smacked Bill on the top of his head. "Dammit, woman!" he said angrily. Then he stage-whispered, "Do that again later." She huffed and started to lean forward again like she was going to smack him again but thought better of it.

Now Al reached over the table and slapped Bill on the head. Danny started laughing, and I looked desperately at Callan, hoping he'd break up the bitch-slapping before full-on mayhem broke out in the garden. He simply shifted his weight from one leg to the other, but it was enough to calm everyone down.

"Why are there four sheep here?" he asked.

"Well, we couldn't figure out what happened to Danny's sheep. You know Al's got a dog the size of my car? I thought maybe the dog ate the sheep, but I couldn't find any proof. They were just...gone. I thought Al should make amends by buying Danny two new sheep, and I would try to negotiate a peace offering. Like, two sheep in exchange for not pressing any charges against anyone. I came up with a great plan. Burt and Loni were delivered here, and I was going to give them to Danny today and try to keep Al and Bill out of trouble. But then all of this happened." I raised my arm and pointed in the general direction of the animals. "Four sheep, an extra rooster, and Beryl, who had gone missing last week."

"That chicken freaks me out," said Danny.

"I know, right? It's like she has superpowers!" I marveled.

"Let me get this straight," said Callan. "Two of the sheep are Danny's. Two of them belong to Al and Bill. You've got your chicken back, plus an extra rooster."

"His name is Earl," I clarified.

"And none of this damn zoo is supposed to be in this backyard!" yelled Leona.

Callan lay a hand on her shoulder and she quieted down. Bill looked at the sheriff warily.

"Al, did you have the sheep all along? Don't bullshit me. I can always tell when you're lying." Callan gazed steadily at Al, who began to squirm. That dirty rat!

"No sir, I honestly have no idea what happened to them sheep. They up and disappeared from my backyard, like Bev said. I reckon maybe ol' Smiley dog coulda eaten them, but now here they are."

"And Danny, you knew nothing about this?"

"This is the first I'm hearing about any of it. I had no idea who had taken my sheep or that Bev was involved. Yet somehow, I'm not surprised." He turned and looked at me. I was afraid he was mad, until I saw the sparkle in his bright blue eyes.

"So," said Callan thoughtfully. "We have no idea how the sheep disappeared or how they got back here."

"Well, we got one good possibility," Bill reminded everyone. We all looked at him expectantly. "Bigfoot," he said slowly. We all nodded, thinking this over. It was just as good as any other explanation.

"We do know that he likes your chicken," said Danny.

"You're not helping." I elbowed him in the ribs.

We sat in silence for a minute. We were at a stalemate. Al and Bill were in trouble. I was in trouble. Leona was mad at me and Bill. Danny was confused but didn't seem too angry. The sheriff looked like he was resentful of having to babysit us all. I felt like I was five years old.

Finally, the sheriff started outlining a possible peace accord. And after what felt like an eternity of negotiating, we reached a tentative agreement. Danny said he wouldn't press any charges and would take his two original sheep, but he refused to take Burt and Loni as apology gifts. "They're not mine. And you don't want to mess with farm karma," he explained. "That's kind of a big deal around here."

"So...don't mess with big farma?" I asked. Al, Bill, and Leona looked at me blankly, Danny looked confused again, and Callan did everything he could to keep from laughing.

Al then suggested he take Burt and Loni, since he had bought them. But I pointed out that his monster of a dog would swallow them whole like they were a couple of *amuse-bouche*. Leona reminded me that I was forbidden to keep them and that she was also considering evicting me over the whole mess. Bill then very sweetly convinced Leona that I had only been trying to help, so she decided she'd think it over a little longer before deciding. I hoped our newfound friendship would count for something when she made up her mind.

The sheriff put his hand on Leona's shoulder again, and solemnly told her that Burt and Loni would be staying with me and the chickens for now, but that he would personally vouch for me, and would make sure I wouldn't give her any trouble as a renter. He gave me a stern look, which I knew was for her benefit. I wanted to kiss him really bad right then.

Finally, we all pledged to keep Bill and Leona's budding romance a secret, at least until Leona said it was okay to make it public. I couldn't imagine why she didn't want people to know.

At this point, I went inside and brought out six glasses of iced tea, and we all toasted to our agreement, and threw one back in honor of our negotiating skills. I told everyone I had enough tuna salad to make us each a quarter of a sandwich if they wanted, but they all declined so I just brought out the fresh-baked cookies and we declared them lunch. It ended up being a pretty nice garden party, once we agreed no one would get arrested.

———

I had to break up the garden party shortly after we finished off the cookies; I was expected at the bookstore. I graciously thanked everyone for coming over, like a good hostess would, even though I had only invited one of them. By design, the sheriff was the last to leave. I was glad to be alone with him, but also a little scared. He'd agreed to vouch for me, but that didn't mean he wouldn't still want to stop seeing me. It was easier to pull a weed when it was still small.

We watched Leona leave through the garden gate with Bill in tow, and I felt myself being able to breathe a little easier. I sat down heavily at the picnic table.

"You're my hero," I said, trying not to swoon.

"Aw shucks, ma'am. All in a day's work," he said.

"Stop mocking me. I'm serious! I don't know what I would have done if you hadn't shown up when you did."

"It was looking a little grim," he admitted.

"I don't know how I get myself into these things," I sighed.

"Yeah, that was weird," he admitted. "And I've seen some pretty weird stuff."

"I'll bet!"

"I'm guessing this is just everyday life for you," he said, sitting down next to me.

"I'd like to say it's not, but yeah, it kind of is."

We sat next to each other, not saying anything. I imagined he was trying to think of a way to tell me thanks, but no thanks.

"I understand if it's too much weirdness for you," I began. "I mean, there's only so much weirdness a person can take, and if it's—"

"Nah," he said, "it's kinda fun."

"Well then, you're in for a whole lot of fun," I said.

One of his eyebrows went up. "I certainly hope so." He was good at the double entendre and I liked that. A lot.

"So you're not going to arrest me for harboring fugitive sheep?" I asked.

"Not today."

That was all I could ask for.

"Can I give you a ride to the bookstore?" he asked.

"But that means you'd have to give me a ride home," I said. He just looked at me. "Oh."

I accepted the offer of a ride, and we left soon after. He stopped at Hoboken so I could get a coffee and then dropped me at the shop, where I took over for Chuck and Julie.

Business was brisk at the store, and when Callan walked in at closing time, it had felt like only fifteen minutes had passed. He drove me home, but turned down my offer to stay for dinner, as he had to take care of some top-secret sheriff stuff. Which was just as well. Technically, I still had to write an article about Bigfoot. But I did invite him to Sunday breakfast the following morning, and he accepted.

I was tired, hungry, and full of questions. What had actually happened? Would I ever be able to fill in the blanks? Did it matter? We were all curious though.

As I fixed myself some dinner, I wondered if it truly could have been Bigfoot that orchestrated all this. If so, he—they? she? Lord only knew how many of them were involved—knew where I lived. I wasn't sure how I felt about that. So far, however, Bigfoot had returned my chicken twice and brought me some sheep. My dad had a saying that he would tell me as often as he could: "One cannot escape one's destiny." Then I would tell him that was a big load of hooey, but today I found myself thinking there might be a kernel of truth in it. If Bigfoot knew where I lived, I'd have to trust that he would respect at least some of my personal boundaries. In any case, I decided I'd invest in some better-quality window coverings.

Maybe they were my protectors, I mused as I walked outside to eat a cookie and check on all the animals. In any case, I was sounding like someone who was starting to believe in Bigfoot. Maybe there was a better explanation for everything that had happened, but it hadn't presented itself yet.

The old me would have been stress eating my way through the

pantry right now. But there was a new me that was emerging, and this new me was okay with stress snacking instead of stress scarfing. The new-ish me understood that I didn't need to control everything that was going on. There was no way I could anyway, so I'd just have to lighten up a little. This was the stuff that they made quirky Netflix series out of, after all. Go with it, my gut said. Also, my gut said I should get another cookie.

The afternoon had been sunny and surprisingly warm. The forecast for the following day looked like more of the same, which was nice. Maybe Callan and I could go on a walk after breakfast. I was looking forward to his visit and to cooking for him. I'd never been all that domestic while I was in New York, preferring a stroll down to the corner deli for breakfast, grabbing coffee and something that came with a schmear of cream cheese. But these days I didn't mind making breakfast. Maybe it was because I was getting older and had a newfound appreciation for the little things in life. Maybe it was because of who I was preparing breakfast for. Maybe it was because I felt so self-sufficient, being able to walk out the door to grab some fresh eggs.

But what if I wouldn't be able to keep my chickens? I was still in danger of being evicted, or even worse, being forced to get rid of the birds. Leona would have every right to do it, but I hoped she wouldn't. I'd have to wait and see, I supposed. *Lighten up, Bev.*

Noticing it was dark now, I stood up to go back inside. As I walked to the back door, I heard a distinct string of words in my head. *Beverley, honey,* it said, sounding suspiciously like my mother's voice, *you don't have to have all the answers. Half the fun in life is coming up with the questions. Have some damn fun!*

Some people are really good at picking up on the subtleties of life. I, on the other hand, had always needed a more literal approach, such as big flashing neon signs, or something falling on my head. Something like a self-help book. But eventually, I did receive the message. And I was finally starting to get it now, too.

I had been stressing myself out thinking I needed to know exactly where I wanted to go and exactly what I wanted to do. I was pinning all of my hope, blame, and power to a magic plan that would tell me where to go, who to be with, what to do, and how to do it. I was looking for an easy way out. I had been waiting for someone else to tell me what I should be doing.

And what happened? The more I waited for my magic plan, the more I was giving up my ability to change anything for myself. The more I gave that up, the more out of control everything had become.

In New York, I had been going through the motions and I hadn't even realized that I was unhappy because it had been my chronic state. And now I'd changed locations, but I hadn't changed my outlook.

Instead of fixing anything, I had come close to ruining everything. But I could figure this out. I left New York because I knew in my gut it was the right thing to do, and I moved to Guthrie for the same reason. It might have looked to everyone else like I'd done it on a whim, but I knew better. I could trust myself to know what to do. I didn't need a life plan; I needed faith in myself that I'd find whatever step came next, and the answers would be there when I needed them.

And that's what Callan was telling me that day at the bookstore—all I had to do was continue to course-correct. And enjoy the ride. Damn, he was good. It looked like I was going to have to give my parents credit for a good match after all.

But first, I had a few things to do.

I went in the house and made a beeline for my office, where I took the little PIG sample bags full of weird hairy bits and tossed them in the waste basket. No particulate analysis necessary this time around, I decided.

I proceeded to look up a few things on the internet, and then wrote the best Bigfoot story that the Guthrie *Ledger* had, or would ever, publish. I had told Mark I wasn't going to do it, but both he and I knew I would eventually do it. All this time, I was resisting being the Bigfoot Lady. But now, as part of my new outlook, I decided I should embrace it. If I was going to be the Bigfoot Lady of Guthrie, I was going to be the best dang Bigfoot Lady this town had ever seen.

Guthrie residents were getting quite a story. They were about to discover that our local Sasquatches were not violent, carnivorous monsters who terrorized local women and children, but rather caring, vegetarian Samaritans who found new homes for mistreated animals. Part fact, part fiction, as usual. But no one would care because in the end, that's what life was—part fact, part fiction.

I put the finishing touches on that perfect story, and I sent it to Mark with no explanation whatsoever. He'd love it.

It was late now, but I went outside one more time to check on the kids. Burt and Loni were quiet, but they were milling around like they were hungry. I'd have to get them some real sheep food tomorrow, before they revolted.

All the chickens were quiet and locked up tight. Beryl and Earl were sitting on top of the coop together; she looked happy. Normally I'd be suspicious, but maybe she truly was happier with a "special friend." Maybe I needed one of those, too.

I said goodnight to everyone and went back in for the night and called my parents. I thought I'd see if I could bring anything to dinner the following evening.

"Beverley, honey, is everything all right?" my mom said by way of a greeting.

"Hi, mom," I said. "Yeah, everything is fine. Why?"

"It's Saturday night. Shouldn't you be out on a date or something?"

"Oh, not tonight. That was last night."

Silence. She had expected me to get mad or deny doing anything social. I'd thrown her for a loop. "What was that?" she asked, as if on cue.

"I went out last night, so I'm staying in tonight." I knew she was just dying to ask me who I had gone out with. I'd let her wonder.

"Oh, uh, well that's nice..." She was flustered, and a tiny part of me enjoyed it, even though I knew it was completely juvenile. She brought it out in me sometimes. I stifled a giggle.

"Are we still on for family dinner tomorrow night?" I asked.

"Yes, of course, dear. I'm fixing your favorite," she answered brightly.

"Oh yeah? What's that?"

"Catfish!"

We both burst out laughing. After our laughter died down, she spoke again, her voice quiet, almost thoughtful. "Is everything really okay, Beverley?"

"Sure. Why?"

"You seem—oh I don't know. A little softer, somehow."

"And this is cause for alarm?" I asked.

"Well, maybe. Are you on drugs?"

"No mom. I guess I'm just—I don't know. Happy?"

"Why?"

"Do I need a reason?"

"There's always a reason," she said, suspicious of my overly-simplistic answer.

"Maybe I finally realized I've been making things more complicated than they need to be," I admitted. "I've been trying to control everything for so long. But when everything finally got so far out of control, I realized that I had to give up, and—"

"And things have been better since you did that," she finished for me.

"I think they're headed in that direction," I admitted. We were silent for a few seconds. Everything did feel so much more...easy. Like everything was falling into place on its own. All I'd needed to do was stop trying so hard.

"I'm happy for you, Bev. That's all your dad and I want for you, you know."

"I know, mom. Thanks."

18

WRITING a book is a lot like having sex.

It's also like a lot of other things too, but they're not as nice. Like trying to figure out where to buy pants, or that day every January when you have to sit down and calculate your mileage for the entire previous year for your taxes. Yeah, sex is a better metaphor.

Planners say things like, "It's Tuesday night so that means it's cuddle night!" and, "I will fill all available wall space with sticky notes outlining each and every scene in my novel!" Non-planner types say things like, "I know we're in a public elevator, but the music they're playing is totally getting me in the mood," and "I have no idea whodunit in my mystery novel until I write the last chapter."

Regardless of which approach you prefer, there is room in this world for it all. And unless you pay someone else to do it (which is okay *sometimes* in the writing world), almost all of it's legal.

My point is that there is no one way to write a book. What works for one writer may not work for another, and whether we're talking about sexytime with our favorite person or outlining a book, we're all gonna get there in a different way.

So, when I found myself waking up on Sunday with my mind

full of even more thoughts about the novel outline I'd started, I knew I needed to start writing before I lost them again. Because story ideas could be as elusive as those perfect hot-lovin' moments. When opportunity came knocking, I was no dummy; I opened the damn door.

I took my laptop outside and sat in the early morning sunshine. It was as if my writer's block had disappeared. If I didn't know better, I'd say it happened right around the time I gave up trying to make a big stupid life plan. As soon as I let go and stopped feeling like I had to control everything, the story idea started to take shape. I just kept typing; now I was on a roll. Those Novel Police didn't have anything on me, by golly!

And I was still on that roll when Callan showed up at my house for breakfast. I was still sitting in the backyard, typing as fast as I could when I felt a hand on my shoulder.

"Bigfoot!" I yelled, standing up without thinking. I turned and saw that it was in fact not Sasquatch coming back for his sheep; it was just Callan.

"You need to stop mistaking me for Bigfoot," he said casually. "Am I really that hairy?" He looked down at himself, and we both inspected his appearance.

I smiled as I thought back to him standing shirtless in my kitchen the weekend before. "Not that I recall," I answered. "You're about as tall as a Sasquatch, though. And at this point, I wouldn't be surprised if a Bigfoot showed up for breakfast one day."

"True," he agreed.

"You're supposed to tell me that's silly and there's no such thing as Bigfoot, but even if there was, he wouldn't come to breakfast."

"Sorry," was all he said. Not much appeasement.

I sat back down at my laptop to finish the sentence I'd been writing when he'd scared the living Grape Nuts out of me and noticed the last word I'd typed was *wepoigjvaweifc*. I deleted it and saved the document. "One sec," I said.

"Sure. Where's breakfast?"

"Oh, sonofabitch," I moaned, slapping my palm to my forehead. "I..."

He laughed. "It's all right. I brought donuts."

"Once again, my hero!" I cried. I closed my laptop and put it aside, swinging one leg over the picnic table bench.

"That's right," he said proudly. I was all for girl power and being self-sufficient and strong, but it was also exceedingly okay to have someone around who liked to do nice things for me. I could get used to that.

"I can make us some scrambled eggs right quick, no problem," I said. Before I could get up, he straddled the bench too, and sat down to face me.

"That would be great," he said, reaching out and pulling a curl away from my face.

"There's one thing I have to ask you," I said, looking at the ground.

"Shoot."

"How did you know to come over yesterday? Was it a coincidence? I mean, your timing..."

"Don't sound so surprised," he said casually.

"But...how?"

"I just know things," he said cryptically, raising an eyebrow playfully.

That wasn't good enough for me, and I scowled at him. But he didn't volunteer any information, and I knew he wasn't going to. Police business, I supposed. Or, he had superpowers. Most likely the latter.

"You knew what was going on all along, didn't you?"

"As I said before, it's my business to know what's going on in my county. And sometimes I decide whether or not something is worth making a big deal out of or not. When I found out you were involved in all of this, I decided to wait and see what you came up with. Your negotiating skills are impressive."

"It still blew up in my face," I said morosely.

"It could have been worse," he offered.

"But we're all off the hook now?"

"I wouldn't go that far. If Al and Bill so much as think about stepping out of line, I'll be all over them like honey on a hot biscuit." My stomach growled on cue again.

"How do you think the sheep got from Al's place to my place?" I asked. "Do you think Bigfoot could have done it?"

Callan took a deep breath in and let it out slowly. "No comment," he said.

"Oh my *god*, you're impossible!" I laughed and smacked him on the arm. It was a very muscly arm.

He shrugged.

"Well, I don't know what else could have happened," I mused. "Even Danny thought it was mighty strange."

"Some things are better left unexplained," he said cryptically. We sat and pondered that for a few seconds.

"I had a chat with Danny yesterday evening," he continued. "He seems to be okay with getting his sheep back. He wished me luck with you."

I smiled. "Do you need luck?"

"Well, you have to admit, you *are* a handful, Beverley Green."

I nodded. "Word. So...you're not going to arrest me?"

"Do you plan on collecting any more livestock by dubious means?"

"Well, I don't have any immediate plans to, no, but I can't speak for Beryl. That chicken is crazy. And I don't know what Burt and Loni could get up to, for that matter."

He opened his mouth to speak, but remained silent, looking confused.

"Burt and Loni, the sheep."

He nodded. I had to hand it to him; he took things in stride like a champ. I sure did like that in a man.

"I just hope Leona doesn't kick me out. Maybe she'll be happier now that she's getting some."

Callan's left eyebrow raised slightly again.

"What, are you jealous?"

"Come on now, Bev. You know I only have eyes for you." It was a sweet thing to say and I hoped it was true.

"So...you like me?"

"Of course, I do." He ran a hand over his stubbled jaw, and I had a hot flash. "I like you an awful lot," he said quietly. "You're funny, smart, and sexy as hell."

"I like you too," I said. "but I was scared. I'm still scared that something will go wrong. I don't know where this is all going." I flailed my arms in space, indicating I had no clue about anything anywhere.

"It's kind of early to be worrying about something ending before anything has begun, don't you think?"

"Depends." My eyes lowered as I thought about this. "I'm an expert worrier."

He reached out and lifted my chin, so we were looking each other in the eye. "Let's just take this one step at a time. It's pretty simple; we don't need a plan. But I do know I want to get to know you better."

It was true. We didn't need a fancy plan. They were overrated and got you nothing but extra work and visits from Bigfoot. We would take things as they came.

He kissed me then, and I felt a calmness come over me that I hadn't felt in a very long time. Yeah, maybe this was going to be all right.

He pulled away and looked at me closely. I smiled.

"How'd you like to come with me tonight for dinner at my parents' house?" I asked.

He looked like a deer in headlights. It was so cute.

LIKED THIS BOOK?

If you enjoyed this book and would like to support the author, please consider leaving a review on Amazon or Goodreads - your help is appreciated!

Amazon: amazon.com/author/andreaneil

Goodreads: goodreads.com/andreaneil

ALSO BY ANDREA C. NEIL

Beverley Green: Sasquatch Hunter - Book One of the Beverley Green Adventures

Beverley Green's First Territorial Christmas - Book Two of the Beverley Green Adventures

Visit **acneil.com** for short stories and updates on new projects!

FREE BEVERLEY GREEN SHORT STORY!

Get "Bookstore Confidential: A Short Story in the Beverley Green Adventures" when you sign up to receive my newsletter! You'll receive updates, special discounts and exclusive content with each email. Sign up today!

acneil.com/newsletter

ABOUT THE AUTHOR

Andrea is a writer, editor, and yoga instructor. She balances all of this out with the help of coffee, chocolate, and plenty of irony. Not to be mistaken for ironing. She doesn't do any of that.

She is part of a ridiculously creative family, who have all been wonderful mentors and role models. Her mother loved handcrafts, and her father, always one for details, has excelled in everything from jewelry making to woodworking. She has an uncle who is a world-famous painter. She is the niece of Eleanor and Francis Coppola, and they and their entire family have always been a source of inspiration and encouragement.

Telling stories has been a lifelong passion and pastime. Andrea loves the process and the journey, and the destination is always a bonus.

She lives in Tulsa, Oklahoma but was born and raised in Southern California, where she still visits regularly to recharge her creative soul by the sea.

Sign up for her newsletter at acneil.com and receive a free Beverley Green short story!

facebook.com/andreacneil

twitter.com/andreacneil

instagram.com/andreacneil

amazon.com/author/andreaneil

bookbub.com/authors/andrea-c-neil

goodreads.com/andreaneil

ACKNOWLEDGMENTS

Thanks to my Popster, for being so much like me that it's scary sometimes, and to Magda Neil, for providing a home base away from home.
Cynthia – you are a true unicorn and an amazing artist and I have a total girl crush on you.
Ren – invaluable literary advisor, pop culture maven, super nerd, huzzah!
Marcus – I am currently expressing an appropriate amount of pragmatic gratitude for all the technical support.
Francis & Ellie – thank you for your insight, inspiration and encouragement.
Michele and Breann – HUGE THANKS for all of the word things.
Deepti – you are a sounding board extraordinaire.
Dayl – truly super, truly amazing.
Hope at Esperance Bakery - because bakery!
Thèresé, Erika, Jennifer – thank you for taking the time to beta read this baby.
And finally, eternal appreciation for the muses, who keep my heart open and my voice clear.

64977614R00146

Made in the USA
Middletown, DE
31 August 2019